Lavender's Tangled Tree

JOANN KEDER

Lavender's Tangled Tree

Copyright ©2021 Joann Keder (www.joannkeder.com)

Edited by: Debbie Lombardo See and Benedict Brown
Cover Design by Molly Burton with Cozy Cover Designs

Publisher: Purpleflower Press

ISBN: 978-1-953270-01-6 Paperback

First Edition April 2021

Other books by Joann Keder

Acknowledgements

Thank you to Doug Keder for your support, love and never-faltering confidence in me. Laurie Raphael, you are an impressive well of knowledge. Debbie Lombardo See, your many hours of work to make this book and many others a success are appreciated beyond simple words. I'd like also like to thank the Keder Readers for their time and energy in reading each and every piece of fiction I release. As always, love and appreciation for my family worldwide.

"If you can't get rid of the family skeleton, you may as well make it dance."

—George Bernard Shaw

For all the families that are broken. May you find your pieces and your glue.

Characters

Lavender's World

Rose Ladieux–Lavender's adopted mother

Charles Ladieux–Lavender's adopted father

Minnie Ladieux–Lavender's sister and caretaker

Frances Ladieux–Lavender's eldest sister

Billy Nash–Frances' fiancé

Gavin Anders, Lavender's high school history teacher

Bryla Abernathy–Lavender's school friend

Mrs. Abernathy–Bryla's mother

Pastor Tompkins–the Pastor at The Church of the
   Woeful

Ralph–doorman at Lou Kowalski's Dance Hall

Mr. Morris–principal at the high school

Lou Kowalski–the owner of Lou Kowalski's Dance
   Hall

Jeannie Kowalski–Lou's daughter and Lavender's
   schoolmate

Lanie's World

Cosmo Hill–Lanie's husband-to-be and owner of
   Cosmic Cakes and Antiquery

Berit Campbell-Lanie's Sister

Marveline Pherson–owner of Sassy Lasses Winery

November Bean–Lanie's best friend

Piper Moonlight–a friend of Lanie and Cosmo's who runs Cosmo Cakes and Antiquery

Gladys Petrie–Lanie's elderly friend who runs Piney Falls Public Record

Boysie Lumquest–Gladys's son-in-law and the police chief in Piney Falls

Finnegan Lowery–owner of Cheese with Your Burger

Faythe Lowery–Finnegan's twin sister

Cedar Hill–Cosmo's sister

Royal Granger–Piney Falls local

Naybor Manor–previous owner of the Sassy Lasses Winery

CHAPTER ONE

The Wedding, Part One

Lanie Lavender Anders

AND

Cosmo Orion Hill

REQUEST THE PLEASURE OF THE
COMPANY
OF THEIR FAMILY-OF-CHOICE AND
CLOSEST FRIENDS
AS THEY CELEBRATE THE NEXT LEG OF
THEIR JOYOUS JOURNEY

AUGUST THE TWENTY-FIRST
FOUR O'CLOCK IN THE AFTERNOON

SASSY LASSES WINERY
228 NAYBOR WAY, PINEY FALLS
*IN LIEU OF GIFTS, DONATIONS TO PINEY
FALLS WOMEN'S SUCCESS CENTER WILL
BE APPRECIATED*

⫸⫸⫸⫷⫷⫷

"FORTY MINUTES PEOPLE! Look alive!" Marveline's assistant barks.

I pull the straps up on my ivory, lace-covered dress, thankful that I've not gained any weight – I actually lost five pounds – in these last nine, incredibly stress-filled months. Piper's friend Faythe did my makeup and I have to say, it's the best I've ever looked. There is a small, tasteful veil covering my head; something my friend, Gladys, insisted was necessary for every first-time bride, no matter how "long in the tooth" she appears. Wisps of my newly highlighted blonde, feathered bob peek out from underneath the veil on my forehead, just as we'd planned in our many dry runs.

The bouquet of lavender, roses, eucalyptus, and white hydrangeas sits on a small table in the bunkhouse's corner. This recently refurbished property is the home of our friend, Marveline Pherson, and rich in local history. A location with a few battle scars perfectly represents us as a couple. The historic property boasts some of the best views of rolling hills, and the gentle ocean breeze filters in to keep the temperature at a steady 68 degrees. If I were the type to fantasize about my wedding and at the place to have it, this would have been it.

"I never saw this for my brother. Never." Cosmo's sister, Cedar arrived from San Diego late last night though there are no signs of fatigue in her bright blue eyes. "You are every bit the fairy-tale ending he deserves."

I place my arms on her shoulders. "Growing up, I dreamed of having someone to share my secrets with. And now I have you. I'm so glad you're here, Cedar, to act as Cosmo's best person and to present us both at the altar."

"You'll have to show me your new property tomorrow. Cos has been telling me all about it. Speaking of which, I'd better go check on my brother. The last I'd heard, he was a mess. Blubbering like a baby." She giggles, squeezing my arm. "Hard to imagine our Cos so broken up, but that's what genuine love will do to a good man."

Though I don't have any biological family here, the residents of Piney Falls have become my family of choice. From my beautiful dress, to the flowers, to the cake, they've all pitched in. I can't wait to share this very special afternoon with them.

My best friend, November Bean, has been practicing for months to officiate our ceremony. She became ordained as the Goddess of *The Church of Stretch and Moan* in February, giving her five months to hone her skills. Today she's prepared a ten-minute speech on love and commitment that she very generously pared down from its original forty-six-minute form.

"Lanie, do you think I look alright?" Piper, Cosmo's second-in-charge at the bakery and my dear young friend has braided her rich auburn hair into intricate plaits that all come together on the top of her head to form a tight bun underneath her garland of white hydrangea flowers. The lavender, satin dress pulls in tightly at her waist and she has painted her nails a pretty shade of light purple to match.

"Just stunning, hon. Really." I kiss her lightly on the forehead. "You're still on board for our surprise later?"

"Oh, Lanie. Don't make me cry now. Faythe's already redone my makeup twice. The first time was after I saw how handsome Cos looks today." Piper wipes her cheek lightly, smearing the top layer of her makeup a little bit.

"Go see Faythe again and get a touch up." I look at my watch. Thirty minutes until I marry the man of my dreams. The man I didn't even know was in my dreams until the day we met. It all seems surreal.

I feel a tight grip on my shoulders. "Just thought I'd come back and see if you needed anything ahead of time. Nice that you took my advice and cut out the scones for a few weeks."

"Thank you, Gladys. You were right, as usual." I turn to see my octogenarian friend, who runs Piney Falls Public Records as well as the local gossip mill.

"I'm so touched you came, after you swore you wouldn't attend any events outside of the city limits." I take a step back to look at her. She's wearing a pale peach dress with a lace overlay, and her normally flyaway gray hair is curled and sprayed to perfection. "You look positively stunning, friend."

"Harrumph." She grunts. "Wanted to see how the new wheels felt on the highway. Besides, I was told there'd be food here. You promised."

"There is a tent set up on the other side of Naybor Manor. I'm sure they wouldn't mind if you snuck over and had a nibble ahead of time. Tell them I sent you."

Gladys turns to leave, but I catch her hand. "I just wanted to thank you again for coming. It touches my heart that you would come all the way out here for our wedding. I know it's a long drive and you're adjusting to that new car."

"Boysie did the driving. Guess you were plannin' on shenanigans if you invited the chief of police."

"He's a friend." There's no use arguing with Gladys. About anything.

Marveline Pherson, owner of the winery, approaches looking especially regal herself. Her flowing caftan – her normal attire – accented today by chunky gold earrings and a matching necklace. She is wearing deep red lipstick, making her large brown eyes appear dramatic.

"Lanie, we're thirty minutes from showtime. Is there anything you need? May I bring you a glass of wine? You're resplendent, dear."

Knowing Marveline doesn't hand out compliments with ease, I smile appreciatively and nod. "I'd love a glass of wine. Is everything on schedule?"

Marveline squeezes my arm. "Not to worry, dear. This isn't like one of your mysteries. I've instructed the chamber orchestra to begin playing in exactly five minutes."

Cosmo wanted a local blues band to play, so we compromised. They will play during the reception while the small chamber orchestra plays during the actual wedding so I can hear violins as I walked down the aisle.

"Guests are arriving and are being seated in the lawn area," she continues. "When you put me in charge, I took my duties seriously. This will go off without a hitch."

"Thank you, Marveline. I know we're in expert hands. It's just that, you know, with me there is always some kind of chaos that follows me around."

Marveline turns to walk away. "Not today, dear. I'm going to find you a glass of our Losmo Special Wedding Blend and I'll return shortly."

When she offered to have a wine bottled especially for our wedding, Cosmo thought it was too much. Marveline convinced us it was just as much for her enjoyment as ours.

"Twenty-four minutes, people, look alive! Howooo!" November Bean lets out a loud howl, startling Marveline's new assistant, the only other person left in the bunkhouse. I snap my head around quickly.

She didn't want me to see her outfit until today. Now I understand why. When I told her the colors were lavender, sage, and pale pink, she took it to heart. Her puffy-sleeved one-piece jumpsuit is bright green and purple, dotted with light pink flowers. Her frizzy hair is sculpted into a dramatic ponytail high upon her head; the ends plastered with hair product so they stand tall. Uncharacteristically, November Bean is wearing jewelry. Lots of it. Her neck has at least 18 chains wrapped around it, while bracelets of every color line her arms. Over the top of this ensemble, she is wearing a thick, striped robe of lavender, pink, and green. As per usual, her glasses frames her tortoiseshell glasses in purple and green.

After a moment of thinking, I sputter, "This is a – fresh – look for you!"

"I thought it was just the right amount of serious for this occasion." She says with satisfaction. "I did have some thoughts about my speech, though. Just a few notes–"

"Vem! You promised! We worked hard to get this down to ten minutes! Cos and I want it simple.

Just enough time to say our personalized vows before Gladys eats all of the appetizers in the reception tent."

She sighs. "You don't appreciate a well-done ceremony, Lanie. This is how it's performed professionally."

"Maybe today we keep it less formal? For all involved? What if you have to go to the bathroom and you're in the middle of that big speech? What then? How will you get out of all of your – finery?"

"Oh," she puts her finger to her chin. "I hadn't thought of that. I am on a schedule now. To prepare for the Marathon Howl class I'm going to teach next month. Yes, we'll stick to the original then." Vem pulls up a chair and sits down at my side, leaning in far too close. I can smell the garlic from the six helpings of linguini she enjoyed at our rehearsal dinner. "Are there any pre-wedding confessions you need to make? Get something deep and dark off your chest before your big moment? As the ordained Goddess of *the Church of the Stretch and Moan*, I'm here and ready to listen."

I giggle. "I think you already know all of my deep and dark. Especially after this past year. I do have a couple of favors to ask, though."

"Foot massage? I brought some squirrel dung just in case." She tugs at my leg, trying to move it to her lap.

"First, did you bring any of that wonderful homemade gum? You might want to try a piece before the ceremony. You know, to freshen up."

She opens up a pouch sewn into her robe. "Already on it. I brought three packs of Bev's Bodacious Birch Bark so I could warm up my jaw before the ceremony." She smiles with satisfaction. "What else?"

"Would you and Marveline's assistant step out and give me a few moments? To reflect a bit?"

Vem stands abruptly, causing my leg to flop to the ground. "Why didn't I think of this sooner! I should've made a chant for you! Do you want me to lead you in a moan? I have one for special occasions."

"No, thank you. Just give me a few minutes of peace, please."

Vem shrugs. "Okay. If that's what you want. I'll be counting down the minutes for everyone."

When I am alone and there is blessed silence, I turn back to the mirror, searching the face known for its uncanny resemblance to the famous actress, Tulip Sloan. Like me, she spent many years without a serious relationship. At first, by circumstance, and then by choice. Today, our paths diverge forever as I commit to a life with the other half of my soul.

For a minute, I think about my mother; a beauty in her own right. Every girl, no matter her age, wants her mother by her side on the most important day of her life. Lavender L. Anders should be here today, eyes shining, as her only child walks down the aisle. Instead, our relationship soured and her life ended tragically.

If only I'd understood then what I know now. In spite of my rocky start, I've become the strong woman my mother struggled to portray. "What did I do to deserve such luck?" I ask my reflection.

"You did quite a lot," a voice says from behind me. It's one I never thought I'd hear again.

"What are you doing here?" I gasp. "This is my wedding day. Can't this wait?" My eyes scan behind my reflection for a way out.

"Call it luck or fate, but there won't be any wedding today."

CHAPTER TWO

Lavender Ladieux
1944 – Tredford, Connecticut

"**Y**OU'RE SURE YOU *don't want to see her? Most people want just a glimpse."*

"No, darling. She's going to a suitable home. Just give her a kiss on the head and wish her well from me. I only hope that she keeps her name so that she understands the beautiful flower she is."

＞＞＞＜＜＜

LAVENDER LILAC, A squealing seven pounds of baby, arrived at 24 Melody Lane at approximately 4:00 p.m. on a blustery Saturday. Rose Ladieux, a statuesque, brunette woman with large features and a particularly long nose, closed the door and put the basket containing Lavender on the kitchen table. Her two equally brunette daughters, Minnie and Frances – ages, aged five and ten, respectively – eagerly hugged and kissed the discontented infant.

"Found her in front of the market. With a note

attached. 'Please take care of my babe.' So, I brought her home." Rose didn't bother to look her daughters in the eye.

"What will we call her, Mother?" Minnie asked. "She's so beautiful. Like a little flower." Minnie offered extra kisses to the top of her round head and gently ran her hand across her cheek.

"She already has a name. Lavender Lilac. That's the one given to her before she came to our charge, and that's what it will stay." Rose patted the baby's leg until she stopped fussing. "We won't be addressing the circumstances of her arrival with anyone. From now on, Lavender Lilac Ladieux is your little sister brought here by the heavens above."

Minnie and Frances both shook their heads dutifully. Their lives had been quiet up to this point: Sunday school; sewing lessons on Wednesday; and if they were extra good, roller skating on Friday nights. A little excitement in the Ladieux home might be a good thing.

"Will I be in charge of her, Mother? I can arrange my homework so I'm available to help you whenever needed. You know, I'll be taking a babysitting class soon in school," Frances asked earnestly.

"I'm old enough to help, too," Minnie added eagerly. "I know how to change a diaper. I watch our neighbor, Mrs. Chester, change Howard's diaper all the time. I want to try it."

Rose smiled. "I knew I could count on my girls. I suppose I'll be relying on you both. Taking care of a baby isn't easy, and I wasn't planning on doing it again. Your father and I were glad when the children in our household reached the age when you were self-sufficient. We do what we must. Remember that, girls. Always do what you must."

"Yes, Mama," they replied dutifully.

Charles Ladieux hung his hat beside the door at 5:15 p.m., sharp. He walked over to the basket and glanced at the new arrival. "So, this is it, then?" he remarked without emotion. "The new family member?"

Rose, who was at the stove warming up last night's pot roast, wiped her hands on her lace-edged apron and moved to her husband's side. "I'm sure she won't be a burden. The girls have already offered to help."

"Humph. We don't need more noise in this home. See that it's quiet." He turned and left the kitchen, headed for his office where he always spent approximately twenty minutes reading the afternoon paper before dinner. Rose slipped her fingers around the small, silver container in her pocket and took a sip, almost daring him to turn around. He didn't.

Lavender was exceptionally fussy at night. Not just the first night, but every night. "Stop that infernal racket!" Charles bellowed. Rose covered her ears, refusing to get up when she could take the exhaustion no longer. Minnie crept from bed, warming a bottle and feeding her sister without complaint. The next night, Frances did the same. Rose didn't argue.

Rose began writing notes to excuse Frances from some of her classes so she could come home and care for the baby in the afternoons. Rose took to her bed with her sick headaches and her remedy was a bottle of the cheapest Scotch found in Tredford. She knew just how long she had for the "cure" to take effect before her husband arrived home, expecting dinner.

As soon as Lavender could hold her head up, Minnie propped her up with pillows on the floor so she could watch while Minnie did her homework. By the time Lavender was ready for kindergarten, she thought of her sisters – especially Minnie – as her maternal figures. Charles barely acknowledged his biological children during his rare appearances with the family. Lavender was just another piece of furniture to him. When she reached her arms out begging for affection, he swatted her on the head with his newspaper. It was the way he treated the dog the girls had for a brief time, before he decided that, too, was a nuisance. The dog disappeared one day while the girls were at Sunday School.

Rose dropped her off on the first day of school with a sense of relief. As she turned to leave, the teacher grabbed her arm. "Mrs. Ladieux, the other parents are staying until their children are comfortable. Would you like to stay as well?" Rose shook her head. "The child will be fine without me. She's not that attached."

Another mother whispered, "Your daughter is stunning. She'll either be famous or get herself into real trouble." Rose paused for a moment. No one had ever commented on the beauty of her other two, big-boned daughters. "Ladies, your gossip is rude. The child is not responsible for her face any more than I am. She is not mine, you know."

"What a kind, caring woman you are. Taking in a foundling!" one woman remarked.

Rose sniffed. "We all do what we must. Remember that." She pivoted and left, tired of their nattering.

She spent the long morning going through Lavender's room. She removed everything that would make her think she was special because she looked different from the rest of the family. When it was time for Lavender to come home from school, all of her pink blankets and little-girl things had disappeared, and were replaced with Minnie's more grown-up hand-me-downs.

Lavender's eyes grew wide as she explored her drawers. "Where are my pink dresses and ruffly socks, Rose?" she asked.

"You don't need them anymore. You're grown. From now on, you'll wear whatever your sisters outgrew. Take care you don't eat so much they don't fit. You have the look of a child who will balloon easily. From now on, there will be no dessert for you."

When Rose left, Lavender cried into her pillow. She knew it wouldn't do any good to fuss and complain. If Charles heard her making noise when he came home, he would make her sit in the corner while they all ate. She vowed to never let herself feel that way again.

After a dinner of half-portions, she went to bed with her stomach growling. There was a knock on the door. "Lavender? I brought you something." Minnie entered, carrying two golden-brown cookies in one hand and a glass of milk in the other.

Lavender sat up and took both food and drink, devouring them eagerly.

"Take care you don't leave crumbs in the bed or Mother will find out. Then I can't bring you any-thing else." Minnie watched her delicately-featured sister gobble down with a touch of jealousy. She would never be called "clown nose" the way Minnie had in school.

Lavender nodded. "Minnie, could you tell me the story again? Of the woman who was a performer?"

"Oh, yes." Minnie leaned back and took hold of

one knee. "There was a beautiful woman who grew up in the poor section of Tredford. Lita Travers was her name. She had gold hair the color of yours and had the happiest childhood. She grew up and got a job in vaudeville as a magician's assistant, but she dreamed of becoming a famous actress. One day, a handsome man came to see her show and fell in love with her. They were married soon after, and Lita left her dreams behind. Instead, she threw herself into making sure the children of Tredford were just as happy as she had been. She started the first city park and gave money to the library. Poor Lita never became an actress, but just like mother says, 'We do what we must.' "She's famous now, for what she gave the community. Everyone knew and loved her."

"Did you know her?" Lavender finished one last bite of cookie as Frances wiped a milk mustache from her lip with the corner of her sheet.

"I didn't. I just know the story. Everybody does."

"That's what I'm going to do one day. I'm going to be an actress like Lita, but I won't marry a man and give up my dreams." Lavender smiled as her thoughts wandered off to somewhere much better, where she was universally loved.

"Lie down now," Frances commanded. "Did you say your prayers?"

Lavender scooched down in her bed and pulled the covers up tightly under her chin. "Yes. I remembered. I ended with, 'we do what we must.'"

"Yes, we do." Frances kissed the top of her head. "You'll be whatever you want, Lavender Ladieux. If I have anything to do with it, you'll grow into a woman of such power and wonder. People will stop and stare as you walk down the street. As long as you follow the rules, you'll grow up to be whatever you want to be."

"Thank you, Minnie," Lavender said as she began to drift off, comforted by the nightly affection of her sister.

CHAPTER THREE

Lavender Ladieux

1952

MELODY LANE WAS a clean, four-block area of square, two-story homes. The street was filled with well-to-do children who took their expensive toys onto well-manicured lawns and played quietly while their nannies hovered; with clean towels at the ready to remove any signs of childish mess.

"Mother, I'd like to play with the neighbor children. May I?" Lavender was a precocious eight-year-old girl with large, blue eyes and bouncy blonde hair.

"No, I think not." Rose stirred the onions she was preparing to add to their Friday night meal of liver-and-onions. "We're not like them. You'll not give them any ideas to the contrary."

"Why are we different, Rose? Because they have women to do their laundry and make their meals?" Lavender pulled a small, metal stool close to her mother and sat on the top step where she could watch closely as Rose cooked. She knew she wasn't allowed to stay long. Rose didn't want anyone staring when she took drinks from her flask.

"You know why, Lavender. Don't be impertinent. We're here because of the generous nature of a family member. That could end at any moment. We all do what we must." Rose stirred harder, bringing the flask to her lips for the first time in full view of her daughter. "You'll stop talking about the neighborhood children and you won't mention it again. Especially to your father."

"What is the child to keep from me?" a voice boomed from the doorway. A frigid blast of air made its way through the kitchen until it forced a chill down Lavender's back.

"The girl is asking foolish questions again." Rose sniffed. "Get down now, Lavender." She nudged the stool with her foot. "I have to finish cooking and speak with your father. You can sit in your room until you're called for dinner."

Lavender hopped down and moved the stool back to its spot in the corner, making sure she didn't look Charles in the eyes as she walked near him. Sometimes that made him particularly angry and she'd have to eat in her room, if at all.

Instead of going to her bedroom, she sat on the third step of the staircase, gazing, out over the sparsely furnished living room. A small couch and a single rocking chair barely took up a corner of the large, cold, living room space. The coal-heated room had a dusty smell and a film of black coating everything Rose left undusted. It always felt unhappy to Lavender, though she never knew why.

"She's a busybody is what she is. Always wanting to share our business with others. I wouldn't be surprised if she was sneaking over to the neighbors and telling them all about us. The other two were never like that. They knew our situation but had the sense to keep it to themselves."

"You spent more time caring for them, Rose. You've neglected your duties this go round," Charles admonished. "Teach her to be a young lady instead of spending your days in bed and you'll see better results." He loosened his tie and walked out of the kitchen, not waiting for a response.

Lavender scampered up the stairs as she thought guiltily about the friends she'd made during those long days when Minnie was helping at their new place of worship, The Church of the Woeful, and Frances was studying for her secretary exam. Two doors down at the Williams' palatial home, their maid brought her own daughter, Bryla to work with her during the summer months. Bryla was a loud girl with a bulbous, crooked nose; freckles; and a smile that enveloped her entire face. One day, Bryla recognized Lavender from the school playground. She was playing by herself in a neighboring yard and invited her over. The two soon became giggly, steadfast friends.

"Does your mother know you're out of sight?" Bryla's mother asked one day as she hung the family's wash on the line. "My mother has a sick headache. She locks the doors until 5:00 o'clock." Lavender replied. Bryla's mother took the wooden clothespin from her mouth. "What, now? She's got you running around the neighborhood all by yourself?"

Lavender nodded solemnly. She'd been to other homes before, collecting their kitchen scraps with the same face. It always worked.

"You come in and eat lunch with Bryla, then. The Williamses don't mind another mouth." Bryla's mother bent down to her level and pulled on either side of her dress; Minnie's from second grade. "Now I understand why these clothes are falling off you. We'll put some meat on those bones."

Lavender agreed happily. From that day on, she spent time with Bryla and her mother as often as possible. She hoped Rose wouldn't notice her new habits; Rose threatened to measure her waist every day to assure she hadn't been sneaking into the cupboard for food. Usually, she forgot.

Wearing Minnie's hand-me-downs wasn't that bad; luckily Minnie's physique was much thicker than hers, allowing space for lots of hidden desserts and meals from the soft-hearted cooks around the neighborhood.

Bryla didn't understand Lavender's strange parents and told her so. "Those people are just bananas," she'd remark, biting off another piece of her mother's warm cinnamon cookie. "Bananas."

The two girls became fast friends at school as well, giggling as they walked home every day. By the time they got two blocks away, Bryla had told her the same knock-knock joke over and over, until it was no longer funny. They'd say their goodbyes before Lavender headed to her oversized house, and Bryla walked down a different street leading to her tiny, two-bedroom home. Lavender's mouth fell into a straight line, removing all evidence of joy by the time she reached her porch steps. She was somber enough to be a Ladieux.

Understanding how important it was to have Bryla in her life, Lavender began to wonder about her sister's social world. "Minnie, do you have friends?" she asked one day.

"Yes, I do."

"Why don't you go play with them? Don't you want to laugh and be silly? I've heard Frances with her friends before." Their older sister whispered with her companions in her bedroom; taking care the friends were gone before Charles walked in the door.

Minnie touched her recently-acquired hair ribbon. "I don't need friends, really. I'm much too busy with The Church of the Woeful and school. Don't you like me to be here with you?"

Lavender felt embarrassed for asking. "No, I appreciate that you're always taking care of me. But you should have friends, too. We should both have friends. Mother wouldn't notice if you left during one of her sick headaches and spent some time with Cathie."

Minnie blushed. "How do you know about Cathie?"

"I've seen you talking to her at lunch, under that tree. Your eyes light up when you two are gossiping."

"Lavender Lilac Ladieux, I don't know how you find the time to gawk at me, what with all the boys chasing you. Honestly, if Mother or Father knew of your behavior, it would appall them. And I will not sneak out. You push things to the limit. One of these days, you'll get caught and be in real trouble," she scolded.

Lavender's eyes teared up. "I'm sorry. I can't help it. I try to act like everyone else in the family, but it never quite fits me."

Minnie kissed the top of her head. "Don't display your emotions now. Mother will be down for dinner soon, and you know how she gets annoyed when you're being dramatic."

She tried, for the rest of the week, to be good. To play with the boring girls at recess and ignore the boys pulling her braids and begging her to chase them. She didn't sneak out while Minnie was doing her homework and Rose was resting.

After seven days, she could take the stifling boredom no more. She quietly crept out the back door and ran to the Williams' home. Spicy smells emanated from the kitchen.

"I'm so happy to see you, princess," the cook, Mrs. Rossi, said in her thick, Italian accent when Lavender knocked at the back door. "Spaghetti and meatballs tonight. You wait to test the first batch, no?"

Lavender nodded eagerly. She watched with wonder as the cook rolled out the noodles and cut them into strips, before placing them in boiling water. Her mouth watered when the simmering sauce was placed on freshly made pasta.

"You like?"

Lavender smiled eagerly and didn't complain when a second helping was placed in front of her. She looked up, belly full, and realized her friend was nowhere to be found.

"Where's Bryla?" she asked as the cook wiped her face on her apron.

"Downstairs with her mama. Helping sort the Williams' old clothes for the poor. It's getting dark.

You should go home before your own mama wonders where you might be."

Lavender looked up at the clock. Half-past five. Dinner was at five-thirty and there was no way Rose hadn't missed her absence. She jumped down from the table. "Thank you, Mrs. Rossi." She ran all the way home despite the sick-sloshing feeling in her stomach. While she was an expert at making up stories to remove herself from sticky situations, this one would be hard to explain.

She stood at the back door for a moment, thinking about her speech. Like a speech Lita would give in an imaginary movie Lavender had never seen because movies weren't allowed. "I'm so sorry," she announced. "I saw a butterfly and followed it into another yard."

There was no smell of boiled meat and spiceless side dishes. Only the scurrying of feet. Frances frowned when she saw her sister. "I'm packing for Rose. You'll need to go up and hold her hand until Father arrives." When Lavender looked at her helplessly, Frances pushed her back slightly. "Mother needs us all to pull together. Don't give me any back-talk. Go sit with her now."

Lavender trudged up the stairs, half-wondering if this was a new type of punishment she hadn't yet encountered. She opened the door to Rose's room and the familiar scent of alcohol mixed with vomit hit her nostrils. Her stomach wanted to release everything she had just consumed, but instead she swallowed hard and sat on the bed next to her mother.

"I'm here, Rose – Mother," she said as sweetly as she could muster. "To be your comfort."

Rose's eyes fluttered. When she opened them fully, she gasped. "Sister? You're here to torment me? Haven't I shouldered enough of your burden?"

Lavender had experienced this before. Apparently sick headaches caused Rose to become forgetful of her circumstances and just who was with her in the room. "It's me, Lavender. I'm here to sit with you until Father comes home."

Rose looked around the room and again at Lavender. She rubbed her face and then took Lavender's hand in hers. "I thought you were someone else. Sit beside me."

Lavender moved onto the bed, trying to find a spot that wasn't damp from her mother's sweat and tears.

"Do you know what it is to want your sister's love but never receive it? Your whole life, devoted to someone who pretends you don't exist."

Lavender thought for a moment. Frances and Minnie treated her lovingly. More so than either Charles or Rose. "I don't think so," she said quietly.

"Of course, you don't. I gave you everything you

could want. Including sisters. I'm speaking of my sibling."

"I didn't know you had a sister," Lavender replied. "Have we met her?"

Rose sniffed. "No, child. You've never met. My sister has lived a grand life. Far too grand for us to imagine. She was quite young when she went out on her own, and we've only kept in touch by post. We had different mothers but the same father. Throughout her life, she never told a soul I existed. I was the secret."

For the first time, Rose was treating her as something other than a nuisance. She was more like a friend. "Tell me more about your sister."

"There's not much more that can be told without betraying a confidence. I confessed my heart and soul to her in our letters, hoping that one day she would do the same. Instead, she left me with a burden that I promised to bear without complaint. Instead of a sisterly bond, that was my reward." Rose reached for a tissue and Lavender handed her the last one in the box. She blew her nose hard as Lavender rubbed her shoulders, just as Minnie did for Lavender when she was feeling bad.

"She doesn't deserve you. You're too good for someone to treat you so poorly."

Rose blew her nose once again and then looked up at Lavender's face. Her expression was one of wonderment and then anger. She slapped the girl hard across the cheeks, leaving bright red marks. "Don't speak of my sister that way. She did her best. And we all have to do what we must, especially for our families. It is a sense of duty and nothing more or less. Never forget that."

Lavender put her hand to her face, feeling the sting both inside and out.

Rose took a sip of her drink and sat up in her bed. "You know, you are like her in one way: far too pretty for a girl of your youth. Pretty girls always find trouble. If you were homely like your sisters, you would be on the path of a sensible life. A nice, boring man would marry you and give you a decent life." She set her drink on her bedside table and stared at Lavender again, this time with pity. "Instead, you'll always be the object of troubled men. They'll chase you and turn your head, but they won't want anything to do with you when your little mind becomes completely focused on them."

Lavender didn't entirely understand her mother. Not just today, but ever. She spoke in riddles that didn't make sense to a young girl's mind. "Yes, Mother," she replied dutifully.

There was a knock at the door, and Charles entered. Lavender's shoulders sagged with relief. She stood up quickly, placing Rose's hand by her side. "She's feeling sad about her sister. I was just here to comfort her until you came home."

Charles laid his suit coat on the bed and looked at Lavender with surprise. "You know about her sister?"

"I told the child about my sister's unwillingness to establish our bond. That's all. Come sit with me, Charles." She opened her arms to her husband, who lowered his body beside the bed and patted his wife awkwardly on the shoulder. He turned to stare at the girl coldly. "You can go now, Lavender. You're not needed. I'll tend to Rose."

A small part of Lavender wanted Rose to protest, to tell Charles to go away so she could tell her youngest child more of her secrets.

"When is the funeral?" Charles asked as she slowly pulled the door shut. She stood outside, trying to listen further. Rose never mentioned her sister had died.

"On Friday. I'll go by myself. Don't worry, they assured me we'll be well compensated in the will. That will also cover my train and lodging expenses."

Lavender jumped when she felt a hand on her shoulder. "You shouldn't listen outside of their door!" Frances said harshly.

"Her sister died!" Lavender exclaimed, hoping she was the one for once who bore the knowledge others didn't.

Frances sighed. "Our aunt has been our benefactor for years. I'm hoping we don't have to move to a smaller home now that we don't have her support."

"Move?" Lavender asked with concern. "Where would we go?"

CHAPTER FOUR

Lavender Ladieux
January, 1959

T HERE WOULD BE nothing extraordinary about her 15th birthday. At least there shouldn't have been. Lavender's older sister, Minnie, was tailoring clothes part time for the next-door neighbor when she wasn't volunteering at The Church of the Woeful, and didn't have time to make a cake. Frances, who lived in a boarding house, completed secretarial school and completed secretarial school for Dr. Nash. The handsome young doctor was also her beau. She promised Lavender she would stop by later in the week with a gift.

Charles moved out five days prior. He sat the girls down together on the couch, the three of them barely fitting now that they were grown women. "I can't stand your mother's constant weeping. A man needs peace in his home. I'll be packing up my things and moving out. Perhaps I'll come by for some of Frances' homemade pie when the cherries are ripe."

Minnie and Lavender sat emotionless as Charles began filling his large suitcase with things they assumed were family possessions. "Please don't leave the family," Frances begged. "We all need you. Especially the younger two. Your influence is important to them."

Neither Minnie nor Lavender had spent much time with Charles. They looked at the floor.

"There will be someone coming by to take the furniture in two days' time." Charles put his raincoat over his arm and looked at Frances. "Marry that suitor of yours and you'll be fine." He turned towards his middle daughter. "Minnie, look after your mother." With that, he walked out of their lives, not bothering to leave Lavender with any sage words of advice. Two days later, men arrived to remove all but two dining room chairs and the table, making the main floor appear even more devoid of human inhabitants.

It didn't take long for news of his departure to make its rounds in Tredford. The high school was abuzz with the news the following Monday when Lavender arrived. By Wednesday, it was all anyone could talk about. They stared as she walked down the hall, but no one said a word to her face. Not even Bryla. Mr. Anders, an enthusiastic young teacher with daringly long hair and mischievous brown eyes, kept an eye on her throughout class. She could see other students passing notes, and she knew they were about her. She wished he'd be watching them instead of her.

"Would you mind staying after class today, Miss Ladieux?" he asked, as all the students got up to leave. Well known to the student body was Mr. Anders' deep concern for girls who came from unfortunate homes. Last school year he helped junior Helen Beauregard find a new place to live when her family up and left town without her. Lavender hated that she was now in that category. She stood and waited patiently at his desk, trying to think of something much more important she needed to do.

Mr. Anders reached into the locker he used for his personal items. "I've got a surprise for you today, Lavender," he said. "Please pull your chair over to my desk."

"Oh?" she responded uncomfortably. "What would that be?" She straightened her blouse and tapped her foot nervously. "Surprises" for Lavender usually meant finding Rose's vomit in the bathroom, or strange women looking for Charles.

He walked across the room – his arms wobbly – as he carried a lopsided vanilla cake. The frosting looked as though it had melted in some kind of terrible kitchen fire, and was spread haphazardly on the cake. There was one large candle in the middle. He set it carefully on his desk and looked at her sheepishly.

"This is for you. I made it last night. It was my first attempt at a cake – I'm not a baker, but I knew you would appreciate it either way."

Her eyes darted back and forth between Mr. Anders and the cake. "You did that for me?"

She wondered which of the rumors warranted the cake: that her mother was a drunk confined to her bedroom, or that Charles had left them virtually penniless? Maybe Bryla would tell her later.

"I don't know what to say," she continued awkwardly. "It's very kind of you, Mr. Anders."

"Shall we enjoy a piece and celebrate your birthday? I brought silverware from home, too. If you'll excuse me–" He gently reached to open a drawer in his desk. which was close to her leg. She couldn't help it, she shivered when his hand touched her.

Mr. Anders put two plates on the desk and began cutting the cake. "Oh, no. I forgot to sing. Would you like me to sing?"

"Please don't," she begged, knowing there were still students roaming the halls.

He chuckled as he dumped a large slice on the plate in front of her. "I know. Teasing you, of course."

There was something about him that drew her in. She couldn't quite put her finger on it. She mused over whether it was his eyes that seemed so much deeper than any of the boys in her class, or his scraggly beard that Charles would have found offensive, or just that he smelled like no one she had encountered before.

She put a piece in her mouth and chewed slowly, though her stomach was making noises and she wanted to devour the entire cake. She crunched down something hard, maybe an egg shell. "I don't know what to say, Mr. Anders. It's wonderful. Just like my sister, Frances, would make."

"I hope you don't mind having some of your cake. I've been curious how my creation would turn out and if in fact it would be edible."

"Please do!" She regretted that as soon as it came out of her mouth. One thing Rose told her during moments of clarity was never to appear too eager around men. Especially older men.

"Is Rose still taken to her bed?" He put a small bite in his mouth, just the way Lavender thought he might.

"Yes. She doesn't feel well most of the time. Sick headaches." She didn't bother telling him that she was only actually sick when she didn't have alcohol on hand.

"And what about Minnie? How is she doing these days? She was never my student, but I heard good things about her."

"She's doing clerical work at The Church of the

Woeful. She thinks Pastor Tompkins is the best thing since sliced bread, so he's all she talks about."

Mr. Anders laughed. "Easily swayed by a handsome face, I'd wager."

He set his fork down gently and his face became serious. "Are you doing alright? You and Minnie and your mother? I don't want you to lose sight of the road ahead, even with your troubles at home. I have faith that you'll continue to turn in your assignments and graduate with your class, you know."

"Oh, I'm going to become a Hollywood star. Just like Lita Travers was going to. My sister used to tell me all about her."

Mr. Anders nodded and crossed one leg over the other. "You're pretty enough. You look just like Doris Day. Have you seen any of her movies?"

Lavender shook her head. "When Ch – my father was living with us, he didn't allow us to see movies. Now that he's gone, there won't be money for that, I suppose. Our house is dreary most days." Her face was somber. "When I'm up on the big screen, we'll have lots of money."

"Lavender, I must tell you that the story of Lita is just legend. People have been passing that around since I was a young man. Someone made up that story when they wanted to collect donations to build the new city park, so they created an admirable character to root for. She's not an actual person."

"What?" she looked at him, incredulous. "That can't be. My sister wouldn't lie. Minnie doesn't know how to tell a lie. Believe me, I've tried to teach her."

He laughed, covering his mouth like he wished it hadn't come out. "Your sister probably doesn't know it's a tall tale made up by an enterprising fellow, I suppose. The next time you have library time – that you don't skip –" he put his chin down and looked at her admonishingly, "try to look up this Lita person. You'll see she's not there. I'm afraid we've all become victims of this fantasy at one time or another."

Lavender displayed a strained smile, not daring to let him know how horrible she felt on the inside.

"You should think about secretary school, like your sister. Your typing teacher tells me you are above the other girls in proficiency."

"Yes, sir," she replied dully. "Your cake was lovely, Mr. Anders. I should get home now. My mother may need me."

As she walked home by herself, she thought about his words. She'd spent many nights avoiding the growls of her stomach, and the screaming matches between Charles and Rose, by fantasizing about Lita. It got her through her childhood years.

"Hey you," she felt a bump on her shoulder and a tug at her carefully coifed hair that, today, she'd styled in a victory roll like she'd seen a neighbor wearing.

She never dared show anger around her friend, Bryla. Even though they spent all of their time together, there was something dangerous about this girl. She smoked cigarettes and made out with boys. She was the one who taught Lavender to skip class. "Hi, Bryla. Did you know that Lita Travers isn't a real person?"

Her broad-shouldered friend shook her short, chestnut-brown ponytail. "Of course I did, Fancy Pants. Everybody knows. It's just a story someone made up to feel better about themselves. Nobody exciting ever came from this stupid town. Wait, you didn't think it was real, did you? I never figured you for a chump."

"No, of course not," Lavender sighed. "Nobody important comes from this town," she echoed her friend.

"I want to do something special for your birthday. Can you sneak out tonight?"

Lavender thought for a moment. Minnie would be at The Church of the Woeful for choir practice until at least 9:00 p.m. Rose wouldn't be out of bed all evening. "I can do that."

"Wear your nice skirt. The one without any patches."

Lavender smoothed her dress and stared at the

ground.

Bryla shrugged. "I didn't mean to offend you, Fancy Pants. Just to say that you only have a few nice outfits. That's one of them. Come to my house at seven." Bryla kissed her on the cheek as they reached the crossroad, one way leading to the massive properties on Melody Lane and the other leading to Bryla's neighborhood of modest homes.

Minnie prepared a fine meal of beef goulash and peas. It was Lavender's favorite. But tonight, she could hardly eat; excited to see what daring plan Bryla had in store for them.

Minnie slid a small gift in front of Lavender, wrapped in brown paper. "It's not that much. Frances has something else from both of us that you'll get later in the week."

Lavender pulled the string and opened the package to find an evergreen paisley blouse with puffed sleeves and a big bow at the neck. "Oh, Minnie – It's wonderful! It's just like what the other girls in school wear!" She kissed her sister on the cheek, and held the blouse up to her body. "How does it look?"

"You must try it on first, silly," Minnie playfully scorned. "You deserve something new. And with Mother's sickness being as bad as it is these days, she'll never notice." Minnie's features resembled Rose more and more as she aged. Same long nose, same dull brown hair. There was nothing special about her looks; painfully obvious to Minnie when she was around her younger sister.

Lavender began clearing the dinner dishes. "Leave those," Minnie ordered. "I'll get them after choir practice. Everyone ought to feel special for one night."

Minnie long ago gave up trying to force Lavender to go to The Church of the Woeful with her. The boys stared at Lavender there just as much as they did at school and she realized, somewhat ashamed, that she was jealous.

Lavender felt a little guilty, waiting for her sister to leave the house so she could run off into the night. She pulled her coat, or rather Minnie's coat from high school, tightly around her waist. She could almost wrap it around her body twice. The strange fit felt comfortable, no matter how much she was teased at school by the girls who were jealous of her looks. Luckily, she had Bryla to put them in their place if they got too out of hand.

When she got to the back of Bryla's one-story, tan house, she knocked lightly at the window she knew to be the room that Bryla shared with her cousin. When she heard nothing, she knocked again.

"Boo!"

Bryla was standing behind her, smelling of sickly-sweet perfume, and wearing her mother's tall heels.

"You look so different! Are we going somewhere

fancy?"

Bryla pulled Lavender's coat away from her body to inspect her. "Is that a new blouse?"

"Mmhmm. Minnie made it for me."

"Aces! You'll do just fine. My friend is picking us up down the block. We should go before my dad hears us. We don't want to be late."

CHAPTER FIVE

Lavender Ladieux
January, 1959

"THANKS, CAL!" BRYLA'S senior friend dropped them off at the front door of a nondescript, grey building outside of town. Behind the building, a lake shimmered in the evening moonlight.

"That's Strange Lake. You've never been, I assume?" Bryla tossed her coat over one shoulder, knowing full well that Lavender went nowhere without her.

Lavender shook her head.

"All the kids come out here to swim every summer. Practically the entire town. It's so sad Charles never let you experience a town tradition. The Ladieux house must be like living on the moon."

"Charles thought it was crude, and women shouldn't display themselves in public like that." Lavender suddenly felt very out of place. As much as she craved something different, right now all she could think of was her warm bed, and the familiar smells of alcohol and dust.

"C'mon," Bryla motioned. "You're supposed to be eighteen to get in, but I've got a friend who works the door. Ralph's a good guy. He'll be especially happy to see you; Mr. Kowalski wants as many pretty girls on the floor as he can get." She grinned at her friend and pinched her cheeks.

"Ouch!" Lavender was used to her friend's rough ways, but every once in a while, they caught her off guard. "Why'd you do that?"

"To make it look like you're wearing rouge, silly. You're so green behind the ears, Fancy Pants."

They walked together up to the door where a serious-looking young man stood with his arms crossed. He shone a flashlight in their direction. "I'll need to see some identification, please."

"I can identify things on you that shouldn't be mentioned in public!" Bryla snapped.

"Bry? 'Sthat you?" He squinted until they came close enough for him to view them under the lone light on the building.

"Yes, it's me. And my friend–" she paused, staring at Lavender momentarily. "Lita."

"She don't look eighteen to me," Ralph eyed her suspiciously.

Lavender adjusted her new blouse self-consciously.

"She's a young eighteen. Look at her." Bryla

grabbed her shoulders and pushed her toward Ralph. "How many boys'll be buying dance tickets to take a turn on the floor with this one and her movie star face?"

"Hmm." Ralph looked her up and down.

Lavender felt like a piece of meat. Not like she did with the boys at school, whom she shoved aside when they made crude comments. She felt trapped. "It's okay, I can wait out here for you, Bryla."

Ralph smiled broadly. "This one looks like Hollywood alright. A ringer for Miss Doris Day. Let's hear you sing a tune."

"I – don't–" Lavender stammered.

"He's just joshin' ya, Fancy Pants. Move it, Ralph. I'll give you a cut tonight if we get good tips."

The boy moved aside and Lavender walked into a new world. The joyous space was full of men and women, laughing and hugging. At the far end of the room was a small stage with a banner above it that read Lou Kowalski's Dance Hall. There was a band on the stage; seven men with various instruments waiting for their cue.

When they began playing, the place really came to life. Those who were laughing and talking, jumped to their feet and began swinging their hips back and forth. Skirts swirled in colorful rhythm as women lost themselves in the music. Men moved in compliment, pushing the women away and then daringly pulling them back in, so excitingly close Lavender could feel the electricity from where she was standing.

"C'mon!" Bryla motioned with her hand. The two women found their way to the coat check where they left their coats, and each was given a number to pin on her shirt.

"What's this for?" Lavender asked as Bryla pinned a number to her chest.

"Each of these bruisers buy tickets. When they find someone they want to dance with, they give that girl their ticket. At the end of the night, we turn in our tickets for money."

"They're going to pay to dance with us?" Lavender asked, horrified.

"That's how we make money! I'm doing you a favor, Fancy Pants!" Bryla grabbed her friend's shoulders. "If he's real sweet on you, he'll give you money directly. A 'tip' they call it. It's nothing serious. Just fun and games." Lavender's face still portrayed uncertainty. "Try it for a dance or two," her friend said reassuringly. "If you don't like it, we'll go home. I promise."

Lavender remembered Bryla's friend telling her he'd be back at ten. "I'll try one dance. But then I'll just wait outside. You can enjoy yourself."

A man of at least twenty in a sailor suit tapped on Bryla's shoulder. "Wanna dance?" he asked. She looked back at her friend. "You're silly, Fancy Pants. You wanted excitement. I brought you excitement." The man tugged on her arm and she walked with him toward the dancers before shouting back, "At least try it!"

Lavender watched the dancers in awe. She'd never seen so much energy before. It made her feel guilty–for watching, and for enjoying it. She felt a tap on her shoulder. When she turned around, a handsome, brown-eyed man in a wool suit stood before her. "Would you like to dance, Miss?" he asked shyly.

"I – I don't know how," she stuttered.

"That's okay. I'll teach you!" He took her to the center of the room where everyone was throwing their arms up in the air, then alternately down to the floor, on the downbeats. She began copying them. The next dance came on and the movements were more complicated. Lavender stood still while others moved around her. "Watch me!" the man commanded.

He rotated his hips around and around and then grabbed her hand, twirling her so fast the room spun. She felt her skirt rising in the breeze they created. Lavender's heart beat like it wanted to pop out of her chest.

"You're getting it!" he said enthusiastically.

When the song ended, he clapped for her. "Very

good! I'm Steven, by the way. I believe I owe you another ticket."

Lavender felt her cheeks. They were hot. "That's alright, sir. It was a joy for me. My name is Laven – Lita."

Steven put his finger in the air and disappeared for a moment before returning with two glasses of punch. He handed one to her, and they moved away from the center of the room as a slower dance was beginning.

"I haven't seen you here before. I think I'd remember a goddess like you, Lita."

None of the boys who gave attention to her at school said such things. It was always a derogatory remark about her body. She was much more developed than the other girls in her grade.

"This is my first time. Today is my eighteenth birthday, so my friend brought me," she said, remembering their ruse.

"Oh, my. A birthday girl. Well, you shall have a gift worthy of your extreme beauty, then." He pulled a one-dollar bill out of his pocket and handed it to her. "There's more of that if you promise to return next week. This dull building is brighter for your presence." He kissed her lightly on the cheek and walked away.

Before she could process this act of kindness, another man tapped on her shoulder. This time, he was at least a foot taller than she was, with hair slicked back the way Charles' was when he went to The Church of the Woeful socials. "May I have this dance?" he asked in a deep voice.

"Of course." Lavender was halfway through their jitterbug when she began thinking about ways to sneak out the next weekend; how she might procure a ride. The next man gave her two dollars.

By 10:00 p.m., Lavender Ladieux had accumulated fourteen dollars and sixty-four cents in tips. One man only had change in his pocket, but he, too, promised to bring more if she would return to the dance hall the following weekend.

Bryla, face flushed, found her friend as the lights came up for the band's break. "I know your sister's waiting at home, and my friend won't wait forever in the parking lot. Did you have fun?"

Lavender nodded eagerly. "I'm sorry I didn't trust you. This was more fun than I've ever had. Dancing is stupendous."

Bryla threw her head back in laughter. "Oh, you're a pill, Fancy Pants. C'mon. Let's get our coats."

"Bryla? Who's your friend?" An older, balding man covered in sweat and dark, fuzzy hair blocked their exit.

"Oh, hi, Mr. Kowalski. This is Lita. She wanted to see what all the fuss and muster was about."

"Your friend want a job?" He looked directly at Bryla.

Bryla raised her eyebrows. "I doubt Lita wants to wash dishes. She does plenty of that at home. Plus, getting out here from town is a real bear."

"Not askin' for a dishwasher."

His low, gravelly voice had a rhythm to it Lavender had never heard before. Like he was trying to rhyme without using words that rhymed.

"Just what are you asking, sir?" Lavender asked.

"Had three men come up to me tonight and tell me they'd never seen anyone as pleasant as you. Said you were like a movie star. This joint could use some class." He stared over the top of Lavender's head. "My best girls get paid by the hour, not the dance. You'd be making two dollars an hour. Then I'd give you half the tips. That's more'n anyone in town will pay a girl. Secretaries only make seventy-five cents an hour."

"We'll have to discuss this, Mr. Kowalski. Won't we, Lita?" Bryla took Lavender by the arm and walked her out the door.

"Why'd you do that?" Lavender protested. "He was offering me a lot of money!"

"There're rumors about Mr. Kowalski. That he does all sorts of bad things in his back room. I need to make sure you're safe before we agree to this deal. I can't always be watching you, ya know, kid!"

Lavender barely made it in the back door of her home before Minnie walked in the front. She rushed upstairs and pulled the covers tight over her body.

Minnie knocked on her door. "Are you still awake?" She sat on the side of Lavender's bed. "Pastor Tompkins remembered your birthday. Isn't he amazing?"

Lavender smiled, wanting only to lie in bed and think about the fun she'd had.

"He wants you to know you're old enough to babysit now. You could take care of the three- and four-year-old's during our weekly service. He'd even pay you: fifty cents an hour! What a wonderful opportunity for you, Lavender! Just think! Your own spending money!"

CHAPTER SIX

Minnie Ladieux

1959

MINNIE LADIEUX WENT to bed promptly at 8:30 p.m. every evening, after brushing her teeth for thirty-two seconds and washing her face for fifteen. All of this gave her plenty of time to lie in bed and re-read all the verses of Pastor Tompkins' *Words We Live By*. All one hundred sixty-eight pages filled with his wisdom, songs, and important messages for young ladies only.

She read, for the third time, Chapter Two: *The Respectable Lady Finds Favor in Our Kingdom*. Brushing her hair exactly seventy-four times every night seemed a bit excessive, but who was she to question the wisdom of Pastor Tompkins? Smiling as she spoke on the phone was easy. She'd learned to put on a sunny face no matter what was happening at home. At first, it was for her little sister. Poor little Lavender was too young to be without a father, and it was clear she thought it was something she'd done.

Pastor Tompkins always said how much he admired Minnie; taking care of her home and raising her sister at such a young age, all while going to school and working. She confessed to him early on that her mother was quite ill and required extra care. She mentioned nothing about Charles, but she assumed everyone in the congregation knew of his situation since he hadn't been seen there since he left Melody Lane.

The first night Minnie heard her sister sneaking out, she assumed it was Rose, trying to find her way to the bathroom. The girls had long since given up trying to get her to stop drinking. Instead, they grudgingly brought her alcohol and food, most days pretending she didn't exist. When they heard the clunk of her falling in the bathroom, they waited to hear her getting back up before reacting. "Do you need something, Rose?" Minnie called half-heartedly. Not hearing anything in return, she continued her nightly routine.

The more often the noises came, the more Minnie pretended they didn't exist. Just like everything else in the Ladieux household, she could mold her thoughts to be whatever she wanted, as Pastor Tompkins reminded his congregation weekly.

One day, as they pulled weeds together in the backyard, Lavender made a bold statement. "I know you don't like to speak about him, but I don't think we'll see Father again. He promised he'd come back to visit Frances, and he's not been here in over a year. Rose doesn't seem to care."

Minnie wiped her brow with her free hand. "Pastor Tompkins says a woman should never question the ideas of the man in her home. He's been given knowledge far beyond what a woman's mind can hold. Charles needed a break, but he'll return when the time is right."

"I used to hear him through the walls, telling Rose he didn't love her anymore and she smelled stale like a – like a – still. I don't know what that is, but I know it's not the way a woman should smell. He said her sister had provided a pleasant life and that we could all still share the money, but he didn't want to be here ever again."

"Well," Minnie sat down next to her pile of weeds and took her sister's hand, "that isn't the kind of talk a young girl should be worrying herself about. Pastor Tompkins says women will find happiness only if they immerse themselves in their daily routine." She sighed. "Rose has always struggled to do that. That's why she's so glum. That's not us, though. We're two balls of sunshine, now, aren't we?" She playfully poked Lavender in the stomach and they both giggled.

Secretly, Minnie wasn't so sure they would survive. With what Charles was taking from their monthly income, there was barely enough for all three of them live. She was going to ask Pastor Tompkins for more work.

Minnie loved her time spent at The Church of the Woeful. She could organize the office and work by herself with little interference. Pastor Tompkins always complimented her on her grooming skills. That was enough for Minnie. She spent hours each morning winding her hair into the twenty-nine tight curls, before donning the pea-green skirt and white blouse required of her position. For the church elders to recognize that she followed every single mandate meant the world to her.

It was the Sunday that the pastor gave his sermon on the importance of an exemplary mother that things really hit home for Minnie. It was the cornerstone of The Church of the Woeful's philosophy. Pastor Tompkins worshipped his mother, who refused to attend his sermons because her son made up nonsense. But that didn't stop him from praising her every action as a mother from the day he could remember. In fact, his book, *Words We Live By* used direct quotes from his mother.

Pastor Tompkins told everyone that, without a good foundation, a woman could never achieve what she was created to do. "It's never too late to fix that broken foundation." He looked directly at Minnie and winked. Boldly. "Now is the time to gather all you can from your blessed mother figures. They all want to know they are needed and you precious women fill that for them. Don't hesitate."

Pastor Tompkins never gave flawed advice, so Minnie rushed home from church without even pausing for the post-service vanilla twirl cookies and black tea. His words found their place in her mind and she knew what to do. Rose needed purpose. If not for her own sake, then at least for Lavender's. The child still needed her. The closer she got to her home, the more clearly she saw her life. The noises she'd been hearing at night, she knew exactly what they were.

She knocked on Rose's door, mentally preparing herself for the sights and smells she would soon encounter. She had no idea if Rose had bathed this week.

"Mother?" she asked timidly. There was no answer, so she boldly stepped in a little farther. She could hear her mother's heavy breathing in the dimly lit room. She tiptoed to the bed and touched the lump under the blankets. When she received no response, she shook it until she received a response.

"Mother, I know that you're not feeling well at present, but I need your advice," she said bravely. "I think that our Lavender is doing things that she shouldn't. I think that she may be sneaking out and spending time with a gentleman. That is my assumption, because she smells like – Well, she smells like you when she comes home."

There was a grunt and then some movement from the lump in the bed. Rose's feeble hand appeared from the top of the covers and she pushed them down. Minnie gasped at the sight of her mother's haggard face. Even more pale and worn than the last time she'd seen it unobstructed.

"Hmmm?" Rose came to life slowly. "What is it you want, child?" she said in the gravelly voice of someone who hadn't spoken for days.

"I came in to ask you about our Lavender. I'm doing my best to see that she is a proper young lady. But sometimes, she needs a firm hand. And that isn't something I'm good at."

"Of course she needs a firm hand!" Rose said. "She was always trouble. I did my best with her, but you'll see, the troublesome types always end up on the wrong side of life. It's a pity Charles didn't take more of an interest."

Minnie crossed her legs. "Please don't say that about her. It's not her fault that Charles left. You know it's fine that he's gone, really. We are much better off without him."

Rose smiled slightly and grunted. Or maybe she was laughing. It was very hard for Minnie to remember how the old Rose used to react to things. "I wasn't prepared to take on another child –

especially that one. Charles said it was a mistake, but I didn't listen."

"It was awfully kind of you to adopt our sister," Minnie said soothingly. "I suppose she's just acting like every other girl her age. If I'm going to be honest, I had those sorts of inclinations myself but despite that, I started going to The Church of the Woeful." She was beginning to regret her impulsive decision to speak with Rose.

"I don't think going to church is going to save you, Minnie," Rose said bluntly. "You're practically doomed to repeat my mistakes. Poor dear." She reached out and grabbed for Minnie's hand, but Minnie instinctually pulled it back.

When she remembered why she was there in the first place, she put her hand beside her mother's. "I do need some advice though, Mother. I think Lavender has been seeing men for quite some time. How do I put a stop to it?"

Rose abruptly sat upright in her bed, frightening Minnie and making her jump backwards. The stench of her unwashed body quickly filled the room.

"She's going to end up in a family way," Rose said matter-of-factly. "That's how things work for those types. That's how things worked with her mother, and that's why I ended up with her."

"What do you mean? You told us you found her at the market with a note attached. That's what you said." Minnie had always known, deep down.

Rose shook her head. "I couldn't tell you the truth. It was too scandalous, and I'd promised I'd never tell. She was the child of my own sister. My sister, whose life was filled with shocking events, asked me – – no, begged me – to take in this baby and never to tell anyone of her origin. I should have known the child would grow up to become exactly like her mother: always looking for trouble."

"Oh, Mother. I wish you would've shared this sooner."

"She was not a good sister to me and would not have made a good aunt to you." Rose told Lavender differently, but her opinion changed daily. "I'm not sad she's gone."

"Well, what do I do about Lavender?" Minnie stood, trying hard to stick to her task at hand. "It's been so hard, Mother. I don't want our Lavender to go down the wrong path. Will you help me?" Her voice began to waver.

"My poor, sweet girl. Left all alone to deal with this." Rose again reached for Minnie. This time, Minnie allowed her touch.

"You know, I've been waiting all this time for you to come to me," Rose said softly. "Thank you for asking for my help. We won't fail her."

CHAPTER SEVEN

Lavender Ladieux
February, 1959

I T WASN'T JUST the money that was intoxicating to Lavender. It was the excitement of being outside of her home and doing something that wasn't routine. The people who went to Lou Kowalski's Dance Hall were different from the milquetoast residents from Melody Lane.

These people looked like they had been places in the world. Maybe even exotic places where there were interesting smells and animals she'd never seen, not even in her textbooks at school. These were people who knew the world and knew people who had made something of themselves.

She made at least $15 in tips every night she went to the Hall. If she somehow got out of the house on Saturday evening, her tips were even higher, sometimes up to $20 or $25. The first thing she did was purchase an outfit like the other girls at the Hall were wearing. The red tweed skirt, bright blue blouse (that buttoned just a little lower than all the rest of them), and a pair of stockings were hidden underneath her bed and away from the prying eyes of her older sister. For the first time in her life, Lavender Ladieux could actually see herself as a successful woman.

It wasn't hard to find a ride once she figured out a system. She went over to Bryla's street and waited for Bryla's cue: the whistle of the North American Cardinal. Their English teacher, a stern woman named Mrs. Finewald, often got bored teaching the rudimentary tools of the language and would assign her students unique bird calls, so each of these evening calls were a bit of homework.

Both girls delighted in learning the sounds and used them to signal different things. Are you going out tonight? American Goldfinch. *Wheeet oh whe-wheet-whe-weet*. Meet me down the block. Common Grackle *kackackkack*. I'm here. Let's go. Northern Cardinal. *Whodeetwhoodeetwhoodeet*

The doorman at Lou Kowalski's Dance Hall had become familiar with Lavender and always greeted her with a smile. "Evening, Miss Lita," Ralph said kindly. "Hope you enjoy your dances tonight." It turned out that Ralph had graduated a year before Minnie. His dream was to buy Tommy's Fish 'n Chips, a restaurant on an old fishing boat on Strange Lake, where he worked during the day, and spent his evenings working the door at Lou Kowalski's Dance Hall to save for the down payment.

Over time, Lavender became acquainted with Lou Kowalski. Like an evil version of Santa Claus, he had squinty eyes and a bulbous, crooked nose that leaned to the left. His bushy mustache and beard covered most of his reddish, oblong face. Lou was a contradiction in every way. There was something truly terrifying about him, though, at the same time, she found him charming.

"You're the favorite 'round here, Lita. Keep putting on your smile. We'll make a fortune, you and me." He chewed on the end of his big cigar and winked at her.

None of the girls who danced regularly were allowed to go into the locked room at the back of the dance hall, where men mysteriously disappeared for hours at a time. That suited Lavender just fine. She was just there to make tips while dancing, and meet exciting men with colorful stories. One night, she danced with a traveling salesman who was in town visiting his cousin for the night. He had been to places all over the country and found Lavender to be the most stunning woman he'd seen in all of his travels. He danced with her six times and left her a tip of four dollars.

The following Thursday, she danced with the son of the owner of the cigarette factory, who showed up wearing his finest of suits and sporting a mustache which curled up at the ends. He was a very short man who yielded so much power that the room parted when he walked through. When he finished dancing with Lavender, he straightened his jacket and headed for the back room. A large menacing-looking man blocked his entrance until he whispered something in his ear and the brute stepped aside looked around him first before entering.

There was one person who lurked toward the back of the dance hall; a dark cloud in a room otherwise filled with joy. Jeannie Kowalski, a girl with a dull, lifeless face and brown bangs cut straight and low across her eyes, was Lou's daughter. Jeannie was a year behind Lavender in school, and never one to announce her presence. She chose, instead, to skulk in the back of every room, scowling at anyone who entered. While there was always the risk that she might tell someone at school that an underage girl was frequenting her father's dance hall, Lavender didn't waste time worrying.

"Hello, Jeannie! Here for a Lindy tonight?" she said on her way to get a drink of water. Jeannie scowled and didn't respond. Her reason for being there remained a mystery.

When Lavender returned to her bedroom every night at 10:30 p.m., she removed her skirt and blouse and placed them carefully under the bed. She took them out to be washed only when Minnie was at a women's retreat at The Church of the Woeful. The retreats were happening almost every week often, so it wasn't difficult to find time for her laundry.

She got up the next morning and went to breakfast with a smile on her face. Her sister was never the wiser for her evening activities.

"What noise was that outside last night? What did I hear?" Minnie asked, as she spooned lumpy oatmeal into a dish. "I thought I heard bumping against the house. I got up to look after I read Chapter Nine, *Dumpy is Delightful* and recited it out loud, but there was nothing there. Did you hear anything?"

"You know how the oak trees bang against the windows, Minnie. Frances said the next time she stops over, she'll bring Billy with her and they'll see about getting them trimmed." Lavender swirled the mush half-heartedly, thinking about the handsome man she'd met the night before who reminded her of Johnson Hobarth, the screen star who had died tragically some years earlier. She'd seen his photo on the cover of a magazine the last time she was outbuying milk. Her dance partner told her they'd both be in Hollywood someday, and he could say he knew her back when she was dancing the jive at a little dance hall in Connecticut.

"Pastor Tompkins would like you to come on

Sunday. Help babysit in the nursery. You'll do that, won't you? To help those in need?"

Lavender sighed. "I suppose. If you think it's really necessary." Minnie bothered her about babysitting so much, maybe if she went one time that would be the end of it.

"When the service is over, women pick up their children and the nursery attendants join us for a light snack. You might find you enjoy being around such interesting people. They're all devoted to a cause. True devotion brings miracles, you know."

"Mmmhmmm." Lavender looked at the time. Five more minutes and she could leave for school. Minnie's constant lectures on the good people of The Church of the Woeful made her stomach hurt.

"Why, just last week, I had an eye-opening experience of my own."

Lavender looked up, running her transgressions through her mind. Things Minnie suddenly discovered about her – things that would bring about more discussion, and perhaps punishment – might prevent her from going out at night. "What kind of miracle, Minnie? Something that will help us buy a new couch, maybe?"

Minnie studied her sister's face, trying to determine if she was serious. She had a hard time understanding humor, especially since it was frowned upon in The Church of the Woeful. "No, silly. Pastor said I should go in and speak with Rose. Treat her with kindness and she might come out of her shell."

"Oh." Lavender leaned back in her chair. "Did she spill her bottle all over you as she tried sitting up? The last time I was in there, she wanted me to bring her water, but what she meant was liquor. She gets them confused now."

Minnie tapped her sister's cheek lightly. "Don't make fun of her. She's our mother. She's been through more than either of us will ever understand. She told me many things in confidence. Someday you'll appreciate all that she's done. Mark my word; Rose's sacrifice will become the beacon in your life, your example for surviving the hardships of being a woman."

Lavender looked up at her sister abruptly. "Why would you listen to her? Rose is – sick. She doesn't know what she's talking about." She often wondered if Minnie knew what was happening in the real world since. She spent so much time immersed in Pastor Tompkins' words.

"She said you might respond in that manner. She and I have grand plans for you, Lavender."

Lavender's chest ached. Rose and Minnie conspiring against her hurt deeply. "I'm going to be late for school. I have to go." She grabbed her things and left quickly.

When she arrived at school, she told Bryla what

had taken place. Her friend replied calmly, "Don't worry about Rose. I've got an aunt with the same problem." Bryla made a drinking motion with her hand. "They don't remember longer than a day or two."

The following evening, Minnie sat herself in front of Lavender's door with a flashlight and all the socks that needed darning. She began the tedious process with her back against the hard wall, waiting to catch her sister leaving. Rose told her Lavender was sneaking out and the only way to stop it was to catch her.

She began reciting all the verses of Chapter Four – *A Woman's Joy in Hard Work* to herself. Unfortunately, the lateness of the evening proved too much for her, and the next thing she knew, daylight was peeking through the hall window. She opened Lavender's door to find her asleep, still in the clothes she'd obviously worn the evening before on one of her adventures.

Despite what was before her eyes, Minnie convinced herself it really was a tree branch banging against the roof. She didn't want to confront her sister anyway.

CHAPTER EIGHT

Gavin Anders
March, 1959

GAVIN ANDERS COULD be a movie star in his own right. Most of the girls in his class thought about him dreamily as he spoke passionately about tragic worldwide events. He wore thick, black glasses that accentuated his strong jawline and shaggy beard.

Mr. Anders was a man who often took broken birds under his wing. He genuinely cared about the young people who came from troubled circumstances. He thought he could help, or at least he could try. Last year, one girl in his sophomore class didn't have clothing to wear during the cold, harsh winter months. He found an abundance of skirts, tops, and pants for her, donated by a family that had several adolescent daughters and a large income. They were most eager to share the clothing with this needy girl. The next winter, his humanitarian project was a girl in his freshman history class. She didn't have anyone in her life interested in whether or not she succeeded.

In her mind, she just had to get through a few years of high school and then begin her work in the local factory. Life was a series of negative events; neither did she see a way to make it better, nor did she want them to be better. She had never known anything different. Gavin found her a place to live rent free and got her hours at the factory reduced to part time until she graduated. She became a happy, lively young woman who thrived in school and looked forward to every day.

In the fall of 1959, Gavin Anders was taken aback by the beauty of one particular student. She was a broken bird of stunning color. She came to school in ill-fitting clothing that the other teachers said came from her older sisters. It was a stark contrast, this girl with movie star qualities dressing as if she were Cinderella.

Mr. Anders began inquiring about Lavender, asking why she was not well taken care of. Other teachers had worked with Minnie and Frances, and also knew the tragic story of Rose. Charles' abandonment of the family and Rose's subsequent "illness" made tongues wag around the school. What wasn't as well-known was the state in which Lavender spent her life: existing as if Minnie were her mother, and with the ghost of Rose always upstairs in the bedroom.

While others didn't think the girls needed any

kind of help given the fancy home they owned in, Gavin Anders saw beyond the facade. He wanted to give Lavender the chance to have a decent future.

It appalled him to learn, from a student who resided down the street from the Ladieux residence, that Lavender came and went as she pleased. It saddened him to understand she was seen frequently coming and going under the cover of darkness, expertly maneuvering down the trellis that once held bright, pansies.

He began noticing that, despite her natural beauty, the girl had permanent dark circles under her eyes. Her thin body now seemed to swim in the clothing that both of her sisters had filled out during their tenure. Most troublesome: her above-average grades had slipped to barely-passing on her best day.

She fell asleep in his class on more than one occasion. When questioned, she said she had sleeping problems and was working to correct them. He knew better. He had dealt with these girls before and realized that every time one of them presented these symptoms there was an underlying cause even more sinister.

"Miss Ladieux, will you stay after class today?" He touched her shoulder gently, trying not to startle the sleeping beauty as he picked up the tests completed by everyone in the class but her.

"Mmhmm," she sat up and closed her book,

rubbing her eyes and trying to act as though she hadn't spent the last thirty minutes in the most luscious state of slumber.

Lavender stood and straightened her dull, gray skirt. She smoothed her blonde hair and pulled at either side of her thread-bare blouse to make sure she was somewhat presentable. She'd become accustomed to the finery she wore out at night. Lavender found her sisters' hand-me-downs dull and lifeless, though she'd come to view them as a disguise; something she wore during the day, so no one knew her actual identity.

She moved to her teacher's desk, ready with the pat excuse she used in every other class when she was reprimanded. "I'll study harder next time, Mr. Anders. I know you expected us to learn the dates of battles for the French and Indian War. It's just that I've been struggling to sleep at night. We've got a branch batting against the house and—"

Gavin sighed. He thought that after he'd spent so much time baking her a birthday cake, she would view him as an ally. "I was hoping you would be honest with me, Miss Ladieux. I've made it plain all year that I'm here to be your guide if needed. I'm not your enemy."

She opened her blue eyes wide, something she'd learned recently made the gentlemen on the dance floor gasp. "I am being honest, sir. I'm not sleeping well. Our home economics teacher said it can come from too much tea in the evening."

Gavin was immune to her charm. "You may indeed be struggling with your slumber. But that is in part because you spend your evenings out on the town. Most likely with unruly sorts. Those people won't get you where you want to be in life, Miss Ladieux." He had given this speech more times than he could count. These girls all thought they were different; their individual situations unique. Mostly, they just lacked the focus to succeed, and a kind, fatherly figure to offer both support and encouragement.

Lavender blushed. "Please don't tell Mo – my sister Minnie. She works so hard to provide for us. I don't want her thinking I'm ungrateful." She placed her arm on his, on the off-chance this gesture would have the effect her widened gaze did not.

He gently took her arm and placed it on the desk beside him. "If you're concerned about your sister, the best thing to do is change your behavior." He turned to face her. "Miss Ladieux, I have experience working with less-fortunate girls. All I've wanted my entire life is to help others. I wanted to make a place of safety for girls such as yourself, but for a long time, I lacked the means. One day I asked myself if I would do whatever it took to find the funds to make that happen. Sometimes the best answers aren't the easiest." He half-smiled, revealing a perfect row of white teeth. "And now I've acquired the resources to help those in need."

Lavender put her chin in the air, pointing her upturned nose toward the ceiling. "I'm not in need. I'm just fine. I don't know what busybody told you otherwise. The Ladieux family lives in the biggest house on Melody Lane."

"While the exterior of your life sounds impressive, I've reason to believe it isn't all it appears. Your father hasn't been seen in town in several months, and your mother has taken to her bed. I have the resources to help you. Please allow me to do that."

Lavender looked at his face. He didn't have the faraway look many of the men she danced with had. Like they were wishing they could dance with someone they loved, but instead were spending their time with a stranger. Then there were others who stared at her a little too intently, wanting more than she was willing to share.

"Mr. Anders, I've – lessened the burden on my sister. I found a job that pays double what she's making. I stop on my way home from school at the market and fill a bag with fruits and vegetables. She never says a word, but she has to understand she didn't buy them. I think she's grateful."

He leaned back and put his hand up to his chin. "And what job could a young woman of fifteen be doing to bring in an excess of riches?"

"I've been dancing three nights a week at Lou Kowalski's Dance Hall," she blurted out. "I've learned all the dances: – the twist, the hop – It's nothing but good, clean fun. I get tips and sometimes make as much as twenty dollars in one night! Mr. Kowalski is such a nice man. He treats me respectfully and says I'm the brightest spot in his night." Her eyes shone as she spoke, thinking about the world where she was already a star. For a second, her thoughts drifted to the private, back room where men came and went, and how she'd fantasized about what took place there.

"Lavender, that isn't a place for respectable young ladies. If you want to find a husband, or perhaps become a secretary like your sister, Frances, this isn't the way to go about it." Gavin shifted uncomfortably in his chair. "There are other things that happen in those places; besides dancing, you know. It really isn't proper."

"No, Mr. Anders, it's not what you think," she protested. "Even Jeannie Kowalski spends time there. Would he allow his daughter to attend if there was something untoward?" Her voice was hollow. Jeannie Kowalski never looked like she was having fun. She was always trying to get her father's attention, but Lou brushed her aside and told her to "go help with something."

"You should try it! Come for a dance on a Friday night. We do the Lindy, the Pinetown Rag–"

Gavin made a mental note to speak with Jeannie Kowalski. She hadn't been on his radar. Even though she was a sour girl, word was that she had a stable home life. "Miss Ladieux, that's not a place I'd feel comfortable, nor would it be appropriate. My concern is for your well-being." He pulled a sheet of paper from his desk. "Tell you what. I'm going to give you my home phone number. You can call me if you ever need a listening ear or something more serious." He wrote his name and phone number across the top. "These are dangerous games you're playing. I've dealt with more troubled girls than I can count. It's my calling in life. If things are ever so unbearable in your home that you need a way out, I've recently opened the Anders Home for Youth. We have rooms for just such occasions."

Lavender's brow wrinkled. "But I have a home, Mr. Anders. I have a bed and food. Why would I need something different? My sister and I keep our home clean. We're doing just fine."

"Just keep my number. In case the day comes when you feel like you're in trouble. I want to see you succeed in life, Miss Ladieux. There's a whole, wide world out there just waiting for you. The door to it is not located within Kowalski's Dance Hall, I assure you."

CHAPTER NINE

Lavender Ladieux
April, 1959

"SAY, DO I recognize you from The Church of the Woeful? He slipped his hand dangerously close to the dip in her back as they waltzed, a dance Lavender had just recently learned.

"Yes, I've gone there with my sister twice. She asked me to babysit but then we ended up staying way after the service so she could flirt with the pastor. She's hopeless." Lavender looked over his shoulder at the more attractive man dancing with Bryla. She swallowed her jealousy.

"Well, you know that, technically, we're not supposed to be here dancing. In his handbook, the pastor has deemed dancing to be the devil's playground. Any kind of joy we experience should come from his words and his words alone." He looked at Lavender with a serious face for a moment before bursting out laughing. "You know, and I know, that he's full of baloney."

Just the weekend before, Lavender had agreed to work in the nursery of The Church of the Woeful when the regular attendant came down with the flu. Minnie begged and pleaded, reminding Lavender how often she helped her with homework. Lavender relented, on condition that Minnie didn't force her to go again.

The sermon was interminably long; a two-hour speech involving the use of cleaning products. Pastor Tompkins felt there were only certain products pure enough to use if you were to be one of his followers. Sun Shiney floor cleaner was really the Devil's liquid, he said. Women were to go home and throw whatever Sun Shiney remained they had in the cupboard into the trash if they were truly devoted to him.

After the sermon, Lavender stood anxiously by Minnie's side as she spoke to the other parishioners about the pastor's message. It wasn't long before they found a more interesting topic to her ears.

"That dance hall on the outside of town is an aberration. If we could close that down, we could prove to the pastor that we understand his words and are completely devoted to them," a lady dressed all in black said.

Minnie nodded vigorously. "I've heard such things about that place. The loose women who go would do well with a sermon here at The Church of the Woeful – They might find themselves a decent husband and a purpose in the world instead of spending their weekends gyrating."

Lavender chuckled to herself thinking about the women at the dance hall and how full of life they were. They weren't interested in learning about the best cleaning product to use, nor were they going to devote themselves to a man who thought more of his image in the mirror than he did of his congregants.

As the church women stood there talking, the pastor approached. "Good morning, dear ladies. I'm sure you're discussing today's words and not gossiping about the community." He smoothed his fine white-blond hair and winked a translucent, blue eye at the lady closest to Minnie. She blushed and looked away.

Lavender, who had been standing with her arms folded, barely able to contain her frustration over the conversation, nodded in agreement. "You are right about that pastor. We should not be gossiping we should be going home to make dinner. It's a waste of time to stand here and do otherwise."

Minnie and the pastor exchanged glances. "Lavender, your sister has asked that I speak with you. Might we step into my office and have a few words?"

Lavender looked at her sister with a feeling of betrayal. Had the "nursery emergency" just been a ruse to get her to the church? Minnie looked at the floor.

Reluctantly, Lavender followed Pastor Tompkins into a cherry-wood-paneled room. Pastor Tompkins moved behind a heavy desk and seated himself in a tall, leather chair. Lavender walked to a much shorter, simple, wooden chair and sat down uncomfortably.

The pastor leaned back, folding his hands on his abdominal area. He eyed her up and down as if he were picking out a nice steak at the market. "Your sister tells me you have no real purpose in your life. She also says your grades are poor and you need some motivation to make yourself the proper woman for a potential husband."

Anger welled up inside her. This was no business of his, and Minnie should not have come to him with something so personal. "I'm planning to go into the acting field," she announced. "I may move to Hollywood when I graduate." She'd had yet to attend a movie, but it was something she repeated often.

He shook his head in disgust. "A beautiful young thing like you should think about actual plans for your future. There are many eligible men in The Church of the Woeful who would make fine husbands. If you'd come with your sister on Wednesday evenings, I would be happy to introduce you to some of them. You have no father to guide you, so it's not surprising you need extra help to find your way. You'll see: there are many decent men in the world. Not all are like Charles Ladieux."

Lavender stood up and put her hands on her hips. "The Ladieux women haven't needed any men in our lives for quite some time. We've done just fine – Minnie, Frances and I. We've kept the roof over our heads and food on our table. I don't know why people think we need more than that. I will not be coming to your service on Wednesday or any other night."

The pastor stood, towering over her by at least a foot. He moved to the door, trying to block her exit, but she pushed around him. "Your words directly contradict those taught in my booklet, something you would find immensely helpful." He shook his head and stared hard at the whole of her. "You're just a child. I will instruct Minnie to keep a tighter rein on you. I'll give her detailed instructions on what needs to happen going forward. You'll not win a battle with me, Miss Ladieux."

There was no point in arguing further. As long as she was in this building, his heavy words trapped her. She walked away from his office without looking back. When she found Minnie still engaged in gossip with the other women, she tugged on her arm. "Come on, Min," she urged. "I've had enough of this place for one day."

On their way home, Lavender raged about her experience. "The nerve of that man thinking he knows anything about me or our lives. Why would you confide in him, Minnie? He doesn't have a clue. I'm concerned that you're devoting your life to a place that's giving you sore muscles and misery in return. Don't you want to go out and spend time with friends, laughing and having fun? That's never going to happen as long as you're under his thumb. It's like you've given up on having a mother and gone to him for those needs instead." Lavender regretted the words as soon as they came out of her mouth. She knew how hard Minnie had worked to be an adult even before out of high school.

Minnie stopped walking and grabbed her sister's arm. "It wasn't his idea to have that conversation. It was our mother, Rose, who suggested it. She told me to go to him and have him speak with you sternly."

Lavender was dumbfounded. "This all came from Rose?"

"She's been giving me all sorts of excellent advice." Minnie announced proudly. "We've had such wonderful discussions about life. She's told me so much about – Well, things that maybe I can tell you someday, but not today. But she really cares about you, Lavender."

Lavender felt sick inside; her own sister had betrayed her. "You know that Rose isn't thinking right. All the alcohol has curdled her brain. And maybe even before she started drinking, things weren't working right in there. Why would you listen to her?"

Minnie started walking again, and her face tightened. "I will not speak to you about this anymore. Maybe if you would go in and sit with her, she would tell you things, too. She's a wonderful lady."

Lavender realized, for the first time, that she was truly on her own. Rose was sick. Frances had her own life. And her dear Minnie was lost–both to Pastor Tompkins and to Rose. Maybe they were one and the same.

That Saturday, Frances breezed into the stale Ladieux home like a breath of fresh air. She brought a heavy basket containing meatloaf, mashed potatoes and an apple pie. Minnie was washing windows at The Church of the Woeful. Lavender resolved she would speak with her about Minnie's obsession with her church and Pastor Tompkins and maybe even about what was going on with Rose.

"Lavender, you should see some of the women who come to our clinic. Dressed to the nines for a doctor's appointment. In between phone calls, I took notes so I could be sure and share them with you." She pulled out a large notebook and began thumbing through. "Oh, here's one, from a lady who wore a dress the color of a stop sign, barely covering her unmentionables. She had a big, yellow hat on her head that was almost larger than her dress. Can you imagine?"

Lavender forced a laugh, then remembered what needed to be said. "Frances, I need to talk to you about Minnie and her church. Things aren't right there, and that pastor is just downright scary."

Frances took Lavender's hands in her own and squeezed them. "Dear sister, I'm sorry for all of your worries. Poor Minnie, she needs a life of her own outside of this home. She's worked far too hard for a girl so young. On top of the day-to-day concerns, I think she's overwhelmed by the roof problems."

Lavender sat up straight. "What about the roof?" She knew Minnie thought the tree branches against the roof were causing the noise when she came and went. Minnie had mentioned nothing further.

"Didn't she tell you? We need a new roof. Father spoke of fixing it years ago, but there was always something he found more important." Frances sighed. "I had someone come last week, and it's going to cost us close to eight hundred dollars to replace it. I don't have that money, and neither do you girls." Frances jiggled her foot nervously. "It may be time to think about selling this house. Billy knows a lot about those things and he can help us. Billy's parents might allow you to stay with them temporarily. They have an extra room the three of you could share."

The thought of sharing a bedroom with Minnie and Rose made her cringe. Especially now that she had extra-curricular activities at night. "Frances, if you'll give me a week, I might come up with a solution. Would you do that?"

"What would you know about roofs?" Frances said dismissively. "This isn't something you can handle on your own, Lavender."

"Please, just give me a few days. If I can't come up with the money, we'll work on selling the house."

Frances looked at her with skepticism. "We'll see," she said noncommittally.

The following Thursday evening, Lavender went to Lou Kowalski's office and knocked on the door. "What?" he barked.

She entered and lowered her chin, batting her eyes in his direction. "Mr. Kowalski, I have some information for you. Important information. But I'll only share it if there's something in it for me."

Lou's eyes narrowed. Unexpectedly, he let out a loud snort. "You've got more spunk than I thought, Lita. What's this information gonna cost me?"

Lavender steadied herself. She'd never negotiated a deal before. "I need eight hundred dollars for a new roof. I know you have things going on in your back room that bring in money. I want to be a part of that."

Lou leaned forward in his chair. "What makes you think you're worth that much to me?"

"My information could save your business," she said importantly. "Do you want to take that risk?"

He looked at her with skepticism, trying to decide if this young woman was attempting to scam him as so many had before her. "Okay, kid," Lou sighed. "Tell me what you've got. If it's worth big money, I'll see what I can do."

Lavender took a deep breath. "I was at The Church of the Woeful last week. I overheard a large group discussing ways they could shut you down."

Lou snorted again. "Tompkins? He knows better." He put his finger on the cleft in his chin. "How do they think they'll accomplish that?"

She hadn't expected this question. "Well – my sister pulled me away," she stammered. "I didn't hear the rest. But they were serious, I know that."

"I'll talk to him. If there's a real problem, I'll see what kind of compromise we can work out. Again." He looked down at his desk, deep in thought. "Tell you what, I'll give you half now. That was excellent information. You can earn the rest in tips working my poker room. I could use another pretty dame. But you can't just show up whenever you want. You've got to be here when you're scheduled." He put his thick hand out. "Do we have a deal?"

"Deal." Lavender hesitantly stuck her delicate hand in his.

"Did you mention a sister?"

"Yes, I have a sister. Minnie."

He put his cigar up to his mouth and squinted. "Does she look like you?"

"Sort of," Lavender mumbled.

"Bring her. She could earn some good tips too. You'll have your roof in no time."

CHAPTER TEN

Lavender Ladieux
April, 1959

WORKING IN THE poker room wasn't so bad. The uniform was a crushed, red-velvet dress, cut farther down in front than she'd ever imagined was legal. It was far above her knees, leaving her cold every night because Lou kept the back door open. The room was a dimly-lit, wood-paneled square with a cartoon painting of four dogs playing cards on one wall. On the opposite wall was a shiny ax with a spotlight over the top. Underneath it was a plaque with the words *Lou Kowalski, Ax Throwing Champion, Kenowala State Fair, 1949.*

She'd never actually watched people play cards before. Charles didn't believe in games of any sort. Minnie wasn't allowed to play cards according to the latest doctrines of The Church of the Woeful, and Francis was far too busy to engage in something so frivolous. The strategy excited Lavender and she wanted to learn more. Her job was to walk constantly around the room, filling drinks and offering cigarettes to those who wanted them. It wasn't hard.

Lavender recognized many faces from around town in the poker room. It became clear why they wanted to keep the room and the occupants' identities a secret. She saw the man who ran the grocery store where she stopped to get milk and bread on the way home from school. She saw her school principal. Sitting next to him was Bryla's friend who always gave them rides but disappeared soon after arrival. They never entered from the front door like she did, but came in the back way where Lou stood, at the end of each night, watching the trash burn in a big pit.

There were nightly games, everyone throwing wads of cash in the middle of the table to bet on a few cards. More money than the four hundred dollars Lou gave her was just tossed away like it was nothing. Her job was to sell cigarettes to the players, bat her eyelashes, and giggle every time they said something remotely complimentary. The next day when she walked the halls of the high school, or bought milk, these men acted as though nothing out of the ordinary had taken place. At the end of the evening, she received large tips from most of them; tips Lou insisted she keep in the drawer of his desk along with the other girls' tips. He would distribute them at the end of the month.

As she cleaned the room each evening after everyone was gone, she watched as Lou stood by the burn pit, smoking a cigar. She could feel his hard stare as she worked. When she turned to face him, she waved heartily. He turned around and continued smoking without acknowledging her.

By the fifth night she worked as a cigarette girl, she had her routine down. She could push away the handsy men who had grown a little too comfortable touching her. She really liked the tips and knew she wouldn't have to do it too much longer in order to get the money they needed to fix the roof.

Bryla came infrequently now that her father changed jobs and was home most evenings. One night, Bryla waved happily from the dance floor as Lavender emerged from the back room to get more glasses from the kitchen. Lavender tried to scurry by, but wasn't able to avoid her friend.

"I almost didn't recognize you in those racy clothes," Bryla pulled on the sleeve of Lavender's brand-new rouge-colored blouse. "Some pretty fancy duds you got on there. Why haven't I seen you on the dance floor?"

"I've been helping Lou with a project." Lavender refused to look at her friend. "I thought you couldn't come anymore because of your dad?"

"My cousin needs some new orthopedic shoes. Those ain't cheap," Bryla began sheepishly. "Say,

Mr. Anders has been asking about you. He says he's received information from another student that you're doing more than dancing here. He said to say you'd better come to school before you get into real trouble for not showing up. There are people who could go to your house and make noise about it. Maybe even get Rose involved. You wouldn't want her out of her bedroom and interacting with your teacher."

Lavender thought about that. No, she would not want Rose anywhere near Mr. Anders, or anyone from the school. Her slurred speech and erratic way of thinking scared Lavender sometimes. Who knows what Mr. Anders might think of their family if he were to witness it too?

"I've been sick. Headaches. I suppose I should go talk to him. I've been doing extra–" she paused. As much as she liked Bryla, she didn't want to share this opportunity. She needed the money to fix the roof and cutting the tips any further just wouldn't work. She looked at her watch. "Sorry Bryla, I've got to help Lou with something in the back."

"Be careful around that man. He's dangerous," her friend said with concern. "I like him and all, but I've heard rumors from other girls. Don't ever let him corner you."

Lavender couldn't tell if this was just another of Bryla's tall tales, or if she'd, in fact, heard horror stories about Lou. "It's great seeing you. Maybe we'll dance beside each other later." She patted her friend absently on the back and then walked away towards the ladies' bathroom. She felt an enormous sense of guilt lying to her only friend. It was also a bit of a disappointment that Bryla hadn't figured out what she was doing. After all of her time there, a seasoned pro at sneaking out, and it was this easy pulling one over on her.

When she reentered the poker room and placed her cigarette halter over her body, it shocked her to see, not only the familiar faces of her high school principal and the grocer, but also Pastor Tompkins. After a flicker of recognition, he acted as if he'd never seen her. "Cigarette girl?" He motioned for her to come to his side. When she placed the cigarettes on the table in front of him, he grabbed her arm. "We're going to speak later," he sneered.

Blushing, she stood up tall and hurried to the other side of the table. She watched the cards with interest, though Lou admonished her never to show any emotion when she did.

As she moved around the table, filling drinks and laughing as she'd been taught, she noticed something shocking. Pastor Tompkins was replacing the cards in his hand with some he kept in his pocket. Every time he took out his handkerchief to wipe his forehead, he was bringing a new card to his hand.

The extra card was skillfully placed in a pocket sewn into the waistband of his pants.

At the end of the evening, Lavender began her usual cleanup routine. She scooped the trash from the table into the large bin and moved it over to the door, where Lou would retrieve it to burn. She placed the cigarettes in the drawer under the liquor. When she turned around, Pastor Tompkins was standing behind her.

"Did you think I'd forgotten you?" he asked coldly.

"I will not babysit again."

"You're not to tell your sister you saw me here. This is a place of discretion; for gentlemen only, not little girls."

Her first instinct was to punch him. It was something she'd been dreaming about lately; socking him right in his self-righteous gut. He now required Minnie to turn three times in a circle before entering any room. Like a trained monkey. He said this kind of discomfort was the only way to prove her devotion to The Church of the Woeful.

Instead of punching him, Lavender smiled broadly. "I wouldn't dream of it, Pastor. But in return, I'd like a favor."

Lou, who was preparing the burn pit, cocked his head back to see inside the poker room. When he realized it was Pastor Tompkins, he returned to his work.

"You're in no position to ask any favors," Pastor Tompkins continued. "A girl out past her bedtime with no supervision. Not the way young ladies train for their roles in my church. It's too bad you never attend, or you'd learn such things."

"I want you to find other tasks for Minnie. Let her visit the elderly or do something that makes The Church of the Woeful look good in the community. She needs some time outside. Somewhere she can feel like a person and not just your trained animal," Lavender demanded.

"It's a splendid gift I have given her; working in my office every day," Pastor Tompkins huffed. "Do you know how many women come in and beg to do her job? Why would I turn the poor waif away?"

"Because you said you didn't want her to know you were here. That's how you can assure that she won't." Lavender knew he was cheating at cards. That was something else she could hold over him, but she was banking his transgressions to use at a later date, like having a savings account.

Pastor Tompkins had just a hint of a smile on his face; somewhere between amused and angry. "I'll think about it. This is a small town. It won't take long before everyone, including Minnie, knows how you spend your evenings. When that happens, even my good word won't help with your sister." He pivoted and left.

She finished up, placing her tips from the evening in a Lou's desk drawer. She shut off the light, proud of herself that she'd used her position to do something good. Lavender was returning a stray glass to the kitchen when she remembered she'd left her purse in the poker room. When she turned to go back the way she came, another unfriendly face greeted her. "Jeannie? Your dad is burning garbage. He's out back."

"I told on you." She retorted. Her long brown hair hung down over her eyes. The only visible part of her face were her lips, which were trembling. "Mr. Anders is wonderful. He's head-over-heels for you, just like everybody else. It's not right. I told him what you did here at night. How you do nasty things with men."

Lavender gasped. Of all the strange things that had taken place this evening, this had to be the strangest. "Why would you do that? Haven't you been in your father's poker room before? Haven't you seen other girls in there, selling cigarettes? That's all I do!"

Jeannie stuck her chin out defiantly. "I don't believe you. Girls like you are only good for one thing. That's what my mother says. That's the only reason my daddy has any interest in you."

"Well, your mother is completely wrong." Lavender pushed her way past Jeannie. "I'll straighten this out tomorrow. Good grief."

"I'm always going to beat the likes of you, Lavender Ladieux!" Jeannie called threateningly. "You may have the pretty hair and figure, but I've got two things more important in this world: money and brains. Let's call it our own card game. And my suit always wins."

CHAPTER ELEVEN

Lavender Ladieux
May, 1959

"I'VE GOT ALMOST enough money to fix our roof. If you'll just give me another two weeks, I can afford it all." Lavender sat at the kitchen table with her sister, Frances. Although she had a large wad of cash in her pocket, she didn't want to produce it until she had the entire amount. Showing your hand early, as she'd learned during many nights in the poker room, was never a good thing.

Frances looked at her skeptically. "Where would you come up with money like that? You're a schoolgirl. Minnie has never once mentioned your getting an after-school job."

Now is not the time, Lavender. "I've been babysitting the Bombgarten children down the street. Their nanny attends to personal needs twice a week. I've never spent a dime of the money." She smiled with satisfaction. That was a story she came up with right then and there.

"You don't make 'new roof' kind of money from babysitting. I babysat in high school and never received over two dollars for an evenings' work." Frances leaned forward and put her hand on her sister's knee. "I know you want to help, love. This is more of a grown-up problem. If we have to sell the place, then so be it. It's really too much upkeep for you and Minnie. When Billy and I get married, we'll have our own home to worry about." Frances smiled comfortingly. It was something that Lavender looked forward to seeing during their rare time together. "You're very kind to want to help. Really, Lavender."

Lavender folded her arms across her chest, frustrated.

"How is school going? You know it's very important to finish your education, so you can go to secretarial school, like me." Frances put the cup of tea to her lips without looking at her sister.

"Who told you?" Lavender asked suspiciously.

"Your Mr. Anders was in for his annual checkup. He mentioned you have missed quite a few days of school. He thinks you may stay up late, for whatever reason."

"It's fine. I've got A's in every subject." Lavender panicked for a moment, trying to remember if she'd destroyed all the threatening letters from the school, telling her parent she risked expulsion if she didn't attend class more often. Fortunately, she arrived home every day before Minnie and got the mail from the mailbox, finding all of the offending letters.

"You've got more responsibility than a girl of your age should, but school is important. Just a few more years. You can do it!" Frances encouraged.

"I wish you'd move back, Frances," Lavender said wistfully. "Everything would be so much better if you were here!"

Frances touched her face softly. "Sweet girl. As mother says, I 'did what I must' for as long as I could. I'm not as strong as you or Minnie. I can't live in this misery, knowing that my mother is wasting away upstairs. The boarding house is better for me." She folded her hands in front of her. "Lavender, may I ask you a grown-up kind of question?"

She was startled and a bit insulted; Frances had no idea how much "adult" she'd seen. "Yes, I believe I can handle it."

"I'm concerned about Minnie. You were right about her being too involved in her church. The last time I saw her, she had to whisper the word 'blue' seven times before she could speak to me. What kind of nonsense is that? Do you see other worrying signs?"

Lavender thought of Pastor Tompkins and how he cheated at poker. He was pure evil. How Minnie, who used to worry about Lavender's well-being, now barely had the energy to kiss her goodnight at the end of her day. Instead of giving her better things to do as he'd promised, Pastor Tompkins doubled her workload. "Yes, I do worry about her. It's not just Pastor Tompkins. It's also Rose. When Minnie's not at The Church of the Woeful, she's in Rose's room, whispering and giggling. It's hard to know who is the worse influence."

Frances stared at her with shock. "Why would Rose be a dangerous influence? She's not well, but she's still her mother. Your mother too!"

Lavender thought about all the visits Frances had made to their home. Not once did she go up and knock on Rose's door. "We've all done our best to comfort her, but I worry that she doesn't think right, and Minnie may believe the words she's saying are all true."

"I can speak with her," Frances said with reservation. "Minnie has a good head on her shoulders. She's kept this house afloat all of this time. I'm sure it's nothing for you to worry about."

"But I've been buying–" Lavender began. There would be no food in the refrigerator if she didn't stop at the store after school. She thought better of it. "You're probably right, Frances."

Minnie walked in the back door, circled three times and sat down at the table. "Lavender, run upstairs and let me speak with Frances alone," she ordered. Lavender kissed Frances on the cheek and left the kitchen. Instead of going up to her room, she waited on the stairs, straining to listen.

"I've asked the Pastor. He doesn't have money to give me a raise. They're stretched to the bone as it is. You'd think with so many people contributing to The Church of the Woeful, our finances would be in better shape," Minnie said in a hushed tone. "Blue, blue, blue."

Pastor Tompkins always came to the poker room with wads of cash. Probably directly from the collection plate. Poor Minnie worked her fingers to the bone and spouted his nonsense, thinking that agreeing to a pitiful salary was what would keep the place running.

"I hate to bring this up," Frances began, "but can you cut back on the liquor you buy for Rose? I know you want to make her happy, but this is not the way to–"

Minnie stood up. "You know nothing about our mother. You walked out on her long ago. Lately she's been inviting me in to sit with her. She's not drunk at all, Frances. We have the most marvelous talks."

"When you come in to visit with her, do you bring alcohol?" Frances cleared her throat. "Maybe that's why she's thrilled to see you."

"Get out." The tone of Minnie's voice never wavered as she pointed toward the door. "You gave up the right to tell me what to do when you left us. Just like Pastor Tompkins says, a woman who doesn't cling to her home is a woman without purpose."

"You can't solve this problem by ignoring it, Minnie." Frances rose. "If we can't find the money to repair the roof in two weeks, it won't get done until the fall and by then, it will need a full replacement. Who knows how much damage will occur? Billy says we should put the house on the market." Frances quietly walked toward the door. She glanced up the stairs on her way by, nodding to acknowledge Lavender's presence. "It's not just you to consider, Minnie."

When she heard the door close, Minnie sat back at the table and wept. Lavender crept down the stairs and into the kitchen where she rubbed her back. "I'm sorry this falls on you. It's not fair."

"Thank you," Minnie sobbed. "It's not the fault of either of us. It's Charles. If he hadn't left and taken most of the money our aunt willed us, we wouldn't be in this predicament. Pastor Tompkins says he knew all along that Charles was no good. Not once did he contribute to the church's upkeep. Shameful." She wiped her eyes on her apron and looked up at her sister. "You know, Mother and I have been talking a lot about you lately. About the circumstances of your birth."

Lavender felt a knot in her stomach. She hadn't expected this conversation. "I don't need to know anything further about those people. They abandoned me."

Minnie shrugged. "Suit yourself. You may find it interesting someday."

"I have an idea about how to make the money we need." Lavender changed the subject as abruptly as she could. "You will have to help, though. You just can't be judgmental. We do what we must, remember?"

"What could you possibly know about making money?" Minnie cocked her head to the side. "You're not involving yourself in something untoward, are you, Lavender Ladieux? I won't approve of illegal means."

"Nothing illegal. It's a way to make money that won't take long and it's actually kind of fun." Lavender took in a deep breath, wondering if she would get through this entire explanation before Minnie exploded. "It's dancing. I go and dance at Lou Kowalski's Dance Hall. I make tips and have fun. There's nothing untoward, I promise. And after two or three nights, we'll have enough between the two of us to pay for the roof. I've almost earned all of it."

Minnie's eyes narrowed. "How long has this been going on? Pastor Tompkins told us to quit trying to shut that place down. While I trust him, I don't believe it's safe for a decent young lady."

Lavender looked at her sister incredulously. Minnie had to know by now that Lavender was sneaking out. She could hear. There were groceries magically appearing in the refrigerator. But they played this little game, and it suited Minnie just fine. It made her world so much easier to digest.

"My friend Bryla took me once. I've gone a few times. It allows me to buy things we need. Remember last week, when the handle to the soup pot broke? I had enough money to purchase a new one." Lavender held her breath, waiting for whatever came next.

Minnie thought carefully about what was said. "You're telling me that with just a few times at this dance hall, we can solve our problems with the roof?" She ignored Lavender's admission of guilt.

Lavender nodded eagerly. "And if you want to come more, we can build up some savings. For whatever happens next. We'll have a cushion and Billy won't need to put our house on the market."

Minnie's face eased. "While I don't approve of your going to this dance hall, this may be just what we need to solve this problem. It's temporary, mind you."

"Thank you, Minnie! You won't regret it!" Lavender jumped up and kissed her on the cheek. "I have a special dress to wear and a spare in case it gets dirty. My friend Bryla gave them to me." It was too soon to tell her about the trunk of clothes under the bed or the fact that she'd spent over one hundred dollars acquiring them.

"There's just one thing that concerns me: what will the pastor think of me? Although he doesn't want the place shut down, he wouldn't approve of me gallivanting all over town. Pastor Tompkins says activities that don't involve the church or the home aren't needed for the fulfillment of a woman."

Lavender thought again of his nights in the poker room. "He doesn't have to know. I won't tell any of your Church of the Woeful friends. Not even Frances. It will be our secret."

"Frances!" Minnie put her hand over her mouth. "I never thought of her. What will we tell her? She'll want to know where the money came from!"

"We'll tell her the pastor gave you extra work at his home. You mentioned he was looking for someone to paint his study."

Minnie looked at her with relief. "Yes, yes, of course he did. I'll tell her I painted for him all this week."

That evening, Lavender pulled her most dowdy dress from the trunk and gave it to Minnie. It was rust-colored and buttoned all the way up the front. Normally, she wore the top two buttons open, at least in part to stay cool while she was dancing. She pulled her cigarette girl uniform from the trunk, quickly thinking of a way to explain its risqué appearance to Minnie. After she applied a touch of lipstick and pulled her flaxen hair into a barrette on one side, she looked in the mirror with satisfaction; slightly grown-up looking, but not enough to alarm her sister.

She stepped quickly past Rose's room and knocked lightly on Minnie's door. "Here's a dress for you. Something that will compliment your features."

"Oh, my. You're quite stunning. I didn't expect that." Minnie looked her sister up and down.

Lavender dropped her shoulders, relieved to avoid questions about her outfit.

"Won't the young men be expecting perfection like you? I'm not sure they want to dance with a dowdy woman like me."

"Oh, Minnie," Lavender's heart melted. "I wish you saw yourself as the beauty you truly are. They are there to dance and have fun. They aren't they are looking for the next dish soap model. I promise you: you will have a good time, and you'll forget to be self-conscious. And remember, at the end of the evening, we we'll both be getting good tips. I may have to leave the dance floor for a time. I have extra duties to perform for Mr. Kowalski."

They arrived at Lou Kowalski's Dance Hall a little after 8:00 p.m. Minnie parked the car and held her sister's hand tenuously as they walked in together. "It will be fine, I promise," Lavender reassured her.

"Nice to see you brought a friend tonight, Lita!" Ralph the doorman said, tipping his hat to the women.

Lavender blushed, hoping Minnie didn't catch the name Ralph used. "Minnie, this is my friend, Ralph. He's just as cheery as he can be."

Ralph took Minnie's hand in his and kissed it. "What a lovely lady. I only wish I had time to dance with such a vision."

"She's dancing for the first time."

Minnie blushed and looked away. "I'm just here to see what all the fuss is about."

"Well, have a good time, both of you." Ralph opened the door and Lavender grabbed her sister's hand, leading her gently into the large hall She guided Minnie to the desk to get a number to pin on her skirt. When she finished, she nodded with satisfaction.

"Stand here, Minnie. When someone wants to dance with you, they'll know you're ready. I'll be back in a few minutes. I need to check on something."

Minnie nodded.

Lavender went to the game room, where Lou and four other men were already at the table. "You're late," he growled without looking up. "If I can't rely on you, then I'll have to find a replacement. Is that what you want?"

"No sir," Lavender replied, pulling the straps of the cigarette box over her head. "I brought my sister to dance tonight. I had to get her set up."

The game began and, soon, Pastor Tompkins stepped in. Lavender hadn't planned on him attending on a Thursday night. Usually, he came on Fridays when there were no Church of the Woeful activities he needed to attend. Lavender's face fell when he sat down and motioned for her to come to him.

"You look like a trollop with your hair like that," he whispered in her ear.

She shook her head and stood up, saying out loud, "I have cigarettes if you're interested."

After a half-hour, someone knocked on the door. It was another girl who danced frequently. "I need to speak with Lavender," she said frantically.

"What for?" Lou asked, smoke tumbling from his mouth.

"It's about her sister. She's in a tizzy."

"You brought your sister?" Pastor Tompkins yelled. "To this filthy establishment?" He stood, whether to strike Lavender, or to see to Minnie, was unclear.

"Hey, no bad-mouthing my place unless you want to play your cards with a few less teeth!" Lou barked. "Sit back down or lose your hand."

Pastor Tompkins looked around the room, waiting for one of the other men to back him up. When none of them did, he grudgingly dropped back into his seat and picked up his cards.

Lou nodded to Lavender. "Ten minutes."

She hurried to the front of the establishment where Minnie was sitting on a bench, her head in her hands, sobbing. "What's wrong, Minnie?"

"A man," she sobbed. "He touched me."

"What? Did you report him? They aren't allowed to do that, Minnie. It's not that kind of place."

The girl who had retrieved Lavender from the game room touched her arm and motioned for her to talk. They moved out of earshot of Minnie. "I saw the whole thing. It was a regular. Joe Wilson. We were all on the floor, doing the jive. Apparently, your sister has no idea what that is. She stood there in the middle of everyone like a bump. Joe tried to show her how to move and when she refused, he tried to move her out of the way. The crowd jostled them, and he accidentally touched her behind. He didn't mean anything."

Lavender returned to her sister and bent back down beside her. "I don't think this man was trying to bother you, Minnie."

"You don't know that!" Minnie screamed through her tears. "You ran off and left me. We've learned about these things from Pastor Tompkins. Men outside the church are all after one thing!" The music stopped and the energy in the room screeched to a halt. "You promised this would be fun. I'm not having any fun, Lavender! We need to go!" The door to the game room swung open and all the men stepped out into the hallway. As soon as Pastor Tompkins recognized it was Minnie making the fuss, he slunk back inside.

"I can't leave, Minnie." Lavender blushed, embarrassed to have been caught in the back room. "This is my real job. I sell cigarettes and Mr. Kowalski is counting on me. It's the only way we can afford to fix the roof."

Minnie refused to look at her sister. "Help! Anyone!" she called out into the sea of concerned faces on the dance floor. "I've been attacked, and my sister refuses to come to my aid!" The room was quiet as everyone contemplated what came next.

Ralph, came to Minnie's side and offered his arm. "I'll be happy to escort you to your car, Miss Ladieux."

She gazed at him with gratitude. "Oh, thank you, sir. Finally, a gentleman in this place!" She shot Lavender an angry glance before taking Ralph's arm. When they reached the door, she paused and turned around. "Disgraceful! All of you!" she yelled.

When the door shut behind her, the room re-

JOANN KEDER

sumed its normal buzz. Lavender returned to the poker room, plastering a smile on her face. "Sorry for the disruption, gentlemen!" she said cheerily.

"No more chances after this, Lita," Lou warned. "You cost me cigarette sales tonight. This is your last warning. Next time, I tell Ralph not to let you in."

Lavender gulped and nodded.

When the evening came to an end, she did her usual cleanup. She opened the drawer to deposit her tips, excited to see what had accumulated so far this month. To her horror, the drawer was empty. She walked into every room, looking for Lou. When she reached the kitchen, she found Jeannie sitting calmly on a stool, holding a giant wad of cash, and drinking a glass of milk.

"Why did you take that?" Lavender asked as anger welled up inside her. "That's not just from me. There are three other girls who earned that money!"

Jeannie grinned. "But you're the only one who is already in trouble. If Dad thinks you stole the money, you'll be fired."

"I'll tell him the truth. That you took it!" Lavender said defiantly. "He'll believe me!"

"He's not going to believe you," Jeannie said smarmily. "There have been fifty before you, all batting their eyes at him. There will be fifty more after you're gone. He doesn't care about you."

Tears of frustration formed in Lavender's eyes. "I

need that money. I'm going to fix my roof. If I don't get it fixed, the house will be ruined. What do you want me to do?"

"Leave. And never come back to the dance hall. If you were to make that promise, I'd give all of your tips back."

"I can't. I have nowhere to go." Lavender wiped her eyes on the back of her sleeve. "This job was my only hope."

Jeannie took the money and stuffed it into her purse. "I guess this is mine then. I'll leave it up to you to explain to the other girls what happened." She stood up and pulled her coat around her shoulders. "I'm going to buy the best stereo."

There was no point in trying to argue with Jeannie. She was right: whatever she told Lou, he would believe. Lavender stomped over to the coat hook and pulled her coat off so quickly, she tore the sleeve. "You'll get what's coming to you someday, Jeannie Kowalski!" she warned.

The next morning, Lavender left early for school. It was as much to avoid Minnie as to keep her mind on something else. After class, she stayed to speak with Mr. Anders. He was her only hope now. Without hesitation, she told him everything.

"I just need to find the money to fix our roof," she finished. "Please, Mr. Anders, if there's any way you can help me. I don't know where else to turn."

He had been patiently waiting for her to come to him since their last confrontation. In his experience with girls this age, they all came around eventually. He had a speech in his head about redemption and how, in his own life, he'd become someone better. That all went out the window when she told him her dire tale.

"I know exactly what to do. We'll get your roof fixed, don't worry."

CHAPTER TWELVE

Gavin Anders

G ALE ANDERS, A milk delivery man, and his wife, Nora, the school lunch lady, wanted nothing more than to raise a large family. After Nora's sixth miscarriage, they gave up on that dream. The following year, they were both pleased and surprised to welcome a son they named Gavin.

Gavin Anders grew up in a town not far from Tredford. He was an only child and his parents doted on him, spending all the money they had to give him an exceptional life. While he was polite, Gavin expected things without questioning just how it was his parents came to afford them. Gale and Nora went without the basics – skipping meals and wearing tattered clothing – in order to give Gavin a new scooter, or the best books filled with colorful pictures of the world.

In return, their son excelled in everything he did; always wanting to be the best to please his parents. He was the captain of his high school basketball team and won every contest in school, receiving ribbons for his essays on World War I and the Fall of the Roman Empire. All the while, his parents proudly supported him.

When he was 16, his mother developed a disturbing cough. She said it was nothing, and Gavin believed her. Nora stopped attending his games and performances, but Gale always cheered him on. That's why it came as a complete shock the day he came home from his basketball championship game and found his mother lying on the floor. He set the "most valuable player" trophy down as he shook his mother's shoulders. When she didn't respond, he noticed blood on the carpet and in the handkerchief she was holding. He called an ambulance and then his father, thinking perhaps she'd taken a fall while cleaning the living room windows and knocked her head.

Gale met them at the hospital, where a doctor delivered the sobering news: Nora was dying of tuberculosis. "Told her we needed to treat her kidney problems years ago. It may have prevented this altogether," the doctor admonished them both, "I wish you would've taken better care of her."

"What's he talking about, Dad?" Gavin asked earnestly. To him, his mother was slightly ill, temporarily sidelined. It didn't seem possible that the person whose smile never left her face could be sick enough to die. His parents were indestructible.

Gale shrugged. "That medicine he prescribed for her was expensive. She and I decided our money should go to other things." He looked at the ground. "It's what your mother wanted. She's got no regrets."

Gavin's mouth fell open. "You knew Mom was sick, and you didn't say anything? You must not love her the way I do!"

"Love 'r more than you know. All that woman's ever wanted in her life was to see you happy." Gale's face was twisted in pain. "Remember when you asked for those books to study for your college exams last Christmas? We bought those instead of the medicine. She couldn't bear to see you disappointed on Christmas morning." Gale turned and walked away from his son. "I'll bring your mother some things from home."

Gavin had never before considered himself to be selfish, but now he saw that all he did was take. Not once did he offer to get an after-school job to help them, or insist he needed less. The guilt he felt in his mother's last days was overwhelming at some times; depleting at others. When she died, Gavin resolved to be a shining example of his mother's selflessness. He spent all of his extra time volunteering at the soup kitchen, with never-ending lines that wound around each block. The Depression never ended in Sprague, and those who were hungry still needed to eat.

Some days, he would take another volunteer with him to carry a tureen of coffee while he ladled the warm drink into the cups of those who'd been standing in line for hours. He asked for each story, and listened intently as each person or family explained the loss they had experienced that placed them in the embarrassing position of asking for help.

The stories that touched his heart the most were those of the young women left out in the cold. Some of them had been expelled from their homes because of misunderstandings, while others were merely looked upon as a burdensome extra mouth to feed. Even more difficult to hear were the young women who had fallen in love, or so they thought, only to be tossed aside with nothing to their names.

Gavin vowed his mission in life would be to help people. Not just any person, but the young women whose suffering went unheeded. He wanted to skip college altogether and dedicate himself to these women's futures, but his father convinced him otherwise. "The best way to help them is to become a teacher. Guide them, son. Your mother always saw your caring side."

His father died a month before he got his teaching diploma, leaving him their dilapidated home and his milk truck with three flat tires. He had a building to house his dream, but no money to fix it up. To honor his parents' memories, he had to find funding.

As they sat in the Tredford High School teacher's lounge one rainy Wednesday, he told his fellow teachers of his plans to open a home for young women with nowhere to go. He wished to expand from there, maybe opening a community center and more. The room was silent until the French teacher burst out laughing. "And where do you suppose you'll get the money for that?"

Gavin shook his head. "I'm still working on that. This is for my mother. The girls can all pitch in and help once I get enough money to purchase supplies."

Principal Morris caught his arm as he left that day. "I may know a way for you to make your money. If you're willing to put in some time."

For the next six weeks, Gavin spent his weekends at Principal Morris' home, learning the game of poker. Principal Morris taught him when to fold, how to read other people's faces and movements, and how to play with no mercy. The principal took him to his first poker game; a gathering of high-profile men. In addition to Gavin and Mr. Morris, in attendance were the power-players in the community: a banker, a lawyer, and the owner of the nicest restaurant in town.

Gavin followed his instructions to a tee, just as he'd done his entire life. That night, he went home with almost $300. As Mr. Morris took him to seedier places with higher-stake gamblers, his thirst for winning only grew.

When he acquired enough to open Nora's House, a Home for Troubled Teens, he knew he should quit. But there would be operating expenses, and – what if they needed to expand? Soon, gambling was all he thought about. He barely left time to finish his lesson plans each week as he studied the books Mr. Morris found for him. Convincing himself it was for the betterment of the community, he allowed his obsession to grow. It was a well with no bottom.

Finally, Principal Morris took him aside. "Your students are suffering. I gave you the opportunity to get your dream off the ground. Don't make me sorry that I did," he said sternly. "Find a business to support your charity and move on with your life, while you're still young enough to have one. If you don't, I'll have no choice but to terminate your employment."

Gavin looked at himself in the mirror. Gaunt, pale, losing hair. He was a shell of his former self, not the handsome, young man his mother called her "gallant knight."

One night, when he was about to leave for his nightly poker game, there was a knock on the door. A young woman from one of his classes was asking for help. Not for herself, but her neighbor. "I can hear her pleas for help at night when her window is open," she cried. "Please, Mr. Anders. Go and save her."

Gavin Anders had kept a secret ever since junior high. While his mother and father thought his ambition knew no bounds, he was, in actuality, hiding. After-school activities such as sports and chess Hall were ways to stay away from the school bullies who tormented the loner relentlessly. If he spent long enough at school each afternoon, they grew bored and went home without beating him up. Even after the death of his mother, they pursued him; taunting, poking, smacking and laughing at him.

Now that he was an adult, he still carried those scars. Gavin was a champion of the downtrodden, only if they came to him. He hated conflict of any kind. That night, he went to the home of the abused girl and stood on the sidewalk in front, listening to loud, uncomfortable sounds. He couldn't bring himself to knock on the door and save the girl. The next week, she was hospitalized with severe injuries. For five days, he was wracked with guilt and didn't leave his home.

Mr. Morris came to check on him. "You can't save them all, Gavin," he said. "You need to pick yourself up and move on. I've got an idea for your charity. Go to those rich men at the poker games. Make a deal with them that you'll never play again if they'll fund your endeavors. They'll all be relieved."

Gavin did just that and ended his time at the

poker table.

The day Lavender came to him with her plaintive eyes and the same dark circles he knew so well from his own addiction, he realized immediately what his parents would say.

"Please, Mr. Anders. I don't know what to do. I need the money to repair our roof."

"Show up for your job as you always do. I can fix it."

CHAPTER THIRTEEN

Tredford, Connecticut
May, 1959

I T WAS STRANGE for Lavender to walk in to Lou Kowalski's Dance Hall with someone other than Bryla. She was used to being by herself; the fact that she could do something on her own made her proud. She walked behind Mr. Anders as they entered, her eyes focused on the ground in front of them.

"Brought a friend tonight, Lavender?" Ralph asked her, surprised.

"An acquaintance," she said noncommittally. They entered and hurried to the back room, where the other men gathered for that evening's game. All of them, including Lou, raised a brow as Gavin sat down at the table.

Lavender slipped the cigarette holder over her head and pulled the cash from the drawer, as if nothing new was happening.

"Cigarette?" she asked Bryla's friend, Cal.

"Gavin? Surprised to see you here," Mr. Morris

said, pulling out the chair next to him. "Sit. I'm looking forward to having some good competition again." He leaned over as Gavin sat and whispered, "Sure you want to do this, son? You got yourself into a heap of trouble before."

Gavin nodded. "I'll give you a run for your money, sir," he said out loud, a little too enthusiastically.

Pastor Tompkins entered soon after, his eyes widening at the sight of a new player. He took his usual seat and adjusted his pants as Lavender nodded to Gavin.

"Facing north brings me the most luck." Gavin rose from his seat and moved to the chair next to Pastor Tompkins.

Pastor Tompkins shuffled uncomfortably in his chair. "I don't care for new meat next to me. Lou, will you switch with me?"

Lou grumbled as he chewed on the end of his cigar. "Just this once." The two men got up and changed places. Lavender looked at Mr. Anders with dismay.

Throughout the evening, each time Pastor Tompkins removed a card from his hidden pocket, Lavender stood behind him, signaling to Mr. Anders across the table by itching her nose, who noted the hand he himself had and the time. More times than not, Pastor Tompkins won each round. Gavin won two pots though – the biggest of the evening – which relieved Lavender. She knew some of that money would go to repairing her roof.

As they finished, Pastor Tompkins stood just as Lavender walked by, carrying half-empty glasses. He shoved his elbow into her side, causing her to spill the remainder of the drinks onto her dress. "Got to be a little more careful, Miss Ladieux," he sneered.

She picked up the glasses and turned to look for a rag. He grabbed her arm and pulled it at an odd angle, away from her body, causing her to wince in pain. "I know exactly what's happening. You're not going to blow this for me. You're nothing. I can have you disposed of and no one will care."

She refused to look him in the eye. That was his power. Whenever Minnie looked at him, it was as if he had her in a trance. "What do you want, Pastor Tompkins? I won't work for you. You've got your hooks in my sister. There's nothing else you can take from me." At that moment, she felt completely depleted. Every day of her life was a fight for something and she just didn't care anymore.

"I don't know who your friend is, but I don't him to come back," he growled. "There's plenty more games in town. If I see him here again, I'll–" he paused, realizing Lavender wasn't afraid for her safety. "I'll make life miserable for the poor wretch you call a sister. She'll be scrubbing my kitchen with a toothbrush while she sings the alphabet backwards." He let out a roaring laugh, like a lion triumphantly controlling his pride.

Gavin, who had been talking to the principal in the hallway, stuck his head inside the room. Pastor Tompkins immediately released her arm.

"Anything wrong here?" Gavin asked.

"Nothing at all, fine sir." Pastor Tompkins smiled. "Just telling the girl she needs to be less clumsy. I've got some pews need cleaning. That would sharpen her skills a bit, don't you think?"

Gavin cleared his throat uncomfortably. "I've got the car warming up, Lavender. Come out as soon as you can."

Pastor Tompkins put his hand on Gavin's shoulder, as if they'd been friends forever. "You're quite the player, pal. Who taught you?"

"Oh, you know. The locals." He moved into the room and took Lavender's hand. "C'mon Lavender. I'll tell Mr. Kowalski your ride is leaving."

She obediently followed him outside. When they reached his car, she let out her breath. "I don't like that man. He's awful. Poor Minnie is under his spell."

"I got your money. All of it. You never have to go back to that place again." Gavin pressed a roll of cash into her palm. "I forgot how exhilarating that could be. Especially knowing there was a cheater in the room. It really kept me on my toes."

She curled her fingers around the money and placed it in her coat pocket. The thought of never returning to Lou Kowalski's Dance Hall, despite all that had gone on, was disheartening. Having somewhere to go and being treated as an adult gave her purpose.

"Lou's expecting me. He doesn't have any other cigarette girls for the rest of the week."

Gavin pulled the car over. "We made a deal. You wouldn't go back to that place if I got you the money," he said solemnly. "And you would consider moving into the home for girls."

"YOU made that decision," Lavender huffed. "I just asked for your help. I didn't realize there were strings attached." She folded her arms across her chest.

"Lavender, that isn't a safe place for you. That is a place for adults and you are still a child, no matter what you learned at home. You need a chance to develop into a young lady who has—"

"Who has morals? Refinement? The makings of a good wife? Is that what you're saying? I have plenty of morals and I don't need refinement, thank you; more than Pastor Tompkins ever will. Besides, I'm never going to marry. I won't need any kind of help from anyone!"

Gavin looked at her with dismay. "I want the best for you. I can see your future and everything that the world has to offer you. None of it happens in Lou Kowalski's Dance Hall."

"I'll go back – just for this week – and finish out my shifts. But I can't move out. Minnie needs me."

"Fair enough." Gavin put the car in gear. "if you would at least come to the center and see what we do there, I think you would be impressed. Would you join me on Thursday? I'll show you around and introduce you to the other girls."

They rode the rest of the way home in silence. Lavender was thinking about her future. She had no idea what she wanted. Her dream of being a star had been crushed. And whatever Mr. Anders saw for her – – this woman cooking in the kitchen with a baby on her hip thing – was someone else.

The next night, she showed up for her shift as usual. Lou pulled her aside before the men arrived. "I've gotten some distressing news about you, young lady." He put his cigar to his mouth and looked away as he blew smoke rings. "Distressing, indeed."

"Oh?" Lavender gulped.

"Heard from Pastor Tompkins that you brought a ringer in last night. He said it was your boyfriend. And that you were looking at his cards all evening. We can't have that here. My boys gotta trust me or they won't come back."

She hoped her face wasn't flushed, but she could feel it burning. "I don't have a boyfriend, sir. There was a gentleman here that I know from another part of my life. He gave me a ride, and we may have had a conversation or two, but that's all there is to that story."

Lou shook his head. "Well, it's not just that. I don't trust that old Tompkins; there's something wrong with him. But my daughter Jeanie gave me an earful. She said she caught you taking all the cash from the top drawer after she told you she'd heard you were sleeping with some of the customers." He examined his cigar like it was a fine jewel. "Don't like to hear that. I run a clean operation here. You're a pretty little thing and you do a good job. One of these alone wouldn't push my buttons too hard. But you've got quite a stack of transgressions against you, girl. I'm afraid I'm gonna have to let you go."

Something strange gripped Lavender. She was going to quit in two days, at least that's what she had told Gavin. But when Mr. Kowalski said he was going to let her go, she felt as though she'd dropped off a cliff. She couldn't bear to leave with her reputation in tatters because of lies from a hateful girl. "What if we were to make a deal? What if I had proof someone has been cheating?"

Lou raised his eyebrows and stared at her. "Who is that?"

"Deal first?"

"Again, with the deal." Lou chuckled. "You're a

smart cookie, Lita, I'll give you that. Your job for information." Lou folded his arms across his enormous stomach. "Now spill it."

"Pastor Tompkins has an extra pocket in his pants that I've seen him pull cards out of. It's not in the usual spot; it's sewn into the waistband."

Lou squinted. "You sure about that?"

"Yes, sir. I've seen it on several occasions. That's how he wins so many hands, even though he tells everyone it's divine intervention. I let Mr. Anders know that Pastor Tompkins was cheating, that's true. Just so he could win fair and square."

"Well, tonight it's gonna be me you signal to. I want you to let me know every time he pulls the card out. I'm gonna keep my eye on him. Sure hope you're right, because, if you're yanking my chain, you're going to be in a world of hurt. I don't get on well with those who cross me. Don't care who you are."

"Yes, sir." Lavender felt a small sense of satisfaction for calling out Pastor Tompkins. He'd caused Minnie's life to become a drudgery of nonsensical rituals.

All the usual men arrived for their poker game. She handed out cigarettes and got each of them their drink. Pastor Tompkins snickered and attempted to say something threatening into her ear, but she just moved along. Tonight, she wasn't afraid of him.

During the second round, he pulled a new queen

out of his hidden pocket. A moment later, he took a six of Halls out of his hand and swapped the cards. "Bear Brand tonight, Mr. Kowalski?" She asked, just as they'd rehearsed. He looked up from his cards, for a moment with no recollection of their conversation. "Huh? Oh, right. Set 'em here."

Lavender set the cigarettes on the table, touching her nose lightly. She went around to the other players, hoping he'd got the sign. When they finished that round, Pastor Tompkins reached for a new deck of cards, as was their tradition mid-evening.

"Wait." Lou put a sausage finger in the air. "I wanna count the cards first. See if anything's missin'."

The looks around the table were those of collective disbelief. "You think we're cheating? Lou – After all this time–" someone said angrily. They all knew better than to cross Lou Kowalski, so after that, they sat silently as he sorted the cards.

"We're missing a six of Halls. Anyone know what might've happened to it?" He looked around the room at each face, never pausing too long on one. "Maybe look on the floor. See if one of you may have 'dropped' it."

Lou watched without comment as Pastor Tompkins bent down, pretending to look, then placed the card on the table and said, "Must've fallen out while someone shuffled."

The rest of the evening went on uneventfully. When all the men got up to leave, Lou touched Pastor Tompkins back. "Need to visit a minute."

Pastor Tompkins put on his Sunday-ready smile and draped his coat over one arm. "What do you need tonight, Lou? Some words of advice, maybe? Or perhaps you're going to make a donation to The Church of the Woeful's ladies' society?"

"Let's not fool around here, Tompkins. I know what you're doing. I know you've been doing it for a while. I should've caught on, but even a seasoned old buzzard like me can miss a few things."

"I don't know what you're talking about, Lou. If you're insinuating some kind of cheating, well, that's insulting. I'm a man of the cloth," Pastor Tompkins blustered. "There is nothing that I do that isn't for the good of the community. Even my winnings here. I put them all in the coffers of The Church of the Woeful. You're going to take that away from all the good people of my church community?"

"I'm sure we can work something out." Lou put his arm around Pastor Tompkins and guided him out the back door, heading toward the burn-pit. "I'll make a nice donation to The Church of the Woeful in your name."

Lavender was cleaning up the table inside as they were talking. She hoped it wouldn't get ugly. Minnie would never forgive her if Pastor Tompkins spent the rest of the week in a funk.

She watched the two men laughing and talking as Lou started the fire. They stood and laughed while Lou pulled out a cigar and offered it to Pastor Tompkins. Lou put his arm around the Pastor's shoulder as they talked and she let out a sigh of relief. She returned to her cleaning, glancing at them every few minutes. What happened next took only a few seconds, but played in Lavender's head in slow motion for years.

Lou pulled a gun out of his pocket. There was only a split second between that image and the one of him shooting a man in the chest. She jumped, but her feet seemed rooted to that spot and she could not move. She was forced to watch as the force of the blast made the pastor stumble and fall into the raging fire of the burn pit. Lavender couldn't be sure if what she saw was real or if her mind had just played a giant, ugly trick on her. Lou turned to view the open doorway where Lavender stood motionless.

"What will Minnie say?" she mouthed. Lou looked away, stirring the pit to arouse the flames engulfing Pastor Tompkins.

She continued cleaning, numb and in shock. She wiped down everything thoroughly, including the ax Lou kept on the wall. It was so shiny she could see her pale reflection. After she finished, she tried to scurry out of the back room as quickly as she could.

As she was putting on her coat, she felt someone grab her arm. This time, she screamed.

Lou clasped his other hand over her mouth. "I don't know what you think you saw out there. Nothing happened tonight."

She nodded and tried to walk toward the door, but he held her tight. "We're in this together. I own you now. Any word out of your mouth and I put the gun in your hand. The poor Pastor, you thought he was getting handsy, and you pushed him in the fire pit. See how easy that works? Ol' Lou's got some pull in this town."

Lavender said nothing. Her mind was empty, devoid of thought or feeling after all that had transpired. She stood, once again rooted in place.

"See ya tomorrow night, kid." Lou released her arm and dusted off the back of her coat. "Who knows where things could go for us now?"

CHAPTER FOURTEEN

Lavender Ladieux
September, 1959

MINNIE HAD BEEN angry with her ever since the night at Lou Kowalski's Dance Hall, when she felt she was being threatened. Despite this, Lavender and her sister kept up their normal routine.

"I'll be late tonight. Ever since Pastor Tompkins surprised us all by leaving for a mission trip to South America, we've been waiting for a new leader," she began as she stirred the eggs Lavender had purchased. "He left instructions for Alfred Manner to take the pulpit in his stead, only just announced. I've been assigned to instruct him on Pastor Tompkins' ways. Things outside his manual." She hummed happily to herself.

Lavender remembered Alfred; he was one of Lou's henchmen. He stood in the back of the poker room, just to make sure there was no trouble. He was the furthest thing from a minister she could imagine. "Maybe now is the time to start fresh.

You've mentioned several ideas for running The Church of the Woeful more smoothly."

"Oh, I don't mind instructing him. This will be fun!" She scooped a spatula full of scrambled eggs onto Lavender's plate. "It's strange though, I've never heard Pastor mention Mr. Manner before. It's almost like he dropped from the sky." She giggled. "Heavenly addition, you might say."

"Yes, I would imagine." Lavender looked at her, perplexed. There was some relief on her sister's face, no doubt from being out from under Pastor Tompkins' thumb. She didn't seem to mind that the person she'd devoted her life to was suddenly nowhere to be found.

"I won't see you, then. I've got to get to work early." There was no point in hiding it anymore. Minnie knew where she was spending her time. "Did Frances say when they'd be here to start on the new roof?"

"Friday, I think," Minnie replied absently, not bothering to thank her younger sister for coming up with the cash needed for the repairs. "Oh, Mr. Manner says we ought not be judgmental of the dance hall. He says it's just a place for fun. We're going to have a gathering there next month. You should come!"

Lavender nodded uncomfortably and put her plate in the sink. "I need to get to school early today." She kissed Minnie on the cheek. "I'll see you tomorrow."

"Bye, dear. You must be rather important, with all the hours you've been putting in."

She didn't reply. It was too ugly to think about what had happened to Pastor Tompkins, so most of the time she didn't allow her mind to go there. Today, after school, she had a meeting scheduled with Mr. Anders. She had successfully avoided him outside of class ever since the night she promised him she'd quit. It would be an admission of failure if he knew she went back to Lou; and now, he owned her.

Mr. Anders sent a note to her in PE class that said he needed to see her after school. She thought he'd given up trying to contact her. As the hours wore on in school, she contemplated skipping her last class and going to Bryla's house, but eventually her curiosity got the better of her.

Mr. Anders looked up from grading papers as she entered. "Lavender? I was hoping we could keep in touch over the summer. I tried calling your home several times but no one ever answered. Please sit." He pulled a chair next to his desk and observed her as she gingerly lowered herself. "How are things going?"

"Wonderful!" she responded, a bit too brightly. "I'm still working for Lou. He promoted me. I'm the head cigarette girl, so I get most of the tips. We got our new roof and it's dreamy. Minnie and I won't have to move anytime soon. Things are going swimmingly!"

Gavin placed his hands on the desk and stared at them. "The thing is: Principal Morris told me he was there last week, and you weren't in the poker room. He said Lou brought in someone else because he had you busy with 'other things.'"

Her stoicism only lasted twenty seconds. "He makes me dance privately for the men who pay extra. Not with them – for them," she snuffled. "And then when they're gone, it's just me and Lou. If he doesn't have his hands all over me, he's hitting me. He says that's why I make extra money – to be his punching bag. I'm in a prison and there's no way out." She put her hands on the table and rested her head on top of them, unable to stop the emotion from pouring out.

Gavin touched her head gently. "There's always a way out. Why does he have this kind of control over you? The last I knew, you were planning to quit. You're not like your sister – beholden to others – right?"

There was no one else she could tell, and the words came shooting out of her like an open faucet whether she wanted them to or not. "I saw him doing something bad. Horrible. And if I tell anyone, he'll blame it on me."

Gavin sat back in his chair and thought for a moment. "So, what you're telling me is that you were placed in a bad position through no fault of your own?"

She didn't lift her head but nodded.

"If I were to make a guess, would you nod yes or no?"

She nodded once more.

"Lou has been violent before. People have disappeared with no word. No one dares question Lou; he's too powerful in this town. Was he violent with someone?"

She nodded again, not daring to look at him.

Gavin swallowed hard. "Did this violence end in death?"

"Yes," she whispered.

It only took him a matter of moments to figure out who it was. "I only know of one person in our community who hasn't been seen. That's Pastor Tompkins." Gavin stood up. "Lou killed Pastor Tompkins? It makes sense. I don't know why I didn't put that together sooner." He walked over to the large panel of windows and stood, staring at the teens laughing in the schoolyard. "He's good at making people disappear without being noticed, though. Kowalski's been doing it to his enemies for years." He turned around and looked at the forlorn girl. "Lavender, you're in terrible danger. We've got to get you out of town."

"But I can't leave!" she protested. "He'll know! He'll find me!"

"Go to work as usual tonight. I'll take care of everything."

Lavender looked at him with trepidation. It wasn't the first time he'd uttered these words; but, this time, the stakes were much higher.

CHAPTER FIFTEEN

Lavender Ladieux
October, 1959

Lou PUNCHED HER hard enough to knock her off her feet for the hundredth time. The longer she suffered through his abuse, the more frequent it became. She'd hoped Gavin would show up to save her night after night. He didn't. She didn't bother going to his class anymore. Facing someone she thought was her savior but who turned out to be a disappointment was worse than being with Lou. At least she knew where she stood with him.

Her body battered and bruised, Lavender had a hard time dragging herself to the kitchen for breakfast. Minnie found a way to make it even tougher. "You understand, don't you dear?" Minnie set a cup of tea in front of Lavender.

Even though Minnie was spending more time with Rose, Lavender had never expected this kind of betrayal. "Not really. You're saying you don't want me here anymore?" Lavender shakily brought the cup up to her lips.

"Rose thinks it's best. She's feeling better now, but she can't walk about the house freely as long as you live here. She thinks you're working for the enemy."

"What enemy?" Lavender asked incredulously.

"Oh, Rose says you've been working against her all these years. She thinks that's why Charles left. I know that's not true, but if she's going to be healthy again, I have to do what makes her feel safe."

There had been too many harsh things in her recent life for her to feel anything anymore, including shock. She'd known for some time that Rose was filling Minnie's head with nonsense. One day, she asked Minnie to nail her door shut so she couldn't ever come out again and ruin things. Minnie only considered it for a moment.

"Maybe you can go live with Frances and Billy after they marry. They'd be happy to have someone else to keep the place clean. Just until you find a proper husband. You know, Ralph, the doorman from Mr. Kowalski's Dance Hall has been coming to The Church of the Woeful. He's such a nice man. He asked me if I would accompany him out for a soda after Wednesday service, and I think I might go. If you'd come to The Church of the Woeful, you might find an agreeable gentleman too!"

She shouldn't have been surprised that Minnie

would turn her out. It was bound to happen eventually, given her inability to live in reality. Her life consisted of the church where Lou's henchmen ran things, and the words of Rose. "I'm not going to your church, Minnie," she said quietly. "When do you want me out?"

"Oh, a week or two."

Lavender rose to leave the kitchen, but Minnie stopped her. She put her hands on either side of Lavender's face. "Never quit dreaming, dear. Who knows what's going to come of it. Our new pastor told me the other night that our dreams will only come true if we do for others as we do for ourselves. I think he's right. I'm doing what's best for Rose. And you'll do what's best for you." She smiled cheerily. "We all do what we must, as mother always says."

Lavender took one of Minnie's hands and kissed it before placing it in hers. "I'd love for your life to be about more than 'must'. What about doing something enjoyable? Selfish, even? It's time Minnie Ladieux came first."

Minnie sniffed and pulled her hand back. "Not now."

Lavender sat through all of her classes that day as if she were in a dream. She knew what was coming each time with Lou. Soon, she would have to pack up her things and find another place to live. Her world, imperfect as it was, had been predictable these past few months. Now it neared implosion. If she could just get away from Lou, maybe she could start over. There was nowhere to hide, unfortunately. He was right about that.

She was walking down the hall, holding her books tightly to her chest when she bumped into someone. She looked up to see the harsh face of Jeannie Kowalski. "I saw you with my father the other night. You're disgusting. I'm going to tell everyone who you really are. Everyone I haven't already."

"I'm sorry, Jeannie. I don't know what you mean," she looked away, without the energy to fight.

"You and my dad. I saw him kissing you. You're just another floozy. In a month, you'll disappear just like the last one. Poof!" She made a wide gesture with her arms, narrowly missing Lavender's head.

Lavender pushed past her, her heart racing. She skipped Mr. Anders class, unable to face him. He'd let her down just like Charles and Rose and now Minnie.

As she was pulling things from her locker, Mr. Anders stepped out of his classroom. "Miss Ladieux? Could you see me when school is dismissed? We need to talk."

She shook her head firmly. "I'm busy. I have to get to work." She turned and walked down the hall without fear of reprisal.

"I can fix this!" Mr. Anders called after her. He ran to catch up and, when he did, he grabbed her arm. "Don't go to work tonight. Just stay home and I'll take care of everything."

She stopped for a moment, glaring at him. "You've said that before. No one can help me now, Mr. Anders."

"I was – a coward. I made a promise to my mother that I would help others and I let you down. It's unforgiveable. She came to me in a dream last night, telling me to stand up and be the man she expected me to be. That's exactly what I'm going to do. Stay home from work tonight. Do as I say, Lavender and things will be all right."

She wanted to tell him she'd been kicked out of her home, that she needed his home for young women now. The words stuck in her throat. She nodded to him and shook herself free from his arm before scurrying off.

Lavender trudged home, realizing that by asking Gavin for help, she would be exchanging one captor for another. No, she'd find another way. When she walked in through the kitchen, it surprised her to see Rose sitting at the table, drinking coffee. Her hair was fixed just as it had been all those years ago, with a splash of lipstick across her lips. She was wearing one of the dresses from the trunk under Lavender's bed – the lightning blue one with a blue and green plaid tie at the collar.

"Do you always arrive home so late from school? You've got a lovely collection of clothing," she commented, taking a sip of her coffee.

"Did Minnie forget to bring you something this morning? I can get it for you," Lavender dropped her books and walked past Rose, avoiding her as carefully as possible while she plotted what to do next.

Rose followed her, folding her arms and leaning in the doorway. "You're quite the looker. I'd forgotten. You know, Minnie and I have conversations about you. She tells me everything."

"Oh?" Lavender hung up her coat and brushed lint off her skirt, wanting to run upstairs to check her trunk to see what else was missing. "Well, I have homework. I should–"

"You've got quite a thing going for yourself. Working nights at the Hall. I found your money upstairs. I was premature in asking you to leave. You could work every night if you weren't going to school. No more need for Charles. I'm sober now and I can manage the funds."

Lavender gulped. "I have to go." She took her coat off the hook once again and pulled it around her tightly, before dashing out the door. She ran as hard and as fast as she could, blinded by her tears as she passed the large houses on Melody Lane. She turned down Bryla's street and continued running. There was no destination, just a need for her feet to carry her as far away from her misery as they could.

When she reached a diner with bright lights and the welcoming smell of baking cinnamon rolls, she went inside. She sat, drinking coffee with trembling hands trying to figure out her next move. As she brought the warm liquid to her lips, she noticed a familiar figure across the street. Lavender ran outside. "Frances!" She waved furiously as her sister walked up the stairs of an apartment building, not the boarding house she told the family she'd been living in. Frances walked across the busy street and motioned for her sister to join her inside the coffee shop.

"Oh, Frances, you're such a sight for sore eyes!" Lavender held her sister tightly.

"Let's sit down," Frances said tersely.

"I have to tell you about Rose–"

"Well, you've caught me. I suppose Minnie sent you, as some sort of spy for her and our crazy mother," Frances said sharply.

"What?" Lavender had never heard her sister speak so harshly to her before. "I'm not here for either of them." She wanted to beg Frances to take her in, but something seemed off.

"You might as well know." Frances sighed. "Billy

lost his job. His father found out and we don't know what we'll do next."

"Why did Billy lose his job? I'm so sorry!"

Frances looked at her with curiosity. "You really don't know? It's all over town. I've been living with Billy. I never moved into the boarding house. Now we're expecting." She rubbed her belly for a moment before remembering they were in public. "His father said that wasn't the proper way for a young doctor to behave. So, he's kicked him out of his practice. We lost everything. I lost my job too."

Lavender reached over and grabbed her sister's hand. "I'm so sorry. I wish I knew what to say. What will you do?"

"Courthouse wedding," Frances said matter-of-factly. "We'll probably move somewhere else and start over. We all do what we must, Lavender." She squeezed her sister's hand. "At least I won't have to worry about my baby sister. You've always taken care of yourself quite well. I know you've been working at the dance hall to keep food on the table. That's also common knowledge around town." Frances looked at her watch. "I've got to make dinner before Billy gets home. We've got a meeting with a potential clinic in Sprague tomorrow and Billy wants me to help him practice his interview. She stood and kissed Lavender on the head. "Be well, sister. I'll be in touch soon."

Lavender watched her eldest sister walk away confidently. Frances was the only good thing left in her life and she was moving on, too. She sat in the café until it closed, thinking about what came next. Maybe move in with Bryla and go to secretary school, like Frances. Or she could get a job in a diner like this one.

"Who am I kidding?" she said out loud. "I'll never be able to have my own life as long as I'm tied to him."

"Miss Lita?" She felt a hand on her back. When she turned around, she recognized the face as Steven, the man she'd met her very first night at the dance hall. He came regularly, but she didn't dance much, at least publicly, any more.

"Steven? How nice to see you." It was comforting to see a familiar face.

"What are you doing here by yourself? Can I offer you a ride somewhere?"

Lavender smiled. "You're such a nice person. I don't need a–" She paused, thinking about what she'd lost today and the dark road ahead. "Actually, I would like a ride to Lou Kowalski's Dance Hall, if it's not too far out of your way."

"You look like you could use a good, hot meal, if you don't mind my saying so. Why don't you let me take you to Mel's Italian down the street first?"

She could feel her stomach growling now and

realized she hadn't eaten since breakfast. "That would be lovely, Steven," she said with gratitude. "I needed a friend like you today."

As the two laughed and ate, Lavender realized this was the life she wanted: laughing and enjoying the company of others. There was only one thing standing in her way. She looked at the clock. "It's almost ten!"

"You can dance another night, can't you?" Steven asked.

"No, I really need to speak with Lou tonight. Can you still drive me?"

The two left the restaurant and drove out to Strange Lake. "Do you want me to wait here for you, Lita?" Steven asked as she got out.

"There's no telling how long this will take. I appreciate the ride, Steven!" She shut the door before he could continue the conversation.

"Lita?" Ralph asked as she straightened her skirt. "I didn't think you were coming tonight. We're almost done for the evening. You sure you wanna see Lou at this late hour? Maybe you'd rather wait until another time?"

She grabbed Ralph and hugged him hard. "Thank you. I need to talk to him tonight or I'll lose my nerve." He had to know what Lou did after hours. As she walked to the back of the building, she took in a deep breath, letting it out slowly. When she reached the poker room, the usual men were finishing up their game. Lavender looked around the room at the familiar faces: Lou, Mr. Morris, the man who owned the grocery store, and Alfred, the replacement pastor at The Church of the Woeful. They all looked surprised to see her. Lavender's eyes rested on one more person.

"I need to speak with you when you're finished, Gavin," she said boldly.

Mr. Anders shook his head furiously. "Not tonight. We can talk tomorrow." He said firmly. "I didn't think you were coming tonight."

Lou chuckled and eyed her greedily. "Tell your ride you'll be staying late tonight."

Lavender didn't reply, but moved to the hall until they finished. She tried to catch Mr. Ander's arm as he walked by, but he shook her off. She watched the poker room while tonight's cigarette girl finished her cleaning. Lou stood out by the burn pit, smoking his cigar. Lavender thought carefully about her options. She could run away now or she could plan a life with a nice man like Steven. Both options offered a new start. But unless she ended this right here, right now – Lou would always be a threat to her life. She had to do what she came for.

With shaky legs, she walked up behind Lou and tapped him on the shoulder. "I need to talk to you."

He grabbed her and pulled her in close, his hands

moving all over her. "We can talk later. First things first." He put his greasy lips on her neck and she pushed him away.

"Stop!" She screamed. "I'm done! I quit! I can't do this anymore!"

He came at her again, this time with such violence in his eyes, she thought it was the end. She'd never seen Hollywood or New York, but maybe her life was supposed to end without those images. She was once again rooted in place, unable to move as he lunged in slow motion toward her.

When his outstretched arms reached her, he grunted loudly. She felt the weight of his body on her chest. Instead of pawing her, his fingers only twitched against her face. His head slumped against her shoulder and she leaned back, letting his large body fall to the ground. When he did, she had to blink several times to comprehend the sight in front of her.

In this middle of his back was the ax that hung above the *Lou Kowalski Ax Throwing Champion, Kenowala State Fair, 1949* plaque. When she looked around to see who else was taking in this horrifying sight, she spotted Gavin Anders, splattered in Lou's blood, his entire body shaking. His mouth hung open at an awkward angle.

"You killed him?" she whispered.

"I told you I would take care of it. You shouldn't

have come tonight." He put his hands on his knees and tried to steady himself. "I had this planned out; I was going to wait until everyone was gone and shoot him. I've been working up the nerve to do that for months. Then I saw him attacking you and something came over me. The only weapon close by was the ax. I had no choice. I had to save you." He stood up and looked at her hopefully. "Right?"

"There was no other way," she agreed.

"I didn't think about what I'd do with the body." Gavin began pacing, wiping his hands incessantly on his pants. "We'll have to leave town. Tonight."

"We'll put him in the burn pit, the way he did Pastor Tompkins." Lavender said methodically. "And then we'll leave. Can you pack a bag quickly? Gather your money?"

"Yes, yes, that's what we'll do. You're a smart girl, Lavender Ladieux."

"We all do what we must," she repeated the phrase she'd heard in her house a thousand times.

"I'll have to remove the ax. It will need to look as though he fell in the burn pit accidentally. Can you help me drag him?"

Gavin tugged until the ax came free from Lou's back. It took both of them to drag the heavy body over the edge of the burn pit and force it in. She smelled the sickly stench of burning flesh, just as she had when Pastor Tompkins met the same fate. Her nostrils flared as she revisited that horrible night, before pushing it away. As they stood and watched the body burn, the enormity of what had happened hit Lavender. "His goons will be after us. Where will we go?"

"I know a place." A voice behind them said. They both jumped. "Lucky it was just me out here tonight," Ralph said. "The thugs are all out collecting debts for Lou. I have a cousin up in Bownton; two days' drive. You go there and tell him Ralph sent you. He'll take good care of you. Won't say a word. I'll tell the rest of the crew that Lou was on a drunken bender and I couldn't find him. That will give us a day or so. He's usually lost in the woods when that happens."

"And the ax?" Gavin asked.

"I've got plans for that. Git on now. We can't waste any time for someone else to show up unannounced."

Lavender ran to him and hugged him for the second time that night. "Ralph. Thank you so much. You've been such a good friend."

He patted her back. "No time for that business."

"Won't it be suspicious that Lavender is gone too?" Gavin asked, still shaking.

"I've taken care of these things for Mr. Kowalski for years. I know what to do. Once you've settled into your new life, don't ever mention this town or what happened to anyone."

CHAPTER SIXTEEN

Nine Months Ago
Piney Falls

"I'M LOOKING FOR a woman named Lanie Anders. I was told she works here." The short, auburn-haired woman touches her oversized, navy-blue necklace as she looks around Cosmic Cakes and Antiquery. Men and women are jammed in at every table, filling every nook and cranny of the small shop. The noise from their gossip and laughter is so loud, something on the antiques side of the store is jingling with the vibration.

The woman leans over the counter; her expensive, blush-colored blouse absorbing drops of a previous customer's latte. "Excuse me! I don't know if you heard me! I was asking about Lanie Anders. I need to speak with her about a matter of some importance. Can you 'fetch' her, or whatever you folks call it?"

A young, dark-haired woman appears from the back room. Flour covers her from head to toe. "I'm sorry, ma'am. We've had a bit of a mishap. Didn't know the bag was broken when I tried to pick it up." She tries in vain to brush the white specks from her face. "What can I help you with? We're running a special on mini scones today. Four for one dollar!"

The woman stares at her in horror. "Good gracious, no." Someone in the back of the room tells an extra funny joke and the table erupts in laughter. "I'm looking for Lanie Anders." She pauses to turn around and glare at the loud table before returning to the conversation. "I was told she worked in your establishment. I'd like to find her soon, before I lose the rest of my hearing!" she yells.

The entire building falls silent, and everyone is staring at the flour-covered employee and the outsider. A police officer with short, gray hair and an enormous belly approaches the counter. "Is there a problem here?" he asks.

"No, Chief Lumquest. This woman was looking for Lanie." She wipes the front of her apron until a nametag displaying the words "Hi, I'm Piper" is visible. "I was just about to tell her that Lanie and her fiancé, Cosmo, are judging the Gorgeously You; Inner Beauty Pageant."

The woman sighs loudly. "How long might that take? I was planning to do some sightseeing after I take care of business."

Chief Lumquest yanks up his belt, trying and

failing to cover his large stomach with his pants. "If you're in a hurry, I could deliver whatever you need. The police do a lot more than just find the bodies here."

There are uncomfortable giggles in the room and the woman looks at Piper with uncertainty. "Was that funny?" she asks.

Piper nods. "It's a local joke. Bodies seem to be plentiful around here. Don't get me wrong, it's a lovely vacation spot."

"Now, Miss Moonlight, let's not scare the lady away. We've all had our lessons on manners and how to make outsiders feel welcome," the officer gently chides. "Ma'am, glad to be of any help we can." He offers a beefy hand in her direction. "Boysie Lumquest.

She shakes his hand hesitantly and looks at her watch. "What if I leave my card with you? I'm staying at the Spruce Bark Motel, at least for the night. I was supposed to have a reservation at the Inn and Spa at Fallen Branch, but they seem to have lost my confirmation number and are full for the next six nights."

Piper scratches her nose. "I'm so sorry about that. We're in the middle of Piney Falls Proud Days. Lanie's idea, actually. We're celebrating the women who founded our town and women who embody modern Piney Falls." She beams. "Like me."

"That's wonderful, dear," the woman says dismissively. "I'll leave my card with you, then, and you can give it to Ms. Anders when she returns from her appointment."

"She really doesn't work here but–" Piper begins, before realizing it's too complicated to explain Lanie's sporadic presence in her fiancé's bakery to a stranger. "I'll give it to her when I see her next." She picks it up and reads:

Berit Campbell, Attorney at Law, New Haven, Connecticut

Piper looks up at the women in shock. "Why would Lanie need a lawyer? From Connecticut? Is she in trouble? She would have told me if something was wrong. She's practically my mother!" Tears form in her eyes.

"'S'there something I need to know about?" Boysie leans one meaty hand on the counter. "Lanie and Cosmo are fine people. Everyone in this room will vouch for their characters."

Berit tugs at her large necklace expensive blouse uncomfortably. "There's nothing to worry about, Officer. Your Lanie isn't in trouble. I'm on vacation and needed to speak with her regarding a legal matter. That's all. Please give her my card and tell her I expect to hear from her soon. I'm only here for a few days." She turns and walks out the door; her clacking heels echoing in the now silent bakery as she goes.

Piper looks at Boysie with concern. "Should I call her? Why would a lawyer from the other side of the country need to speak with Lanie?"

Boysie shrugs. "You could. But it'd be a shame to mess with the bathing suit show."

Piper shakes her head hard. "It's not that kind of pageant. This is a way for girls to express who they are, not what they look like. No swimming suits allowed. Didn't you read the flyer?"

The door jingles as it opens. The rustically-handsome owner of Cosmic Cakes and Antiquery looks around the busy restaurant. "Looks like we've got a full house today," Cosmo Hill remarks.

"One more'n expected." Boysie takes the card from Piper's hand and shows it to Cosmo. "Some strange lady stopped by. Said she had business with your fiancé."

Cosmo runs his fingers through his salt-and-pepper gray hair. "I knew things had been too quiet around here. Lanie will be in as soon as she drops Gladys off at home."

Boysie slaps Cosmo on the back. "Can't tell you how much my mother-in-law enjoyed bein' your parade queen. Every ten seconds it was, 'Boysie, take a picture of me now.' That woman loves her moment in the spotlight."

Cosmo chuckles. "It was Lanie's idea. She thought there was no better local to be the Grand Marshal of the first Piney Falls Proud Days."

The bell on the door jingles once more. A stunning mid-journey woman sporting a blonde ponytail, jeans, and a light pink shirt that matches her lipstick comes through the door. She sails to the glass display case, where she lightly kisses Cosmo and squeezes his muscular shoulder. "One of the best days I can remember. And that's a pretty high bar."

"Ouch!" he winces. "Burned today, remember?"

"Yes, Cos, I remember. You took off your shirt to do the rope pull and forgot to put it back on. Perhaps because of the positive reactions you were getting from the middle-aged women on the bleachers?" Lanie playfully pinches his forearm. "I have some lotion for that when we get home." She turns to Piper and bursts into laughter. "Did the flour bag attack you? You don't have to tell me who won, I figured it out." She goes around the counter and finds a rag, which she uses to remove the flour from Piper's face.

"Lanie, there was someone just here to see you. A very serious person." Piper reports in a low voice. Lanie continues wiping down the front of her like she's waxing a car.

"Oh? Someone I know? People show up all the time from the corporate office for the hotel. They all have my phone number if they have questions about the marketing, though." She stands back to survey her work. "You look much better. Less ghost-like."

"No, it's a lawyer. You in the middle of a divorce you forgot to tell me about?" Cosmo quips.

"You're about all I can handle, darling," Lanie says absently. "Or would want to handle."

Cosmo hands her the business card and folds his arms across his firm chest for a moment before feeling the heat of the burn and placing them at his side.

"Berit? I think I may have heard that name before. Don't recall where. She must be someone I knew when I did marketing in Chicago."

"Call her back, then. You know we're all going to be botherin' you to find out who she is, so you might as well do it in front of us," Boysie demands.

Lanie looks from his face to Piper's to Cosmo's; all staring at her expectantly.

"Okay," she sighs. "There really are no secrets in this town. At least none I haven't or won't uncover." She picks up the card and calls the number.

"Miss Campbell? This is Lanie Anders. I was told you stopped in the bakery today looking for me."

"Yes. Sure. I'd be happy to meet with you. Tomorrow at ten is fine. Yes, here at the bakery." She hangs up and looks at the serious faces. "Apparently my father passed away."

"Oh, babe. I'm so sorry." Cosmo puts his arm around her and pulls her in close, kissing the top of her head.

"It's alright, really. He left when I was six. I never really knew him, other than through the horror stories my mother told. I didn't believe most of those."

"Do you want me – – us – to be here with you tomorrow?" Piper asks timidly.

Lanie smiles. "No, hon. I'll be fine, really. I'm not sure why his attorney would find the need to fly all the way across the country to speak with me about a will. Can't imagine he left his forgotten daughter anything of value."

Chapter Seventeen

Nine Months Ago
Lanie

I'M RELIEVED TO find the prominent table, the one I asked Cos to place a "reserved" sign on, is waiting for us. I pull out the Piney Falls Ledger and attempt to concentrate on the article about the Water Moan and Move classes now offered at the Inn and Spa at Fallen Branch, while sipping a half-foam latte and eating a Scorpio Scone. My foot taps nervously against the table leg and I adjust my bright-green readers often.

"Miss Anders?"

A short woman wearing expensive yellow jeans and a butter-yellow tank top walks confidently to my table. "I'm Berit Campbell." She offers her hand. "Attorney at law."

I stand and we shake firmly as I smooth my hair absently with my free hand "Berit Campbell – I've been wracking my brain since last night, trying to remember where I might know you from. Did we work together at my last job? I attended seminars all over the country for Work Ahead Office Supplies – The Most Profitable Supply Chain in the World." There is also the matter of the men I slept with while attending these seminars. Hopefully, this Berit was not involved with one of them.

"No," Berit shakes her head as she sits down, inviting me to do the same. "We've never met. I tried emailing you at your old job and your forwarding information had expired. When I finally tracked you down in Oregon, I looked at the pictures and discovered it was a lovely place for a vacation. I thought I'd kill two birds with one stone." Her face twitches slightly.

I smile. "That's how I ended up here. Watch out, you may never leave. It's an addictive place. I met my fiancé and my life changed in many amazing ways."

Berit clears her throat. "I have no intention of ending up in a community of this size. It is an enjoyable diversion, however."

I slide forward in my chair, causing my latte to tip toward Berit, spilling some foam across the table. "Oops! Let me get something to clean that up!"

I run to the back of the bakery and shortly return with a cleaning cloth and several paper towels. After clearing the soaked napkins from the table, I plop down in front of her. "I'm so sorry. I'm a bit nervous. I'm usually well prepared for business meetings and you've thrown me for a loop."

"Perfectly understandable." Berit removes several papers from her designer bag. "As I mentioned, your father passed away. He left you a small amount of money and some land."

I cross my arms. "I want nothing from him. He was never a part of my life, and he left me with a crazy woman. I can't imagine he even remembered my name. Last I'd heard, he ran off with some woman who was just as crazy as my mother. He had a type, apparently," I snicker, intentionally catty.

Berit's face betrays no emotion. "If that's what you want, we can arrange for the sale of the land. It's actually a nice piece–"

"No, thank you. I'm sorry you came all the way out here to tell me this. It's been a waste of your time. I can give you some nice brochures on the history of the area, and places for you to visit." I smooth my mint-green top.

"Your father actually spoke of you often," Berit says softly. "You look just as he described. Like the 1940s actress, Tulip Sloan."

"Oh?"

Berit clears her throat. "At bedtime, Daddy told me about a pretty blonde girl. His first daughter."

CHAPTER EIGHTEEN

Lanie
Nine Months Ago

"I'M SORRY – What?" I can't believe what I'm hearing. "Did you just tell me we share a father? Why is this the first I'm hearing of it?"

Berit sits a little taller in her seat, adjusting her lemon-yellow pants. "I will not speculate on that. Daddy was very diplomatic when it came to stories of his first wife. I knew she had some mental health issues. But he adored his time with you."

Jeb Walters, the owner of Pretty Piney Antiques, walks by and pats my shoulder. "Couldn't have done this spectacle without you, Lanie. What a tremendous success. My business doubled over the weekend."

"I'm glad it all worked out," I say without enthusiasm, hoping he doesn't expect actual conversation today.

"More'n that. Best celebration this town's seen in decades," he calls, thankfully continuing to the door.

"You're a treasure to this community, Missus Hill."

My cheeks turn bright red. "I'm engaged," I explain sheepishly. "For some reason, the people in this town think that means I'm already married."

"You are my half-sister. We are Gavin Anders only offspring." Berit's words sound like they're coming from an informational meeting at a seminar, one of many I attended in my former life as marketing manager of Work Ahead Office Supplies – The Most Profitable Supply Chain in the World. This isn't how the people act in sappy movies when they're meeting long-lost relatives. Even the ones I've watched at 4:00 a.m. that have longer commercial breaks than actual movie.

"What did he tell you about me? How could he remember much of anything? He left when I was six." I try not to sound bitter, but there is no other way for the words to come out.

"That you had drive and spunk, even at your young age. He could tell you would grow up to be someone of exceptional talent."

One seminar in particular, *Give Them the Emotion They Desire,* was led by Terrence Buckhold. He used a person just like Berit as an example of how to lose your audience. I slept with Terrence after the conference, and he displayed enough "emotion" for the both of us. "I'm curious; what did he say about my mother?"

Berit squirms uncomfortably in her seat. "I'm sure you know they ended things somewhat acrimoniously. She kicked him out and told him never to return. She sent all of his checks back unopened. He tried to support you, but she wouldn't allow it."

I know this isn't true. Many times, my mother sent me to the mailbox to make sure she had missed nothing. When he sent checks, we had cake and ice cream to celebrate our good fortune. "He probably told you a different story, just to make sure he came out smelling like fresh soap." I search her face, trying to understand who this person is and why she felt the sudden need for a family reunion. I'm not getting anything from her. Even her perfectly round face is foreign, devoid of any signs of my father's lineage. In my frustration, I sputter, "You didn't know my mother and you certainly don't know anything about me."

Berit shows no emotion. "You had struggles. I can empathize. My mother had some mental health issues, too. Gavin Anders, for all of his incredibly good qualities, chose women with lots of baggage."

This may be as close to human as this woman gets. "Tell me about your mother, Berit. Who was she?"

"Well–" Berit clears her throat, as if she is about to give a lecture. "My mother lost her father while she was still in high school. She and her family struggled after that. She went to college; the first in her family to do so. She was quite motivated to find a way out of her dismal, small-town existence. That's what impressed our father – that she had drive and intellect his first wife didn't possess."

I'm getting it now; she wants me to react to the offensive things she's hurling. I can play her game too. "Did she?" I ask coolly.

"Yes, of course. Where there's a will, there's always a way. While she was in college, she met a handsome professor, Gavin Anders. Newly divorced, he was taken in by her beauty and determination. They were a loving couple for over twenty years."

I gulp. The thought of my father, from the few dim memories I have of him, devoting himself to another woman and another family stings. I hate that. My watch buzzes and I look down at the reminder. I have to attend Piney Falls Proud Days post mortem in 15 minutes. We're going to review all that we accomplished and where we need to improve. "I'm going to have to leave soon, but it seems like a missed opportunity if I don't try to get to know you a little better while you're here." *Does it?* I'm not sure I feel that way about this woman. She's as cold as ice.

"My understanding was that we would have a meeting this morning. I left an extra hour in my schedule." Berit is clearly annoyed and looks over my shoulder at the boisterous children standing at the counter. "Children are an irritant I can do without," she snaps.

"Sorry, I double-booked today, but I wanted to make sure we had some time to meet." I hesitate for a minute, not sure whether to proceed. She could be off her rocker just like her mother. Or my mother. "Would you like to come for dinner tonight? You could meet my fiancé and see where I live. It would give us both a little more time to digest this unusual situation."

Berit takes out a planner and studies it for a minute. "Let's see. I have a phone meeting later this afternoon – and then I'm planning to do some sightseeing for the next few days – I could make that work. I do have important matters to discuss with you."

"Forgive me if I'm reading this wrong, but you don't seem terribly excited to be here," I blurt. "You came all this way, and it seems you'd rather be anywhere else."

Berit leans forward. "There are matters that needed a face-to-face discussion."

CHAPTER NINETEEN

Nine Months Ago
Lanie

"**Y**OU'D BETTER GIVE me a list of approved topics so I don't say something embarrassing." Cosmo Hill is rubbing his salt-and-pepper hair with a towel. His chest bulges with the muscles he's recently developed building our new home.

I pinch his arm playfully. "You could never embarrass me, love. We're fact-finding. You convinced me I needed to see this through. Figure out what I need to know about my father so that I can make my peace with it and live a perfect life."

Cosmo tilts his head to the side. "Now, you know that's not what I meant. If I found out I had another sibling, I'd want to know their experience with dear old dad." He chuckles. "Knowing our favorite cult leader, Zion, I bet I have several siblings out there somewhere. He might've confessed some deep dark secret to them." He puts his arm on the counter and leans forward. "You missed out on a dad. Maybe she can fill in some of the question marks in your head. I'm kind of excited to see this genetic extension of the woman I love."

I lean in and kiss him lightly on the lips. "She looks nothing like me. No movie star vibes at all. I'm going to check on the lasagna. It was the most impressive thing we had in the freezer. Put on your new shirt, please," I call over my back.

"One Tulip Sloan lookalike is all the world can handle!" Cosmo guffaws.

After I've set the table with three rose-colored placemats and a vase of blush-pink begonias, I wander over to the window. My neighbor and best friend, November Bean, is leading a new class of students into her Moan and Stretch studio.

"Phew!" I say out loud with a tinge of guilt. As much as I love Vem, her colorful way of viewing the world wouldn't mesh well with uptight Berit Campbell. She would grill Berit about everything from the color of her underwear to what she eats in the middle of the night.

As I allow myself a short daydream about sharing my secrets and desire with a sibling, the doorbell rings. "Cos!" I call. "She's here. Best behavior!"

"I'm not your crazy friend!" he retorts, adjusting the collar of the aquamarine polo shirt I bought him last week. "This thing makes me feel like I'm going to a funeral," he complains. "You know I'm not the fancy shirt type."

I roll my eyes. "Come here." I pull him in close, smoothing his collar and wiping a touch of jelly from his cheek. Today's snack involved taste-testing a new scone for Piper, no doubt. I stand back and admire my work. "There, perfection."

"If you don't answer the door soon, all of this will be wasted, Lanie."

"Yes, you're right." I take a deep breath and pull the door open, showcasing my best professional smile. "Good evening, Berit. Please, come in!"

The brunette, who is much shorter than I remembered from our earlier meeting, nods solemnly and enters the room. I catch a whiff of her perfume as she passes by: *Je Suis Supérieur*, if I remember correctly. Many women wore that scent to give the impression they were powerful in the seminars I attended for Work Ahead Office Supplies – The Most Profitable Supply Chain in the World.

"Is this your fiancé?" she asks, pointing a finger in Cosmo's direction but not looking at him directly.

"Guilty as charged." Cosmo extends his hand. "Cosmo Hill. 'Fiancé' is only one of my titles. But it's the best one I've had so far." He winks at me, and I blow a kiss in his direction.

Berit takes his hand firmly and shakes it, though she still refuses to look at him.

"Please have a seat, Berit. I can offer you some

local wine. Sassy Lasses Rebel Riesling, or Mandeline Merlot. What's your pleasure?"

She clicks her tongue in disapproval as she sits in the middle of the couch without leaving space on either side for another person. "I prefer French wines. Much superior to American vineyards. But if you don't have that, I'll have a Manhattan. Neat."

My face is bright red. "We're pretty simple here. Local wine is all."

"Or beer," Cosmo adds helpfully. "I've got some Over the Falls Stout from our local brewery. It's a dark beer with a bit of a kick. Much like our little hamlet of Piney Falls."

Berit shrugs. "I'll have that."

Cosmo disappears to the garage, where we've set up a refrigerator and an extra television, so he has somewhere to go and think when he's frustrated.

"Berit, after we spoke earlier, I still wasn't sure why you made this trip. We could have taken care of all of this over the phone or internet." I set a cheese plate in front of her and she shakes her head. "You didn't seem that interested in family ties."

"I don't do cheese," she says matter-of-factly.

This will make dinner very difficult. I glance at my kitchen, trying to think of what I have in my refrigerator. Leftover watermelon salad from Piney Falls Proud Days, and six cream cheese scones.

"I came here to bring news of Daddy's death. I

wasn't sure if he'd been in contact with you or not."

Cosmo returns with two beers and hands one to Berit. "Over the Falls Stout. It's their most popular brew."

"Don't you people use glasses?" she gasps. "Are you animals?"

Cosmo rolls his eyes, and I quickly motion for him to retrieve a glass. "I'm not entirely sure I believe that, Berit. You mentioned earlier that there were other things we should discuss? Face to face?" I stare at her sharply, hoping she will feel intimidated. I'm on my third glass of wine, which has emboldened me past my better judgement.

Cosmo, sensing tension, returns quickly with a glass. "Berit, tell us about your life Back East. Do you have other family there?"

Berit pours her beer expertly, not spilling one drop. She uncrosses her legs and sits back in her chair, taking a long drink. "Just my mother. She passed three years ago. I have a few cousins, but we've lost touch. I don't have time for family picnics and other nonsense."

The timer on my oven is dinging. "I'm so sorry, I have to remove the lasagna from the oven." I get up and retreat to the kitchen, somewhat relieved. This dinner was a mistake; I don't know what I was thinking when I invited her. She is a hard woman with no room for relationships. I used to be the very same type. I can hear Cosmo telling stories about the locals who frequent the bakery. "Old Charlie Thumbs can spill a coffee without even touching it. Piper gets the mop the minute she sees him coming in the door."

"Dinner is served! Berit, I made lasagna, but I have several cheese-less options too," I say with fake cheerfulness. *One. I have one cheese-less option.*

Berit moves beside me, examining the table and the food on it. Folding her arms, she sniffs each dish before looking me up and down as though I'm applying for a job at her law firm. "No, this will be fine. I'll pick around what doesn't suit me. I'm used to making substitutions when the situation calls for it."

"'Nether' beer? It might make the conversation much easier!" Cosmo offers as helpfully as possible.

Berit nods. "I suppose. I'm technically on vacation."

I'm grateful for his suggestion. Maybe with a little alcohol in her system, Berit will loosen up. "Now that you've spent a couple of days in our little neck of the woods, what do you think of Piney Falls? It has a charm all of its own."

Cosmo returns with two more beers and pours one into Berit's glass. "It grows on you like a fungus," he adds. "Sometimes we celebrate the fungus for its uniqueness and sometimes we'd like to find a cream to get rid of it."

"Cos," I chuckle, "you are definitely NOT welcome in the tourism meetings!"

"That's okay. I'd be too distracted by the view to accomplish much of anything." He playfully punches my arm.

Berit stares at us both, her demeanor ice-cold. "I find this town overbearingly sweet. People are odd and not at all appreciative of the introspection your scenery allows."

We begin to eat, Cosmo and I each pushing large bites of food in our mouths to make this nightmare move along as quickly as possible.

"What else can you tell me about our father? I don't have many memories of him, other than reading me stories before bed. He and my mother fought so much; I think he was too exhausted to do much parenting."

Berit takes a lengthy drink from her glass. "This is quite good for a small-town brewery. What did you say the name of it was?"

"Tiny Piney Brewery. They do burgers on Wednesdays, too." Cosmo takes a drink of his own beer, and eyes her suspiciously.

"I can assure you, our father was the kindest soul I've ever known. Even though he was a college professor when my parents met, he felt a connection to high school kids. My mother convinced him to return to his roots. He taught at our high school in Bownton until his retirement. All he wanted was to make things better for others, especially young girls who found themselves in difficult circumstances. Daddy started a runaway shelter for young girls."

The anger rises in me so quickly I don't know if I'll be able to control my words. "He certainly didn't care about my difficult circumstances. My mother only spoke in movie quotes. She dressed me up like a dead movie star and paraded me around–"

Cosmo touches my arm and looks at me with purpose. "Lanie would like to know what made the guy tick. Why was he such a do-gooder? Those types are always motivated by something dark in their lives. I was born into a cult, and now I have a soft spot for people who don't feel in control."

Berit clears her throat and wiggles in her seat, showing emotion for the first time tonight. "He was blessed with the love of my mother and me, and felt the need to share his good fortune with others. Such a loving and kind man – and the best father. He just adored me." She drifts off to another time and place. "Students came to our place at all hours seeking his advice. He was a mentor to so many. Until he got sick."

"How did he die? Overcome with kindness? I can see why you don't like this syrupy-sweet town. You had so much of that from our father you couldn't take anymore," I say sarcastically, unable to control myself. Cosmo frowns and shakes his head.

"Cancer." Her voice wavers. "Lung cancer, to be exact."

I shove my plate away and stand up, turning my back to Berit. I'm jealous of her love for a man I never knew. Someone who showed devotion and kindness to her that he never bothered showing me. "So, your amazing father died of lung cancer after a lifetime of acting like Mother Teresa. I don't understand why either of you would decide now is the time to include me. I was doing just fine by myself."

"He wasn't perfect, Lanie," Berit says in a low voice. "Daddy had troubling issues of his own. I have some hard things to tell you."

There isn't anything I'll learn that will be hard. I didn't know the man. But I sit, pushing my half-eaten lasagna away from me so I can rest my elbows on the table.

"When Daddy started the runaway shelter, the first of its kind in Bownton, he'd just lost a student. She had abusive parents. She came to him for help, and she stayed on our couch for two nights. My mother convinced her to go home because we didn't have the space, and she didn't have the patience for another daughter."

"That sounds like a woman my father would

marry," I retort.

"Lanie! Let her finish!" Cosmo admonishes.

"She went home and, the next day, she was beaten until her last breath," Berit continues. "It was devastating for our community. Daddy decided right then that he would do what it took to start his shelter. Unfortunately, he didn't have that kind of money, had or that kind of connections. We thought the idea was dead – until the morning he turned up with $20,000 in his pocket."

"Who did he kill?" Cosmo asks, half-joking.

"He was gambling. It was his major weakness. The shelter opened the following spring. After that, he helped build a community swimming pool and two after-school daycares. He was a hero in our town."

"I still don't understand how this pertains to me. With all of his money, he could've come back and helped his other daughter. Or gotten my mother the care she needed."

"He didn't come back for you as a child, but he was still very interested in you, Lanie. I'm sure he was trying to come up with a way to reconnect."

"How can you be so sure?" I eye her skeptically. I'm more than ready for this woman to leave.

"Because he spent his last three weeks here, in Piney Falls."

CHAPTER TWENTY

Piney Falls

"MY FATHER WAS – here?" It feels like all the air has been sucked out of the room. "Why didn't he contact me?"

Berit takes one more long drink of beer before setting her glass, partially filled with foam, on the table. "That's part of the reason I came. I wanted to see for myself what brought him to this coast. I'll admit, I was jealous that my daddy would choose to spend his last few days without me."

Cosmo, reading the room, jumps up. "I'll get you another beer."

"No," Berit raises her hand. "That's enough for tonight. A delightful surprise, though." She turns to me. "I was hoping you had some insight. Daddy must've wanted to see you, but changed his mind. That was his nature, unfortunately."

The doorbell rings and my insides tighten. I know who it is and things are already tense.

Cosmo looks at me with apprehension as he heads for the door. "Should I tell her we've got a communicable illness?"

"No, it's inevitable." I turn to face Berit, slightly ashamed.

Cosmo opens the door and November Bean bounds in. Tonight, as usual, she's clothed in matching attire. Her pea-green jumpsuit is cinched with a wide, black belt; her frizzy hair is pulled to the top of her head in a pea-green scrunchie making her look like an industrial kitchen mop.

"You forgot to invite me over to meet your sister, Lanie. I can see how that would happen with house-building, a wedding, and a job on your plate. Speaking of which—" She pushes her way past Cosmo and to our table, where she inspects its contents. "It's lasagna night? You know that's my favorite!"

Berit, now standing, stares at Vem with her mouth open.

"How rude of me." Vem sticks her hand in Berit's, clasping her other over the top so there is no escape. "November Bean. Best friend, maid of honor, and professional moaner. You're Lanie's sister, Berit? You don't look alike. Don't feel bad, some families are like that. I'm sure you're special in other ways."

I move quickly to Vem's side, taking hold of her shoulders in an attempt to guide her sturdy body away from Berit. "I'm sorry. She's very enthusiastic. Vem, can I get you that lasagna?"

Cosmo, always one step ahead, is in the kitchen

filling a plate with the watermelon salad in the refrigerator. The more choices she has, the less time she'll be able to speak. He almost jogs back to the table where he scoops up a generous helping of lasagna. He pulls out a chair and gestures to Vem. "Sit," he commands.

"Berit was just telling us that my father was here recently. Apparently, he felt that it wasn't necessary to contact his eldest daughter." It's impossible to remove the bitterness from my voice.

"He was a sweet, thoughtful man," Berit insists. "Though as I said earlier, quite a gambler. Maybe he found something to distract him. Are you sure no one has approached you recently?"

I run through the last two weeks in my mind. It was a flurry of preparations for our community celebration. I had contact with just about everyone in town, assigning them tasks. No faces I didn't recognize. "He must've been here for the ocean."

Berit looks at her oversized watch. "It's getting late. I'm still on Eastern time. We need to discuss the property he left you at some point. I'll be in town for two more days, though I'd really like to find somewhere else to stay. The Spruce Bark Motel is more like something from a late-night horror movie. The owner doesn't seem to have a grasp of the English language."

"You could stay with me!" Vem spits lasagna all

over my brand-new linen placemats in her zeal to answer. "I've got plenty of space. Cosmo and his friend, Truman, built me a studio, so you won't even hear my students moaning."

Berit looks questioningly at Vem and then at me. "I don't know. Even though I think there are drug deals going on in the next room over, at the hotel, I'm not one to stay in private homes. I like my space and I'm not particularly fond of small talk."

Vem wipes her lips and stands up. She walks over and hugs Berit tightly, pulling the small woman off her feet. "You're Lanie's sister. We're not strangers. We're family."

"Put her down, Vem. The poor woman just ate. You'll pop her." Cosmo reaches around Vem and releases her grip on Berit.

"November lives next door. Her home is a show-piece." I guide her to the window where I point out the large home, just a few hundred feet from our driveway. "She's got a guesthouse around back. Vem, you got rid of all of the chicken feathers, right?"

November rolls her eyes. "*Last month* was Poul-try Awareness, Lanie. Try and keep up."

"I'd offer for you to stay here, but we don't have an extra room," I say, hoping neither Cos or Vem will expose my lie. They don't.

"Well, if you're sure. I'll go collect my things and

be back, Ms. Bean. I'd be happy to pay you for your lodging." Berit moves toward the door, grabbing her large, designer bag from the couch.

"Pssht. There's no need. I'm loaded. I was married to the toilet paper king, and he left me FLUSH with cash. I just love to say that." Vem returns to the table, where she scoops up another helping of lasagna. "It'll be fun. Like a sleepover. I had none of those because I grew up in a cult. I asked Lanie to sleep over but she refused. Some sort of aversion to bat-dung facials, or so she said."

The last thing we need now is for Vem to convince Berit she's crazy. "Berit, we'll let you get your things. Vem likes to go to bed early so she can moan with the sunrise, so you'd probably better head out."

"Thank you both for the – meal." She reaches into her purse and pulls out a folded piece of paper. "This is the address of your property."

I take it from her, reluctantly.

When Berit has gone, Cosmo and I join Vem at the table.

"Am I going to be the first to say it? Berit is kind of strange," Vem announces. "No offense, Lanie. She's nothing like you."

"None taken." I smile, comforted, because Vem is always in my corner.

"You don't ever talk about your family, Lanie. Other than the times your mother dressed you up like Tulip Sloan, I don't know anything. Why not?" she tilts her head to the side.

My shoulders tense. "It's not something I'm comfortable discussing. That time in my life is over and done, and I'd like to keep it that way. But you've been very open with me, and I suppose I should extend the same courtesy." I take in a deep breath – as Vem has taught me – and let it out slowly, lowering my shoulders with the release of air. "Let's see. My father was a high school teacher, at least when I knew him. My mother worked as a secretary for a shoe manufacturing company. I knew my mother wasn't happy, but it was still a shock when my father left. One day he was just gone. After that, my mother slowly disappeared into her world of Tulip Sloan movies. I got the feeling she wished she could have been a movie star. Our relationship deteriorated as I got older; she would only speak to me in movie quotes. I just couldn't take it anymore. When I left for college, I never returned. She died when I was twenty-three. Alone."

Vem puts her arms around me and pulls me close. Her hugs are warm and comforting. "Oh, Lanie. I'm so sorry. You needed someone who loved you for you. Not for your face. And now you have me."

"Thank you, Vem." I pat her on the back, hoping this hug will end before it becomes uncomfortable. "It wasn't happy, but it was the hand I was dealt."

She finally releases me and I take a step back.

"I'm going to cut to the chase here," Cosmo interjects. "I know you're itching to find out why your father was here, but building our home and running the bakery are about all I can handle. That leaves–"

"Why, yes, I'll be glad to help." November unloads the last of the garlic bread onto her plate. "What are we going to do first? Will there be violence involved? I've recently gotten my fuchsia belt in goat-adjacent karate."

"That can't be real," Cosmo says. "Are you making that one up?"

"I was thinking I would ask Berit for his picture," I begin, not interested in Vem's sure-to-be lengthy explanation about a new, obscure class she found. "I have no idea what he looked like after he left. My mother ripped up every photo of him she could find. I kept one of the three of us under my pillow. When she found it, she destroyed that one too."

"I'd be curious to know what your dad looked like. I picture a handsome guy. You know, what with your movie star good looks," Cosmo squeezes my shoulder encouragingly. "Figuring him out could be a good thing, Lanie."

I look at the folded paper in my hand and read what's written. 4405 Dairy Dream Road. "This is a local address!" I say with shock.

﷽

THE NEXT MORNING, I glance out my front window continuously, waiting for Berit to run screaming after Vem's latest antics. I'm alternately jealous because the two of them may have found common ground that I haven't yet with my half-sister. When I'm satisfied nothing is happening, I pour myself a third cup of coffee and sit at the table.

I scour my mind for any traces of my father left hidden. He is fuzzy; someone who fought with my mother and tucked me in some nights. My phone rings and I grab it quickly, smiling when I see it's Cosmo.

"It's your third or fourth cup of coffee. Those beautiful eyes are staring out of the patio window while you wrack your brain trying to come up with ideas about your father. Who he was. What he did when you were just a little kid. Any clues he might've left that seemed like nothing. Did I miss anything?"

"Cosmo Hill. I'll have you know, I'm not staring out the patio window. I'd start thinking about the broken railing on the deck you promised you'd fix by the end of summer." I sigh. "But you're right. For the life of me, I can't find complete memories of my father. Just brief flashes. He sat on the bed and read me stories about powerful women. Never any fairy tales. He bought me ice cream when he was in a good mood. A handsome high school teacher who dreamed of building a rec center right in the middle of town. That's all I remember."

"A guy who wanted to help others. Who wanted his daughter to be strong. That's something."

I can hear dishes clattering and customers chattering in the background. "The bakery is busy today by the sounds of it. I should let you go."

"Okay. I just wanted to check on you." Cosmo covers the phone for a minute and I can hear mumbled voices. "Piper wants me to remind you we're meeting her – and that boyfriend of hers – over for dinner tonight. You still up for that?"

Though my insides are a bit twisted at the moment, the thought of spending time with Piper always makes me feel warm and centered. "Of course. Tell her we'll be there at six."

There is a boisterous knock at my door and then a, "Yoo-hoo! Why are we locked?"

"Gotta go. It's Vem. Love you!"

By the time I get there, Vem's forehead is resting against the vertical window beside the door. Steam comes and goes as she breathes. "Lanie? Are you alright? I didn't bring my key!"

"Sorry." I pull the door open and she storms past me. "It's an old habit from living in the city. When there is a new person in the neighborhood, we double-lock our doors until we're sure they aren't going to strangle us in our sleep."

Vem puts her hands on her hips, her tangerine jump suit crinkling slightly. "Lanie, do I look strangled?" She doesn't wait for me to respond. "While your sister does give off the scent of someone hiding something, she doesn't roll her eyes when I speak. She just sits like a lump. When I finished telling her the history of moaning, she said she needed to speak with you again later today about the land your father left you."

My body eases slightly. I'm relieved she's just as awful with Vem as she is with me. "For a woman who professes that her childhood to be idyllic, she is sure miserable. Where is she? Will she be joining us?"

"No, she says she wants to drive down the coast today. I asked for more information on your father. Berit texted this picture and said she was sorry she forgot to share it with you yesterday." She hands me her bright-pink phone.

I stare at the screen apprehensively. A very attractive man in his seventies, with a thick head of white hair, a strong jaw, and eyes that resemble mine, stares back at me. He looks serene, without a care in the world. I think about the chaos my mother and I experienced daily without him there, and have to put the phone down before my mind goes to dark places.

"Kinda hunky, right? Oh, and one more thing.

Your father was loaded. I mean really loaded. Your sister says he left her gads of cash. Sorry. Does that upset you?"

I wrinkle my brow. "That doesn't make any sense. You know what else doesn't make sense? That he put my name on the deed of a house here in Piney Falls. How does a schoolteacher just pop into town and buy a house in a resort community?" My stomach begins to churn. "It would have been nice if he'd spent some of that money on us, so my mother didn't have to force me to be Tulip Sloan every weekend in order to buy milk and bread."

Vem smiles with assurance. "We'll get to the bottom of this; I promise. I can drive us to the Spruce Bark Motel."

The ten-unit motel has seen better days. When I first arrived in Piney Falls, it was the only place to stay that promised clean towels. That was a stretch. There is still peeling, green paint around the windows, but the parking lot has recently been resurfaced, and the scent of fresh-baked cookies wafts to our nostrils when we enter the office.

A tall man – who possibly hasn't bathed this week – sits in front of a small television, eating a sleeve of crackers.

"Can I help you, ma'ams?" He asks, not bothering to divert his gaze from the television screen.

"Ed Junior, we need to ask you about a man who

stayed here recently."

He looks up from his show, startled. "How do you know my name?"

I've been here many times, and each and every time he acts like it's my first. "I'm Lanie Anders. When we were planning Piney Falls Proud Days, I came here and asked for donations. You gave away one free night of lodging for the winner of the pie-eating contest, remember?"

"Oh, yeah, that's right. You're here to collect?"

"No. We want to know if you've seen this man before. He may have stayed here for several nights."

As Vem hands him the phone, I exchange skeptical glances with her, unsure Ed Junior even remembers his own name most days.

"Oh, yeah. That's Gavin. He's the one who gave me the idea to bake up cookies for the guests. Said it would make the place more homey."

There is a chill running down my spine. The thought that my father was here is one thing. Knowing he actually had conversations with people that I know makes it even more surreal.

"What was Gavin doing in Piney Falls? Do you know? Did he tell you anything about himself?"

"Let me give that a think." Ed Junior scratches his chin. "Well, he said he had a son here. And that he was gonna spend some time with him."

"A – son? Are you sure?" Vem asks incredulously. "Could it have been a daughter? Think, man!"

"Maybe. He was planning to spend time with her after he finished a project. Don't know if that ever happened. He just up and left one day without even saying goodbye."

"What was your last conversation like? Was he upset? Do you know if he talked to other people around town?" I look down and realize I've grabbed hold of Ed Junior, gripping his arm tightly. Slowly, I let go. "Sorry. But could you think about it?"

"Hmm. Let me see." He looks up and unrolls his fingers one at a time. "Talked about the cookies. I even made some for him that night. From the tube, so they wasn't so hard." He unrolls the second finger. "Said he was worried about someone dangerous. Didn't ask him who that might be. And four," he unrolls his third finger, "he had to talk to Gladys one more time. I think that's it."

"Gladys? As in Gladys Petrie? The woman who runs the city records office? What in the world would he want with her?" I run through my recent conversations with Gladys. We crowned her Piney Falls Proud Queen at the parade. We gave her a throne that included an orthopedic pillow, a six-layer cake, and a special crown. Everything she asked for. Why would she keep something like this from me?

"Yup. He got a real kick out of her." He glances over at the television, where credits are rolling over his show. "Aw, man! You guys made me miss the end of *Forest Fundry, Lawman.*"

Vem and I turn to leave and she turns back. "I can tell you need to be centered. Maybe a few less crackers and a little moaning and stretching. I can give you my card–"

I pull sharply on Vem's arm. The thought of Ed Junior being just across the road from me on a weekly basis makes me cringe. "Your ad is online. I'm sure he'll come if he wants."

As we get in the car, I look at Vem, incredulously. "How could Gladys keep something like this from me?"

CHAPTER TWENTY-ONE

Nine Months Ago
Lanie

"WELL, LANIE, GLADYS didn't know it was your father. She was probably just gabbing away like it was any other stranger. Don't be too hard on her," Vem says as we drive into town.

"Maybe," I respond half-heartedly.

After we arrive in downtown Piney Falls, I turn to Vem and open my mouth.

"I know, I know. You want to talk to her alone," she says before I have the chance to speak. "I'm supposed to get you a Scorpio Scone and a latte, half foam. And Gladys's Pluto Peach scone. Anything else while I'm at it?"

I pinch her cheek playfully. "Nope, that's it, dear. I'm forever grateful. I just need a few minutes alone with Gladys. She's easily distracted when someone else is around."

A little time is always necessary to center one's self before having an in-depth discussion with Gladys

Petrie. Vem taught me exercises especially for these occasions, breathing deeply with my eyes closed. As frustrating as Gladys can be, I must stay calm.

When I'm completely centered, I enter the historic Piney Falls Public Records building. Gladys has her feet propped on the desk and she's humming as she listens to her device. She is directing something in front of her, the conductor at the helm of her personal symphony. Both of her saggy arms are moving in rhythm and her body is swaying in the chair. Her eyes are closed, and she is lost in rapture.

I tap firmly on her desk. "Gladys?" She doesn't seem to know I'm there, so I tap again, a little louder. "Gladys? Can you hear me? It's Lanie! I need to talk to you about something very important!"

Her eyes flutter slightly. She returns to her conducting for several more awkward seconds. I pull up the folding chair and sit, leaning my elbows on the desk in front of me. I am close enough to Gladys I could reach out and smack her arm, but I rest my face on my palms and stare intently.

Finally, her eyes open fully and her expression changes from one of pure bliss to one of annoyance. "I knew you were there, toots. Didn't want Marching Band Melodica to end."

I try to control my eyes, but they roll despite my best efforts. "I need to ask you some questions."

"Been meaning to call you. That parade was

delightful. One of the best memories of my entire life. Did you notice I blew kisses to some young, handsome bucks and they blew kisses back? Still have that allure to me." Gladys touches her gray curls unconsciously. "Who says you're not a babe in your eighties?"

I feel a sense of satisfaction, knowing I was a part of giving her that wonderful memory. The city council fought me, wanting Bart Bellowsworth to sit atop the flower-covered float instead.

"He's the founder of the Brewery and invented the Piney Pouty Pickle, shipped nationwide, Lanie. He's a local celebrity." Gladys recites, as if I didn't know.

I was adamant; I organized Piney Falls Proud Days to honor our city's founders and women, specifically. Gladys was the best representation of pluck, spirit, and perseverance our community offered. I even made sure there was a sash that said "Our Queen."

"That's exactly the way I wanted things to work out. People came from up and down the coast. I think we had over one thousand people in attendance at the parade." *People like my father.* He could've partaken in some weeklong activities and I would never have known. Berit never mentioned when he died. A chill runs down my spine. "Gladys, I need to ask you about someone. An older gentleman came in here, maybe a week or two ago. He visited with you several times. Maybe he even asked about me."

Gladys reaches into her drawer and pulls out a hard-butterscotch candy. "Oh, are you talking about Gavin? Such a distinguished-looking man. Really a delight. Thought about asking him over to the house for dinner, but I didn't want to set tongues wagging. You know how that goes, Lanie."

"Did he ask about me?" I ask impatiently. "Was Gavin here to find out private things about me or Cos?"

Gladys looks at me innocently as she pops the candy in her mouth. "Course he did. Wanted to know all about you. You're a celebrity of sorts, ya know. Solving all the local mysteries that come your way; murder and mayhem don't pass you by."

"Gladys! How can you be so cavalier?" I protest. "You would tell things about me to a total stranger? What if he was going to harm me? And why didn't you tell me?"

She shrugs. "Seemed harmless enough. Said he'd followed you from your Work Ahead Office Supplies – The Most Profitable Supply Chain in the World days. Was a great admirer, he said. Discovered through your co-workers and whatnot that you were living here now, and he was wondering what you'd been up to. It wasn't anything a serial killer would be askin'."

I lean back in my chair and tap my toes nervously. There has to be a way to reach her without totally losing my cool. "This handsome man, did you wonder why on earth he would follow me from Chicago to the Oregon Coast? Did that happen to come up?"

"Hmmm–" Gladys leans back as well, mimicking my posture. "Now that you mention it, he did. Said he might be related in some way. A shirttail relative, I suspect. He didn't want me to say anything until he was sure." She giggles girlishly. "Gavin was kind of the shy type."

"You've really got to be more careful. I'm sure if you were to tell your son-in-law, the police chief, he would be horrified," I admonish. "Even though we're a vacation destination, we have to be cautious of strangers. There are all sorts who are out to take advantage of–"

"An old woman?" She huffs. "I know that. I'm not a fool, toots. Besides, Boysie knows. That first night, I went home and says, 'The nicest man came to visit. He's here on business of some sort and thinks he might be related to Lanie.' Well, that was good enough for Boysie. He nodded his head and went about the business of eating a tub of ice cream. Ya' see? Nothing to worry about."

"You told your son-in-law someone was asking about me, but you never bothered telling me?" I look at her incredulously. "Gladys, I'm stunned." I take a moment to gather my thoughts, pushing all of my anger deep down inside, since I know that is the surest way to shut her down.

"Let's try this. We'll re-enact his first meeting with you. Scoot around to my side of the desk and I'll be you."

"What? Are you crazy, toots?"

I move around to her side of the desk and pull her wheeled chair to the area where I was sitting. "Just humor me." I scoot the folding chair to Gladys' normal position at the desk and put my feet on top, clearing my throat. "This is public records. Can I help you, mister?"

Gladys looks at me with uncertainty. I nod my head encouragingly. "I said, can I help you, sir?"

"Well, I'm new in these parts. Just passing through, you could say. People at the coffee shop said you are the lady who knows everyone. Name's Gavin Anders."

I slap my hand on the desk. "Wait, he was in the bakery? Did he talk to Cos? Or Piper?"

"Don't break character, toots," Gladys snaps. "I was in the coffee shop on the edge of town, the one called Beans to Go. The folks there directed me to your office."

I nod and lower my voice to Gladys's octave. "I know Lanie. She's a good friend of mine. Brings me my favorite scone and puts up with my crazy shenanigans."

"I don't say that!" she hisses.

"I can tell you that Lanie is the marketing coordinator for the Inn and Spa at Fallen Branch. She also does marketing for the town of Piney Falls, and she and her impossibly handsome fiancé are planning a wedding for next summer. Right now, she's knee-deep in Piney Falls Proud Days. Not a second to herself."

"Hmm. You don't say. I've been a fan since she lived in Chicago. Followed her career and was surprised she ended up out here. Do you know where she lives?"

"Oh, I can't tell you that. Personal safety and all."

Gladys folds her arms in front of her. "That's not what I said, Lanie. I told him right where your house is on Magnificent Drive, then I told him to keep driving up the road to get to your new place, the one Cosmo and Truman Coolidge are building."

"Gladys!" I'm too horrified for words. "I feel so violated. Why would you give him that information?"

"Are we finishing this or what?" she asks, irritated. "I'm just getting into my character. 'Now, Ms. Petrie, I'm seeing some men on business, but I'd like to get in touch with Ms. Anders. Can you tell me the best way to do that?'"

"What men? What business?" I ask, not caring whether I'm sticking to our plan. "Who was he seeing?"

"I asked that. I'm not a total ninny. He said he'd be seeing a Mr. Granger. He also mentioned Piper's beau, Finnegan. Said he had business with the boy."

"Scones and coffee delivery!" November announces as she slams the door shut with her foot. "What did I miss? Dead bodies??"

"Gladys was just telling me how she invites total strangers in and tells them all the personal things she knows about me." I cross my legs as Vem sets my coffee in front of me. "Better watch out, you could be next, Vem. Before you know it, Gladys will have a whole troop of tourists at your front door,"

November looks at Gladys with surprise. "You can do that? I'll leave you information on my moaning and stretching classes. You can tell them whatever you want. I also like to shower outside on Thursday mornings. I don't mind a crowd." She turns to me. "You should try it, Lanie. Another set of eyes on all of your moles isn't necessarily a bad thing."

I grab the paper bag she's set down in front of us and find Gladys's Pluto Peach Scone. I toss it carelessly in front of her, followed by a napkin, before carefully placing my scone in front of myself.

"Be that as it may, she could've put us in real danger. She's lucky it was my father she was talking to and not someone with ill intent."

"Your father? Goodness gracious, toots. You should be happy I gave him your information. The next time he came by, he asked about your daily habits; you know, when you went and where. Told him I didn't know those so much." She shoves the scone in her mouth, crumbs flying everywhere. "At least you can't blame that on me." She scoots her chair back to its rightful spot and pushes me aside. "Done with this game for today."

"And, is that it, Gladys? Please don't tell me you gave him my bank account number, or my license plate."

She sticks her chin in the air, causing crumbs to fly in Vem's direction. "Not talking to you anymore."

I turn to focus my attention on Vem. "She says my father had some business with Finnegan. And – someone Granger."

Vem pulls a giant cinnamon roll from the bag and tears off the outer rim before leaning her head back in order to consume the entire dangling piece. "Oh, I know him. Royal Granger. He lives on the other side of town in a place so far off the beaten path you can't get there without a sturdy truck and a shovel when the roads are wet."

"How is this the first I'm hearing of him?" I lick the last of my Scorpio Scone from my fingers. "What does he do?"

"Nobody knows," Vem replies. "He's just there. He doesn't like visitors, so no one bothers him. You know I'm not afraid of anyone, but Royal Granger is not just anyone."

"Guess you two will be scurrying along then." Gladys makes a waving motion with her hand. "Don't want to keep you."

Vem and I exchange glances before getting up in unison. "If you think of anything else my father might have told you, please let me know, Gladys." I try to keep my voice soft and pleasant, even though I'm feeling anything but.

She shrugs noncommittally. "We'll see."

CHAPTER TWENTY-TWO

With Cheese

"**G**LADYS JUST INFURIATES me!" I pound my hand on my knee as we drive to Cheese with Your Burger, the burger place on the outskirts of town that Finnegan Lowery manages. "How could she just blather to any stranger about me? What if this man meant to do me harm?"

"It's a small town. That's just how people operate here. If she really thought she was talking to a serial killer, she would've had the decency to call you," Vem says matter-of-factly.

"You're right, I suppose. I'm still mad though. At the very least, that's not how you treat a friend. She left me vulnerable to whatever this stranger had planned." We pull into the bustling drive-in where people are waiting for the server to skate up to their cars; a new service implemented by Finnegan.

Vem pauses. "My stomach is growling. Do you mind if I order something while you're working him over?"

I get out and shut the door with Vem following

suit. "You just finished eating! You truly need to be studied."

We dodge the carhops and enter the small restaurant, where I can hear Finnegan arguing with one of his employees.

"Didn't I tell you not to mop in front of the fryer while we're in the middle of the rush? Unacceptable behavior, young man."

"Sorry, Mr. Lowery. It won't happen again."

As we get closer, we can see the office door open. An employee, only a few years younger than twenty-something Finnegan, is sitting on a chair with a large tear on the knee of his navy-blue uniform. Finnegan is leaning back, his considerably long legs butting up against the desk, and arms folded across his narrow chest. His usually bushy, blond hair is pulled back neatly in a ponytail. "We can't afford a lawsuit. I hope you'll keep that in mind. If you want that promotion to afternoon shift manager, you must think like management."

"Yes, sir. I promise you; I won't fail again. This is the first and last time." The employee stands, slapping his torn pants with his white Cheese with Your Burger cap. "Do you want me to finish cleaning up the floor?"

Finnegan nods his head and stands as well. "Yes. And then check the lobby for trash. We don't want people's first impression of Cheese with Your Burger to be marred by garbage." He glances at us and waves. "Oh, and Buck, go into the storage room and see if there are new pants in your size. You always want to look dapper on the job."

As Buck steps out, Finn motions for us to come in. "Lanie and November! Lady Luck has shone on me today! Two of the most attractive women in Piney Falls gracing me with their presence!"

Finnegan has always struck me as odd. He speaks like a man four times his age. I don't understand what Piper sees in this elderly-wannabe. "Do you have a moment?"

"For you two? Always. I think I know why you're here. It's about the heated conversation I had with Piper. I've regretted it ever since." He smooths his hair back with one hand. "I don't talk that way to her. It was like I was possessed by Beelzebub himself."

Alarm bells are going off in my head. "I want to revisit that in a minute. First though, we'd like to ask you a few questions about a stranger who might have been in town the week before last. His name was Gavin."

Finn's already pale face turns a shade lighter. "Not sure I know who that is," he fumbles.

November moves to his side and begins sniffing furiously. "He's lying. Hard to tell under the French-fry grease and cheap body spray, but I can definitely detect that scent."

Finn furrows his brow and looks to me for clarification.

"November has many talents. One of which is her ability to sniff out a lie. She's rarely wrong." I smile at him with satisfaction. My friends are great weapons in my arsenal of truth-finding. "Might as well spill it. We have a busy day ahead."

Finn purses his lips and thinks for a moment before moving behind us to shut the door to his office. "This can't leave this room. I haven't told a soul. Not even Piper."

"I can sniff evil, too. If you'll remove your shirt–" Vem moves forward.

I catch her arm before she reaches him. "No, Vem, that won't be necessary. Finn is going to tell us everything."

He sits down at his desk and motions for us to take a seat in the two chairs on the other side. "You know I've been trying to buy this place. It hasn't been an easy road. The bank first told us they needed collateral in order to secure a loan, but the only thing my sister and I have to our names is the house our grandmother left us. It's a pathetic, rundown, half-painted farm house between here and Tellum. At one point, my folks said it was pretty grand."

The bank recently hired new people to replace those with ties to the former Fallen Branch cult who tried swindling customers. Cosmo says they have a reputation for being hard-nosed with locals who've lived their entire lives in the area.

"Cos and I would be happy to go in with you, if it would help. We can vouch for your character." I swallow hard. "I'm sure there are people in town who would help you come up with the collateral you need."

Finn taps a pencil on his desk. "Thanks, Lanie. That's considerate of you. They weren't interested in my grandparent's property, or at least that's what they said. Later they admitted to me they thought I was too young and it would be far too risky to loan me that much money." His eyes narrow. "I realized I needed to come up with a large down payment, so they couldn't turn me away. The only way for me to get that kind of cash was to sell the farm and the farmhouse." He puts his chin down and looks at both of us with reservation. "I mentioned to a customer I was looking to sell my grandparent's farm and needed top dollar. He told me about this guy, Gavin, who was here to purchase property."

I lean forward in my chair, squeaking with every jostle. "And this 'Gavin,' why was he buying property?"

"The customer told me not to ask a lot of questions. Made it sound like Gavin was a shady character. But once he and I sat down, he was a nice man. Told me all about the community center he built Back East. He said he came out to reconnect with his daughter and found the place charming."

The more I hear about my father, the angrier I become. Making friends in Piney Falls – MY community – and establishing himself like a local. All the while never really intending to see me.

"So, this Gavin person, he bought your grandparent's property? The broken-down farmhouse?"

Finn snaps the pencil in half. "Affirmative. My eyes popped out of my head when he showed me the offer. He said he was giving me a fair deal; that houses cost twice that amount Back East. I ended up with more than enough to buy this place and a car for me and my sister to share. I owe everything to Gavin."

"Did Gavin say what he intended to do with the property? When was the last time you spoke?"

He chuckles. "'No questions,' remember? I just assumed he would fix the place up and move in. Since he'd found his long-lost daughter and all."

I let out an accidental snort. This time, it is Vem who steps on my toe. "You saw him again after you made this deal, then?" she asks. "This Gavin the Wonder Man? I'd be asking for free burgers, if I was him."

"He dropped off the money; all cash, can you believe it? And that was the last time I saw him. He said he had to go back home to work something out, and he'd see me on his next venture to the coast. Do you know him? I'd like to thank him again."

Vem opens her mouth to reply, but I beat her to it. "I'm afraid we don't," I snap. "Just what we've heard about him from Gladys, and now you. And what about your customer? Who was it that guided you to this angel on earth, Gavin?"

"Oh, that was old Mr. Granger. He comes in on Thursdays for his double patty, extra cheese, and no bun. He's kind of a grouch with everyone else, but he thinks I look like his nephew and he treats me like we're related."

"Royal Granger? Who lives outside of town? I didn't think he had anything to do with Piney Falls residents." It's hard to imagine my father would come across the country to spend time with a crotchety old man who shunned even the most basic pleasantries.

"Yeah, that's him. Royal has the skinny on everyone. He said he knew of this guy wanting to buy property and he gave me his card."

"Do you still have it? The card?"

"Let me see–" He digs through his drawer and pulls out a beige business card. "This is it."

In bold black letters, I read the words, G. Ladieux, Real Estate, with a phone number below. The phone on Finn's desk rings and he looks at the caller

ID. "This is about our bun order. We've got a new supplier and I fear I must take it." While he chats, Vem leans over and whispers in my ear. "What's this last name? Sounds foreign to me! Maybe your father was a spy!"

"No, that was my mother's maiden name. Ladieux. I have no idea why he would use it. We need to see Mr. Granger."

When Finn finishes his call, he looks at us expectantly, as if he's willing us to leave on our own.

Vem starts to rise but I grab her arm. "You mentioned there was an issue? With Piper?"

"Oh, yes." He clears his throat. "We had an altercation last night. It was really childish. I told her it was time to change the Moonlight name. She's still tied to a family that caused her nothing but heartache. She became defensive and said she's never had a genuine family, and how dare I throw the fact that I did in her face. I assumed she'd come to you with all the gruesome details."

For the third time today, my blood boils. "You don't have any idea what that girl has been through. Both of her parents, the only ones she knew, are dead. Her brother is off who-knows-where, and she hasn't heard from him in over a year. She has no family other than–"

"You and Cos. You're her family," Vem interrupts. "I'm willing to bet you're ten times better than her parents ever were to her. She's like your third soul mate, after myself and Cos."

This catches me off guard. "Of course, she means the world to me, Vem. That's not the issue." I pivot to Finn. "If you're going to continue dating her, I'm going to have to insist you remember this girl is tough on the outside, but she's got a delicate heart. She's not to be toyed with." I make a "V" with my fingers and point at my eyes, then his. "I'll be watching you closely. No more talk about changing anything. Being a Moonlight is her identity. She is perfect as is."

Finn nods and smiles his business man smile. Vem and I rise to leave and are almost out the door when Finn grabs my shoulder. "If you come across Gavin, will you tell him how much I appreciate what he did for me? He probably doesn't realize the impact he's had on our lives."

"That's not likely," I say with just a hint of sarcasm. "Oh, Finn–? Can you give me the address of your grandparents' place?"

"Sure. It's 4405 Dairy Dream Road."

CHAPTER TWENTY-THREE

Royal Treatment

S INCE PINEY FALLS sits between the hills of the Oregon Coast and the ocean, there are many places, such as mine, that sit on a cliff overlooking the water. Some have been built dramatically close to the edge of the cliff, daring an act of nature to destroy them. Others, like Royal Granger's house, are small fortresses, settled away from the road and far enough back from the cliff-side that they won't slip into the ocean when the next big earthquake comes. When we pull into Royal's driveway, there are no discernable signs of life. The sun is dipping below the landscape, and there are no lights on in the home.

"What do we do, Lanie?" November stretches her arms. "I'm a bit tired today. I don't know if I have it in me to take him down if that's what's required of me."

"We're going to handle this gently, Vem. We're not threatening-looking. I'm sure he won't mind having a brief conversation." As I get out of the car, I turn my body away from her. I don't want her getting a whiff of my fib.

We meander up to the door of the mud-brown, one-story home. The windows are covered in foil and there is no lawn to speak of. I take Vem's hand and clench it. She squeezes mine in support. I ring the bell. Nothing. I ring again.

"Knock this time, Lanie," Vem insists.

I knock once, then twice. Vem pushes me out of the way and bangs hard on the door. "Yoo-hoo, Mr. Granger! It's November Bean! Local record-setting moan and stretch teacher! Here to offer you a free class if you'll only–" She is mid-bang when the door flies open. She almost hits him squarely in the nose, but catches herself in time.

"Oops, so sorry, Mr. Granger. You're quick for an old guy."

A grizzled, squinty-eyed man wearing an unbuttoned, red-flannel shirt, with a stained undershirt beneath, stares at Vem hard. "How do you know my name?" he snarls.

"Everyone knows Royal Granger. You're the man who walks around town with a permanent frown on his face," Vem says proudly.

"We spoke with your acquaintance, Finnegan Lowery. I'm Lanie Anders. My fiancé Cosmo owns the bakery in town and I'm the marketing–"

"I know who you are. Your face is in the paper

every other week. You just did that festival or some garbage." He clears his throat, taking time to produce a considerable amount of phlegm before spitting it directly between us.

"We, um – we're here about Gavin Ladieux. We were told he was an associate of yours."

"Yeah, so?" He squints at me even though the sun is nowhere to be found, and pulls his greasy cap down over his eyes.

"He is a relative of mine. We never chatted while he was here, and I was hoping he gave you some insight into his visit."

He crosses his arms and moves his feet into a wide stance. "I'm sure if he wanted a reunion, he would've contacted you, Miz Anders. Likely he wasn't interested."

That stings, even though I'm certain he has no idea Gavin is my father. "How did you meet him, if I may ask? As the marketing director for the city, we're always looking into how people connect?"

In a marketing seminar I attended while working for Work Ahead Office Supplies – The Most Profitable Supply Chain in the World, I learned that people want to solve a problem. During the seminar *Give Them What They Didn't Know They Wanted,* Bradley Forst suggested every person has an answer to a question that hasn't been asked. I asked him to sleep with me afterward. He said yes.

He shrugs. "At the bar, I guess. The way you meet anybody. You ladies need to move along. I've got things to do."

"We'd like to ask if you discussed–" I begin, as the door is shut abruptly in my face.

"That went rather well," Vem announces.

I look at her, incredulous. "How can you say that? We got nothing from the man!"

"He didn't shoot at us, or threaten to skin us, or drag us into his house for torture," she offers. "It's a good day on a case with Lanie Anders when there's nothing life-threatening taking place."

I suppress a smile, knowing there is truth to her statement. "Okay. I get your point. Maybe I can think on this and we'll visit him again. That's enough for today. Piper and Finn are coming for dinner and I have no idea what we're having."

➤➤➤◄◄◄

I'VE BECOME THE chef I always knew I could be since moving to Piney Falls. Well, sort of. Piper has patiently taught me to bake and I've poured through cookbooks learning to make complicated dishes, but I've still not mastered coming up with anything impressive on the fly.

I stare into my cupboards, finding a can of cream of mushroom soup and a bag of pasta. I feel a warm set of lips on my neck. "We can call out for pizza. You know the kid doesn't mind."

"I know, Cos." I turn and put my arms around his waist. "It's just the principle of the thing. If she were inviting us over, she'd prepare five courses. We're supposed to have it together at our age. I should have this kind of thing down. You can make anything with pasta, right?"

I put a pan of water on the stove to boil before opening the refrigerator. Three apples, two sticks of celery, cheddar cheese and ketchup. Grocery shopping is another area where I could use some work.

After chopping and mixing my ingredients, I stick my finger in and taste. "Cos? Do you have the number for pizza delivery?"

The doorbell rings, and Piper Moonlight enters without waiting for us. She is carrying a savory-smelling casserole dish and sets it down on the counter. "Cos said you were out searching for information on your father today. I thought you might not have time to cook anything, so I made a sausage and potato casserole. There's some bread, salad, and the pumpkin cake that didn't sell yester-day in my car. I hope you don't mind."

I grab her dark head with both hands and kiss it. "You are a sweetheart – Cos!"

"On it!" he says enthusiastically, heading outside

to her car to grab the remaining items.

"I've had a small glimpse into your world, feeling unsure about my roots." I take three plates from the cupboard and set them on the table, before stopping to stare at her admiringly. Her sweet, round face, lavender eyes, and slight frame always make her appear so vulnerable to me. "You've overcome so much in your short lifetime. And here you are, making your way all alone. Never a word of complaint."

Piper blushes and looks at her flour-covered shoes. "You make me sound like a hero. I'm just a girl who decided not to be a victim. That's it."

Cosmo comes barreling into the kitchen, carrying three containers and a folder. "Saw this on your front seat and thought it might need to come in, as well."

"Oh, that." Her voice lowers. "Yeah, I want to talk to you about it."

"What's wrong, hon? I had a conversation with Finn today. He says the two of you had some problems yesterday." I open the containers and place serving utensils in them before setting them on the table, motioning for Cos and Piper to sit.

When we're all seated, she takes a deep breath and folds her hands on the table. "Finnegan and I may have broken up. At the very least, we're not talking for a while until I can figure things out.

That's some information he downloaded from the internet and printed off for me."

"That's rough, kid. Anything we can help with?" Cosmo asks, taking a heaping serving of her casserole and plopping it on his plate. "You know we're always here for you."

Tears surface and she shakes her head, trying to force them away, before giving in to the flow of emotion. Immediately, I rise and rub her back. "Oh, hon. Tell us what's the matter."

"Finnegan wants me to change my name. He's afraid – he and his parents, too – that it's bad for business." She sobs. "If people connect the name Moonlight to Finn and he and I are together, they will assume that Finnegan is connected to the cult. He wants me to erase my Moonlight past. Become someone else for him." She puts her forehead on the table.

Cosmo slams his fork down. "You've been working for me and no one has uttered a word. That kid has his head screwed on backwards."

"That's just because they're afraid to cross you, Cos." She mumbles. "They know about your past, and in your shop, they have to respect you. Out on the street, without your protection, my name is poison. It's the reason Finn couldn't get a loan to start his business."

"Doesn't matter. You've done nothing in this

community to raise red flags or any other color. That kid doesn't understand how the business world works. Money doesn't have a reputation. You have it, you're in."

I think back to my conversation with Finn, doing business with Gavin as if he would own the world soon. I grab my phone off the table and open it to the picture of my father. "Have you ever seen this man before?"

"Mr. Ladieux?"

I gasp.

"Sure. He came in twice. Just visiting from out-of-town. Why do you have his picture? Do you know him?"

"Piper, that's my father; the man I spent the day tracking. He made connections all over town. Even with your Finnegan." I'm wondering if there was another reason the bank wouldn't loan Finn any money. One that will take me some time to sort out.

"Oh, Lanie! I didn't know! He never said a word about being your father. I always try to make conversation with the customers and he was especially friendly. That's all! Ugh! I'm so sorry!" That makes her cry even harder.

"Not to worry, dear." I pat her back. "We'll figure this out. I'm sure there was a reason he didn't tell you who he was. Right now, let's enjoy our dinner together."

Piper reluctantly picks up her fork and begins moving the food around her plate.

"Do either of you know anything about Royal Granger?" I ask.

"He's banned from the bakery," Piper and Cosmo say in unison. Piper puts her hand over her mouth and giggles. "Great minds think alike."

"What happened? Did he threaten someone?" I imagine him pulling a weapon on someone, or deciding to take over a corner of the bakery and not allowing other customers to sit near him.

"He used to come in and read the paper every day. Ordered nothing, just picked up the paper from the stack beside the door. It was irritating, but I figured he was harmless. You finish it, Piper. I've got to stay focused on this casserole." Cosmo guides an overburdened fork into his mouth.

"After a few months of this, he started spending the afternoon doing business deals," Piper continues. "Some shady types came and went until closing time. Royal never spent a dime. I saw him pocketing large amounts of cash, though. I had a real bad feeling about him."

"Did you call Boysie?" I ask.

She nods. "I did. He said he'd had issues with Royal before. Never actually caught him doing anything illegal, but he knew he was up to no good."

"I watched him one day, conducting business like

it was his personal office," Cosmo continues the story. "Closing time comes and I finally went over to the man and said Cosmic Cakes and Antiquery wasn't the place to conduct his business, whatever that may be. Told him if he came back I'd have to look deeper into his comings and goings. And that was it." Cosmo wipes his face with a napkin. "Never came back. The shady types, as Piper calls them, never came back either."

"Did you know any of these people who came in to see him?" I lean over and wipe a spot Cosmo missed with my finger.

"Just one."

CHAPTER TWENTY-FOUR

The Mystery Deepens

C OSMO GETS UP from the table to cut some pumpkin cake. "Want some?" he asks.

"Who did you know, Cos?" I ask impatiently. "Was it my father there with Royal?"

He carefully slices a piece for himself, as if he was in his bakery preparing an order for a customer. "I think it might have been. I wasn't really paying attention, to be honest. One day I'm cleaning off tables and this man tells me he's seen all of our great reviews on the internet. He's impressed by them and wants me to know I've got a good business going here."

"My father contacted you?" I gulp.

"Well, like I said, I think so. I didn't really pay attention to him. We were busy trying to get ready for the festival and my mind was in ten places. I was trying to figure out what we might need for the plastic salmon toss as I was sweeping, and I didn't really study his face. He sat down at the table with Royal and they started talking like old friends. What they were talking about, I don't know."

"All the important people in my life, with the exception of November, have met my father?" My legs are wobbly, so I head for the couch. "This is unreal."

Cosmo comes quickly to my side, stroking my hair and touching my face. "It's okay. We're going to figure this out. I promise." I dissolve into tears and Piper comes to hug us both. It is a position we've displayed frequently, our little family of choice.

"Lanie, tell us everything you know. Three heads are better than one," Piper says, offering me a tissue.

"Well, I've told you about the people he contacted: Gladys, weird old Mr. Granger, and Finnegan. Oh, and Finnegan offered me this business card." I pull it out of my pocket, wrinkled but still legible.

Piper takes it from my hand and studies it. "I thought your dad's last name was Anders, like yours?"

"It is. This is my mother's maiden name. She never used it. In fact, she was somewhat ashamed of being a Ladieux. I never learned why."

Piper looks at me with curiosity. "You've never said much about your mother, other than telling me that she was off her rocker."

"That's because she was a mystery, even to me. She lived in this fantasy world, where I was Tulip Sloan, most of the time. She'd never tell me anything about herself, even when she was lucid. I still don't know if she had any extended family." I stand and put my hands on my hips, leaning my head forward the way my mother did every time I asked her simple questions like where she grew up. I clear my throat so I can lower my voice to the almost-baritone sound of hers. 'Beware of men, Lanie. They'll break you. That's all the history you need from me.'"

"So, we know your mother didn't like men, and yet she slathered you in makeup and suggestive clothing to parade you around like an actress five times your age. She was a woman of contradictions," Cosmo observes.

"What happened to her? I know you left for college and never returned. But did you stay in contact?" Piper asks as she finishes the last bite of pumpkin cake.

I let out a long sigh. "She ran in front of a city bus. It was a strange way to commit suicide, but there it is." I haven't allowed myself to think about this unpleasantness in almost two decades.

"I can't believe that hasn't come up before now," Cosmo remarks, touching my hand. "I'm sorry I haven't asked you. We've been so consumed with my family issues and I've never returned the favor to ask about yours."

"It's okay, really. After I escaped – and that's the way I thought of it – I never wanted to feel like I was related to that woman again. She didn't have the skills to parent a chicken. Other than teaching me about Tulip Sloan, she wasn't a mother at all." I stroke Cosmo's muscular arm and place it around my neck.

"There has to be a reason your dad used your mother's maiden name, though. It's an unusual one. Did he have contact with her family?"

I shrug my shoulders. "I doubt he even knew who they were."

"That's where you need to start this thing, Lanie. Find out more about her background. I'll do what I can to help."

"I'll go speak with Berit tomorrow if she's back from her trip. I'm sure she's tired of Vem's noises by now."

"You and I are going dress shopping tomorrow on my day off," Piper begins, "and we can work on both things! I've always marveled at your mystery-solving abilities!"

With news of my father popping up, I've barely given a thought to my upcoming wedding. I scheduled it so carefully, making sure I'd given myself enough time between Piney Falls Proud Days and the event itself to make it perfect. "Oh, shoot. I'd forgotten about that. We need to look for dresses, you're right."

Cosmo looks at me with mock surprise. "You're

not excited about getting married? To your irresistible, over-the-hill Hill?"

"Don't be silly. Of course I am. My mind is spinning in all directions right now. That's all I meant."

≫≫≪≪

VEM'S PHONE GOES to voicemail each of the seven times I call. *This is Novvvvvember Bean! I'm currently rewarding my body for its service to the world. Please leave a message and I'll call you back when I've meditated on a reply. (Howl)"*

"Vem, pick up!" I implore. Many scenarios swirl around in my head. She could be injured, or tied up, or–

"Lanie? Are you in there? Yoo-hoo, neighbor!"

I run to the front door and pull her inside, hugging her tightly. "I was so worried when you didn't answer. What with your strange house guest and all." I feel silly after saying that out loud. Berit is my sister, albeit a new one.

"Oh, no need to worry." Vem bats a fly away from her face and then studies it when it drops on her shoe. "She's gone."

"What? I thought she was just going for a little drive down the coast!"

Vem sniffs the air. "Do I smell scones?"

"You know Cos brings home leftovers every

night. Go help yourself, you know where they are." I step aside and let her find her way to the kitchen. "You were saying something about Berit?"

Vem sticks half of a Big Bang Blackberry scone in her mouth. "I tried calling her to apologize. The morning she left, I was in the middle of a good howl and I couldn't quit to say goodbye. I wasn't sure if she understood how important that was." She spits crumbs all over the counter and the floor that I just finished cleaning.

"Did you leave a message? Maybe she doesn't have service."

"Oh, you're right. She doesn't have service. It says the phone has been disconnected."

"What? Are you sure? Maybe you called the wrong number."

Vem pulls her phone out of her pocket and shows me the list of numbers she's dialed. Berit's number comes up four times, once the night Vem invited her to stay.

"What is Berit Campbell's game?" I ask in frustration. "She had all of these things to tell me, and she just ran off."

"You can always ask Gladys to search the dark web. She'll find something."

CHAPTER TWENTY-FIVE

The Perfect Dress

PIPER AND I head to the only wedding shop here. Fairie's Wedding Wonderland is in the second-oldest building in town. The owner, Fairie McGee, has cleverly converted this two-story building into a main-floor showroom, and an ornate loft for trying on dresses.

"Miss Anders! Right on time for your appointment." If ever there was a person aptly named, it was Fairie. Her voice is tiny and angelic, her body frail and elfin. Today, her wavy, blonde hair bounces as she walks, giving her the illusion of floating as she moves. "I've got some libations from Sassy Lasses for you lovey ladies to drink while you try on dresses. Your little companion is of age, is she not?"

Piper glances at me and rolls her eyes. "Yes, I'm well past twenty-one."

"You'll miss these days when your cherubic looks are gone, and no one asks you anymore," I chide.

"If you say so," she replies half-heartedly.

"I've taken the liberty of picking out a few pieces

to get us started. If you'll follow me–" Fairie glides up the staircase and we trail behind, gazing at all the extravagant and complicated dresses in the store for young brides. "Will we be dressing other family members? Your mother, perhaps?"

"My mother passed many years ago," I say firmly. "I'm looking for something a bit simple. I'm over fifty and I don't need to pretend that I'm younger. Piper will pick out her own dress."

"Mmmhmmm–" Fairie says absently. When we reach the fitting area, there are two lemon-yellow couches and a series of curtained areas. "I've placed some options in the first dressing room for you, Miss Anders. Your companion can sit out here and wait. Let me go pour the Champagne while you assume your respective positions."

"It's really only called 'Champagne' in France," I begin. I've spent enough time at the Sassy Lasses Winery to consider myself something of an expert. "Other wineries call it, 'sparkling wine.' But I'm glad our local winery has produced something comparable."

"Lanie, she doesn't care," Piper whispers. "Go try on your dresses. I know you have been dreading this, but let's make it fun! I can't wait to see you in your bridal gown!"

"It's really not going to be a bridal gown," I protest, but Piper has already found her way to the couch and pulled out her phone.

The sight inside the fitting room shocks me: dresses with full skirts and frilly things. I can't even imagine Piper wearing one of these. But I know the day is as much for her as it is for me. I want to enjoy every single minute with her and I won't let Fairie's taste in dresses ruin that.

After I've found my way through multiple unnecessary buttons and layers, I open the curtain. Piper has a glass of sparkling wine in her hand and she is sitting with her legs crossed, telling Fairie about a day at the bakery. "You wouldn't believe how many people ask for things we don't have. I can't tell you how many times I've turned people away who asked for pizza." She turns her head when I pull the curtain back. "Lanie! Oh, my gosh!" Piper begins to giggle uncontrollably. She covers her mouth and leans forward, putting her elbow on her knee as she tries to stop the sounds from escaping.

The dress Fairie thought appropriate for a middle-aged woman has a long train; long enough that most of it is still in the fitting room as I step out. There are large swoops of material thickening my hips, like ornate icing on a healthy-sized cake. It droops off my shoulders like the jowls of a sad hound dog, and the worst part is that it is see-through on the top.

"What a majestically lovely lady!" Fairie exclaims in her tiny voice. She comes to my side and begins pulling and twisting things, making this train wreck somehow better in her eyes.

"Fairie, I'm afraid you and I have different ideas of the comfort level of someone my age."

"What?" Her eyes grow so large she looks like an insect. "Just last week I helped a lady who was almost forty. I think I know exactly what's trendy for people your age."

"I'm not almost forty. I'm over a decade past that. I want something simple. For me, this will not be about the dress. It's about finding the man I never thought would be a part of my life. That and spending the day with friends."

Fairie holds her hand to her mouth. "That's just darling. Let me check around for a few minutes. You two enjoy your Shameless Shampagne."

I can hear my phone buzzing in my purse, rattling against my keys. Piper quickly retrieves it and tosses it to me. "Hello?"

"Lanie? Is that you? Sounds like you're in a barrel. Is that a new sport you and Cosmo are trying out? You young ones are more daring than me."

I wriggle against the tight confines of this ridiculously froofy dress and signal for Piper to undo the buttons on each side. "No, Gladys. Piper and I are just trying on some dresses. For the wedding."

"Whose wedding?"

"Mine, Gladys. We've been over this. Cos and I are getting married this summer. I put the date on your calendar already." I occasionally wonder if she's losing her memory. There was a day when she seemed confused by my presence. Sometimes I have to wonder if it's me, experiencing confusion between actual memory loss and plain old irritation with her.

"Of course I know you're getting married, toots. What kind of a doddering old fool do you take me for?" She clucks in judgement. "You've been so slow with this I thought I might kick the bucket before you actually tied the knot. I thought maybe it was a dress for someone else. You know, someone with an actual plan?"

Piper has reached the bottom button and all of me can finally resume its natural state. "Was there a reason for your call, Gladys? We're kind of busy."

"There's always a reason for my call. I'm not about the nonsense and natter, you know that."

Piper hands me my glass and I swallow the remaining champagne in one gulp. "Okay. Let's hear your non-nattering."

"Well, I looked up that Berit like you wanted. Not much about her, but I found her mother's obituary. Interesting that it said nothing about the daughter. Listed some other woman as next of kin. She lives in a retirement community in New Mexico. Got the phone number right here if you want it."

I motion to Piper for something to write on and she hands me a scrap of paper that was sitting on the table and a pen from my purse. Gladys's voice is loud enough that she's heard the entire conversation.

"Thanks, Gladys. Anything else?"

"Well, I'm just glad you're going through with it. The way you two think you have all the time in the world irritates me. Get it done!"

Fairie returns to the loft area, her arms full with cream-colored options. "Here are two dresses I think will be perfect!"

"That woman and her squeaky voice. She needs a lozenge," Gladys growls.

"Thanks for your help!" I hang up quickly and take the selections from Fairie.

"Something for us to investigate?" Piper asks hopefully. She never stopped questioning me on the way here. I don't understand why she's so invested in this.

"A number to call. But I do want to visit Finn one more time. I just don't know the status of your relationship. We never got to the bottom of it last night."

She helps me step out of the dress and into the next one, a silky number that hugs my body tightly, leaving no mystery as to every earned curve and indentation. "I like him a lot and I thought we were getting serious. But if my last name is that much of a problem for him, then I don't know where we stand."

I rub her arm sympathetically. "I know, sweetie. You deserve someone who treats you like the princess you are. I can go another time, when it's just me and Vem."

"No, I want to go with you. I want to help you solve the mystery surrounding your dad." She starts zipping the dress and stops when the zipper reaches a point where it can't move any farther. "I'm sure we can make adjustments," she offers hopefully.

Fairie pushes her aside. "Let me see," she says, taking each side of the fabric and pulling it tightly against my back. "Hmmm. We could probably work with that. All the young women are wearing things a little snug these days."

"I am definitely NOT young!" I huff. "And I'm not interested in pretending I am. This dress will not work unless I decide not to breathe for the duration of my wedding day. Maybe I should just look for something online. I've got plenty of time to send it back if it doesn't work." I attempt to extract myself from the dress, wishing I had use of a buttered spatula.

Fairie laughs uncomfortably. "We're not out of options. I've got this one and then I can search the floor for others, Lanie."

As little as I want to continue, I don't want to let

Piper down. She was so looking forward to this time together. "Okay. Unzip me as carefully as you can, Piper. I'll take this one in the changing booth and look at it before I torture my body with another human-in-a-sausage-casing scenario."

My phone rings again and I see that it is Vem. I put it on speaker while I hold the dress to my body, not as offended by its first impression as I have been by the last two. "Trying on dresses today, Vem. It's not going well," I declare loud enough so that Fairie can hear my displeasure.

"I still don't understand why you didn't want my help designing something. My first wedding dress had hand-pressed beetle dung in the bodice. Startling in its simplicity. I really communed with Mother Earth."

"It was your ONLY wedding, Vem." It's hard to imagine the high-strung toilet paper king being okay with beetle dung that close to him. But to be a fly on the wall at their nuptials. Oh, my. "Was there a reason you called? I was planning to bring a bottle of wine over later. I appreciate your changing roles from maid of honor to officiant. I know that decision was a difficult one for you."

"Not really, Lanie. It came to me in a vision while I was in my pop-up sweat lodge, eating salmon sliders. But that's not why I called. I was deep cleaning the guest room and found something interesting."

There is dead air. Too long. "Vem? Are you still there?"

"Yes, Lanie. I wanted you to know I'm behind you. I thought there was something off with her scent from the start. She wouldn't eat my casseroles and barely said a word when I asked her to moan with me. She didn't outright refuse, but her moan was pathetic. Like a cow who's given up hope of living."

Impulsively, I slip the dress and on and zip it comfortably. It fits like it was made for me. "Vem!" I say impatiently. "What did you find?"

"I think she is searching for a way to get rid of you. She wrote down two phone numbers that she left on the nightstand. One I searched and it came back to your father. The other was–"

Piper pulls the curtain back and gasps. "Oh, Lanie! This is it! This is the one! Come look, Fairie!"

Fairie flits to her side and puts her hand to her mouth. "It's perfection." Fairie pokes and pulls at me again. "There's very little to be done here. Really. It looks like it was made for you."

I stare in the mirror, shocked for a moment. I look exactly like Tulip Sloan in the movie, *The Bride Wore Satin*. She never lived to my age, dying of a drug overdose in her thirties. But if she had–

"Lanie? Are you still there? I've got to tell you something."

"Sorry, Vem. We all got distracted. What were you going to tell me about the number? One was my father and the other?"

"Yes, Lanie. It was Royal Granger."

CHAPTER TWENTY-SIX

Ties That Bind

"THIS IS LANIE Anders. I'm a relative of Gavin Anders. I found your name in his wife's obituary and – well, it will be easier to explain on a live call. Some serious issues have surfaced and I'd appreciate it if you'd call me back at 503-555-5432. I hope to hear from you soon." I put my phone in my purse.

"Don't worry. She'll call you back." Piper takes a long drink of her soda and eyes the room, trying not to be obvious when her eyes rest on her boyfriend at the front counter of Cheese with Your Burger.

Eventually, Finnegan finishes with the lunch rush and sits down in our booth, next to Piper. She scoots in the opposite direction, taking care not to look at him. He fidgets nervously, glancing over at Piper before looking at me. "I wasn't expecting to see you again, Lanie. The other day you seemed kind of perturbed."

"Did I?" I'm surprised he's that aware. "I have a lot on my mind. I wasn't completely forthcoming with you when we spoke last. This Gavin, the man you sold your farm to, is – rather, was – my father. Did you know that?"

Finn sits up taller in his seat. "Seriously? I think I'd recall that. He was just a nice elderly gentleman. Didn't he tell you what he was doing?"

"I haven't had contact with the man since I was a child. Apparently, he spent time with everyone in this town, other than me. It's confusing and hurtful."

"Our families are important to us. Warts and all," Piper snaps, grabbing my hand and staring sharply at Finn. "We all need a sense of identity. Even if it's not the one others want us to have."

Finn moves nervously, causing the French fry in Piper's hand to fall on the paper wrapper. "Finn! Really!" she says with exasperation.

"Sorry, darling," he replies, then turns to me. "I just don't understand, I guess. Do you have any family members you can ask? Maybe they have more information. I told you everything."

I think back to my childhood. My mother made it seem as though we were alone in the world. I was an adult before I realized living so removed from everyone wasn't normal. "As far as I know, neither of my parents had living relatives, other than Berit. I'm still investigating that part. That's why anything you can tell us is of utmost importance, Finn."

"Well, I already told you everything. Thanks to

Royal, this guy just showed up like he'd dropped from heaven. Never saw him before and never saw him again since."

"Who did you tell that you needed to sell the house? Any friends? Anyone else who might've known Gavin? What about your sister?"

Finn's face is blank. I can't tell if this is because he's lying to me, or he's just devoid of personality. "Nope. Nobody. Me, the bank, and Royal. We were the only ones who knew about this. I didn't even tell my sister until she had to sign her name on the dotted line."

"Lanie, it's obvious he doesn't know anything. And I mean ANYTHING." Piper rolls her eyes. "Couldn't be less aware if he tried."

"Why are you being unkind to me? I made a simple suggestion the other night, my precious flower. I really care about you. Changing your name is just as much for your benefit as for mine. We both have a professional image to protect." Finn taps me on the arm. "Lanie can tell you; that's really important, especially in a small town. I bet she's always worked hard to make sure she appears squeaky clean to the business world."

I slept with almost every seminar leader in the seventeen years I worked *for Work Ahead Office Supplies* – The Most Profitable Supply Chain in the World. It might have been a good idea to concern myself with my public image. "I see the point you're trying to make, Finn. But it has nothing to do with Piper's past, or who her parents were. It's about establishing yourself as a trustworthy business owner. Reliable, friendly, and willing to be a part of your community. That's what counts."

The young couple has reached a stalemate. As annoyed as I am by Finn, something about him seems so vulnerable. It's hard not to feel a little bad for him. Just a little.

"Don't we have somewhere to be?" Piper asks impatiently. "I don't want to be here anymore."

I slide out of my seat and Finn does the same. "Please call me if you think of something else, Finn."

"Yes, of course. My interaction with him was truly minimal."

I shake my head and begin walking toward the door. I can't help myself when I blurt out, "Think about what's more important to you: your image, or your relationship! Both can disappear."

Piper gives him the stink eye as we continue to my car.

"It's hard to believe I'm saying this, but I think he genuinely loves you."

"Not now, Lanie." Piper is fighting tears as she opens the door to the car. "I'm too angry. The one other time in my life I let myself be vulnerable and fell for someone, he broke my heart. From that day on, I vowed I'd never put myself in that position again." She bites her lip and takes in a few shaky breaths before continuing. "But then, I met you and Cos. I saw what love was supposed to be like and I wanted it for myself. I guess I should have known things would never work out that way for me."

"Lasting relationships are like a roller coaster. You both have to be willing to hang on tight, no matter how wild the ride. I know you'll find someone to be there for the entire unpredictable experience." I pat her hand. "If not with Finn, then with another young man who can appreciate you for the dynamic woman you are. Not a name; a force to be reckoned with."

My phone rings and I can see it is the number I dialed earlier. "Here goes nothing," I say under my breath as my pulse quickens. I sit down in the car and put the phone to my ear. "Hello?"

"Miss Anders? This is Minerva Jensen," a frail voice on the other end of the line begins. "You called earlier about my sister."

"Yes, Mrs. Jensen. Thank you for returning my call." I clear my throat and try to prepare my words carefully. "I wanted to ask you about your brother-in-law. From the obituary, it wasn't clear you were Mrs. Anders' sister."

She is silent and for a moment I wonder if this is the right number.

"Gavin? He was one-in-a-million. Do you know, he built a home for troubled teens as well as a community center? The man was a saint. It was a pity when he got sick."

"Yes, I heard he had passed."

"For the last five years he'd been fighting lung cancer off and on. Didn't slow him down a bit though. He still did everything he could to support his community."

"I live in Oregon, Mrs. Jensen, and apparently he spent time out here recently. Do you know why?"

"Can't say as I do. We last spoke about a year ago. He sounded upbeat. That man worked as a teacher for decades and somehow saved up enough money to help all of the organizations he supported and still have enough for a vacation. A marvel."

"I know that he taught high school, but maybe he had another, more lucrative job? Did you know anything about that?"

She takes in a deep breath and lets out a raspy cough. "Well, Gavin had a gambling problem, but I thought he'd long since recovered from that. You know how those addicts are. It can take a while."

"And what about your niece, Berit? Do you have a close relationship with her?" I hope this isn't a sticky subject for her, since Berit wasn't listed as next of kin for her mother.

She laughs, causing her to cough once more.

"Oh, Berit. She's kind of a pistol. She calls me every now and again for a painful conversation. The girl isn't exactly full of warm fuzzies. True to form, she didn't bother calling when Gavin passed."

"That's just awful, Mrs. Jensen." I glance at Piper and shake my head in disgust when she catches my eye. She nods. "Why do you think she didn't call?"

"I'm guessing they were still on the outs. She and Gavin didn't speak for several years."

"But she said they were–" I begin, but then think better of it and stop. "Why didn't they speak? Do you know?"

"Families can be complicated. That's really all I want to–" Minerva stops talking abruptly.

"What can you tell me about Berit?" I ask quickly, not wanting the conversation to end. "I've recently discovered we're related through Gavin and I'd like to get together with her if possible."

"Didn't see her own mother for a decade. She decided her mother was the enemy. In Berit's mind, everyone is her enemy. She's nothing like her sweet father was. Even her mother couldn't believe she'd raised such a devious little thing."

"What do you mean by 'devious'?"

"Anything Berit wants, Berit gets by whatever means possible. Gavin put in an offer on Berit's mother's home when she passed. When Berit found out, she took him to court, claiming her mother signed her house over to her before she died. Gavin wanted to start another charitable thing, you know. When she sued him, he gave up that pursuit." She sighs heavily, causing a deep cough. "That's Berit. She'll do whatever it takes to come out on top."

I see it all clearly now. She didn't come to Oregon because she wanted to be with family. She wants the property my father put in my name. She needs to win.

"That's why her mother put me in charge," Minerva continues. "We're not blood sisters, you know, just very close friends. We called each other 'sister' because we felt a kinship. She thought I would take better care of her affairs than her own daughter."

"Thank you so much, Minerva. You've been helpful. Oh, what do you know about Gavin's first wife? Did your friend ever mention anything about her?"

"I knew her. There were stories; you know, the second wife gets all the dirt. Gavin tried inviting company over for dinner on several occasions. He was a very social man, especially when it meant he could network and help others. Well, every time he invited guests, she'd do something crazy. One time she went into the bathroom and stripped off all her clothes. Came out naked as a jay-bird, acting like nothing was out of order. She asked if she could fill their drinks, and all of the guests left after that. She had her reasons for being crazy, I'm sure. I'm not one to judge."

"I'm not surprised," I say quietly. This next question is harder to ask. "And what of his daughter with her? Do you know anything about her?"

"Never knew there was a daughter. Gavin didn't mention a thing, and neither did my friend."

I gulp. "I know her. She feels very abandon by her father and–"

"The good folks are here with my dinner. I need to go now, but feel free to call me any time. Before four p.m.;.; that's when the action starts here."

"Thank you, Minerva."

I turn to Piper, who is waiting impatiently for news. "Well?" She asks. "What did you find out?"

"Berit wasn't trusted by her own mother. And my mother had a reputation, even in Gavin's second family, for her bizarre behavior. But there was one thing that really caught my attention."

"And? Lanie, don't leave me hanging like this!"

"My father had a gambling problem. Maybe, after purchasing Finn's house, he was going to extort money from me for his next adventure."

Piper wrinkles her nose. "I'm not the expert here, but wouldn't he call you in person and try to get money from you? Leaving town without speaking to you doesn't seem like the way to charm you."

"You're probably right."

My phone rings again, this time it is Cos. "I know you wanted me to buy a slinky, nightgown of a dress, but thankfully Piper talked me out of it." I wink at Piper and she gives me the thumbs up.

"You need to come home now, Lanie." Cosmo's voice is serious. "Something really weird just happened."

CHAPTER TWENTY-SEVEN

Eight Months Ago

"COS, I CAME as fast as I could. What's happening here?" I'm still out of breath from running up the hill from the home we currently share, to the one he's been working so hard to build. Cosmo is constructing our dream castle with Truman Coolidge, a U.S.-president-loving friend who lives out by Sassy Lasses Winery. They are just beginning the interior work, putting up sheet rock and insulation.

Truman pushes Cosmo aside, wiping his sweaty brow with a red-white-and-blue handkerchief on the way. "We found something of interest this afternoon. This might panic you a bit, so Cosmo here is at the ready for fainting spells."

I bite my tongue, wanting to tell Truman women of this century don't faint unless forced into a corset or the mindset of someone from corset times, but I smile politely. "No need to worry, Truman. I'm quite sturdy on my feet. What was it you found?"

Cosmo turns me to face him. "Truman was over

in the master bathroom finishing up the sheetrock there. I was here, in the second bedroom, working on some trim. We usually talk through the vents about this and that. Nothing too exciting. Football scores, local gossip, you name it."

"And there I was, mouthing off about the state of the world and whatnot when I dropped a nail. There, on the underside of the vanity I put in last week, I found this." He pulls something black from his pocket that looks like it used to be a zip drive for a computer. Now it's as flat as a pancake.

"A workman left something from his computer? I don't understand. Why did I need to come all the way back here before Piper and I could enjoy a mid-afternoon coffee?"

Truman leans close to my ear. "It's a listenin' device. Like them spies use. Figurin' it's the Russians who left it."

I raise my brow. "Cos?" None of this makes any sense. "Are you sure that's what it is?"

He nods solemnly. "We looked it up online and then I called the computer shop in Tellum to make sure. They verified. Truman took it out and ran over it with his truck numerous times. Pretty sure it's nonfunctional now."

"I don't – this makes little sense at all. Who would want to listen to your conversations? And why?"

"I keep tellin' you, Lanie. It's the Russians." Truman wipes his nose twice to the left, twice to the right and puts his handkerchief back in his pocket. "They do that kind of thing, just to keep track of ordinary Americans."

"No, Truman, I can guarantee you that isn't the case." I look at Cosmo and he nods his head toward the door.

"We're going to step out for a minute, buddy," Cosmo says, escorting me outside.

"We still gotta burn that thing, Cosmo!" Truman calls after him.

"Later!" Cosmo replies. When we reach the barewood front porch, safe from Truman's ears, he looks at me for direction.

"I do have some ideas," I begin.

"I thought you might."

"Today I spoke with a friend of my father's second wife. She said he was into gambling. He may have had a debt to pay. Maybe those people were keeping track of me, thinking they would have a better idea of where my father might be."

Cosmo folds his arms across his dirty, gray, t-shirt. "That's kind of a stretch. Why would they even know about you? No one you've met so far had any indication you were his daughter."

It hits me, as usual, right in the gut. I think for a moment. "Unless they were contacts from back East who followed him. Who knows how deep of a hole he'd gotten into?? Gavin Anders seemed to have quite a lot of money. He had to roll with the big boys in order to be bringing in large amounts of cash for all of his charitable funds."

Cosmo puts his hands in his pants pockets and begins to rock back and forth. His usual behavior when he is nervous. "You really think they'd come all the way out here to track him down?"

"He was a dying man. Maybe he was at a point of desperation where he didn't care anymore; he got sloppy, or lazy, and didn't pay his debts. That could make someone really angry."

Cosmo shrugs. "Maybe we're making too much of this whole thing. Could be some dumb kids came out here to party and left that as a joke, thinking they'd listen in and find some really stimulating conversation instead of two old guys talking about their aches and pains."

"That could be," I say with resignation. If I'm being honest, I'd like it if my father cared enough to put me in danger. At least then I'd know he was thinking of me, as twisted as it sounds."

Cosmo smiles warmly. "Let's go have a beer and think this over. I'm about spent for the day. Truman said he's got a presidential library special he recorded that he'd like to watch, so I'll just send him home."

Even though there is more that I planned to accomplish today, I must admit, all of this has worn me out. I head down to our current home to find something for us to drink while Cosmo heads back into the new house to tell Truman of our plans.

When he returns, I motion for him to remove all of his house-building clothes. "You're probably right, Cos. I'm overthinking this," I say, as he drops his shirt haphazardly on the floor. The designated house-building clothes-hamper, placed by the door for just such items, sits completely empty.

"Here." I hand him an Over the Falls Stout and sit down at the table with my glass of Rebel Riesling. "There has to be something I'm missing. Do you know how many birthdays I waited by the window, hoping he would show up with a gift? I wrote him letters more than once, begging for that one day together. He never responded. To spend his last few days here, so close, makes little sense."

Cosmo touches his beer to my wine glass. "Cheers," he says absently. "Maybe your dad never received your letters. What if your mom took them from the mailbox and they were never mailed?"

I think back to that time when my mother was working two jobs. "Her mind was so many places and most of them were not rooted in reality. But – maybe. Even so, he had to remember that was my birthday. He never even spoke of me to his new wife's family. Then suddenly, as he's dying, he visits my remote town and doesn't even call? And what about his creepy daughter? What was she thinking, coming all the way out here?"

"Yoo-hoo! Neighbors?"

I'm exhausted from today's activities, and the thought of entertaining my enthusiastic best friend is the last of my wishes. But Vem has never turned me away, even on the days she's in a complete funk.

"Would you like a glass of wine? We were just talking through this weird story of my father."

"My Moaning for Memory Makers class was exceptional today." She puts her hands in the pockets of her sky-blue jumpsuit *and* bounces on her toes. "There were fourteen in attendance and not one of them expelled bodily noises."

"Sounds like it was a success! Congrats to you! I'll pour you a wine." I get up and move to the kitchen before she has a chance to respond.

"No thanks, Lanie. I'm currently doing Wine-Free Wednesdays. Toss it Back Tuesdays became too much for me, so I needed to add a day of cleansing."

"I've never known you to turn down a glass of wine before," Cosmo remarks. "Sure you're feeling okay?"

November flops down on the pea-green recliner closest to Cosmo, flipping out the footrest and causing him to pull his feet uncomfortably close to his body. "No, to be honest, I've had a massive headache ever since my class ended. I can't shake the sense that something bad is about to happen."

More times than not, November's premonitions come true in some way. There is the beginning of a knot forming in my stomach. "What do you think is going on? My father is dead, Berit has disappeared, we should be safe, right?"

"I don't know. Old Pete Riversworth, the resident coffee-shop gossip, was chatting with me while he waited for his ride this morning," she begins. "He's not allowed to drive since the squirrel-chasing incident. I'm glad he lost his license. He ran over two fences and almost hit a small child trying to run down one particular squirrel."

"Ummhmm," I say, trying to pretend I'm interested.

"We were short on conversation, so I started telling him about your situation, Lanie."

Leave it to Vem. "This is a delicate matter, Vem! I wish you'd keep it to yourself!"

"You'll be happy I didn't keep this to myself." Vem rolls her eyes. "Honestly. I don't understand why you don't trust me."

"I'd like to hear the end of this story before sundown, November Bean," Cosmo chides impatiently.

She jiggles a bit in her chair, finding just the right place to rest her normally active bones. "Well, Pete said this stranger approached several people about purchasing property, for nefarious purposes, one can only assume. But–"

"Please get to the point, Vem."

"He said he met your father."

"Of course he did," I say sarcastically. "Say it with me: everyone met Gavin, except Lanie."

"Your father came to him asking for connections. Underworld, to be exact. He wanted to get rid of someone in his family."

"Vem, that can't be–"

Before I can finish that thought, a tremendous explosion shakes the house; something too intense for my ears and brain to comprehend. I'm caught for a minute in a timeless dimension where I can see those around me, but the rest of my senses don't appear to be working.

When the sound of the explosion is gone, we all look at each other, waiting for someone to snap back to the present and take some action.

Cos jumps out of his chair and runs to the window. He puts his hand on his forehead and begins rocking back and forth. "This is bad. This is real bad."

Both Vem and I run to his side from where we can see a voluminous cloud of black smoke filling the air above the pine trees. It's coming from the site of our new house.

CHAPTER TWENTY-EIGHT

Piney Falls
Six Months Ago

TRUMAN COOLIDGE IS a reluctant patient. He's spent the last two months with us since being released from the hospital. It has become apparent that nothing in our home meets his standards. The food, the bed, even the slippers we brought over from his place. For a man who's spent his entire adult life living alone, he adjusted quickly to people waiting on him daily.

"I'm not one to complain, Miss. But this soup needs more salt and a touch of hot sauce. I'm not one to complain, Miss. But these blankets are a tad scratchy for my taste. Not one to complain, Miss. But the volume of the television isn't loud enough unless I can feel the walls rattle. That's when I know I'll be able to immerse myself in Presidential Snacks and the Staff Who Made Them."

It's fortunate for me that I don't have time to think about what happened. In my old life, my house in Chicago burned to the ground. The trauma I felt from that took years to overcome. Exhaustion from caring for Truman has at least left me unable to revisit that horror, thank goodness.

"Can you get Marveline on the phone, Lanie? I'd like to check on my dog." Truman's voice quivers. "Grover hardly knows who I am anymore. Nobody to feed him his favorite treats, neither."

His phone is within his reach, but I grab it for him anyway. It's much faster than insisting he do things on his own. "Cos thinks you can go home this weekend. Your injuries have healed nicely and Marveline promised she'd check on you every day." There is a twinge of guilt when I think about pawning Truman Coolidge off on that poor woman. She's got a winery to run, after all.

"Not sure about that. What if I fall, or forget how to cook things in my kitchen? I could start a fire!" He makes a feeble attempt to reach his toe, knowing I'll scratch it for him either way. "Little to the left, please."

"There is that private nurse Vem offered to hire for you. She would be there all day long, ensuring your safety."

Truman shakes his head. "What am I gonna do with another person in my home? How will I feel comfortable sitting around in my starred skivvies while a stranger is watching?" He asks stubbornly. "No sirree. That's not how I do things."

I stare in frustration at his well-clothed body. He has refused to wear anything but his normal striped overalls – albeit slit up the leg to accommodate his cast – every day of his stay. "Well, you have plenty of neighbors who offered to step in and help. There are many casseroles in your future, Truman. And Cos and I will come out when we can." If I never have to prepare another canned-meat casserole or watch another episode of Presidential Pets, I promise I won't complain ever again. Cos and I lie in bed at night and recite the words from that evening's episode to each other until we fall asleep, giddy with exhaustion.

"We'll be busy, of course, so we can't come often. We have to get back to our lives too. Cos will have to rebuild–" My voice trails off. Neither of us have the heart to start over.

"When is the policeman coming back? He said he'd want to question me again about what I saw." Truman reaches half-heartedly for a bowl of peanuts, which he insists we keep beside every place he sits. He looks up at me pleadingly and I rise to scoot it closer to his gnarled fingers.

"Boysie will be back when he has more to ask. They've never found the turquoise car you saw earlier in the day. He's still waiting for the explosive experts from Portland to come." I purse my lips. "They didn't think a half-built residence that exploded was a priority."

"Coulda killed me. Didn't they know an old man wasn't there to hurt anybody? Coulda killed me." Truman falls into his usual routine of reliving the explosion. He is traumatized, as we all have been.

"I know, Mr. Coolidge." I whisper. "We're so very lucky you weren't more seriously injured. A broken leg and arm and a few cuts; that's miraculous. And we'll never be able to express to you how sorry we are." I repeat these words as often as he needs to hear them, but it's holding us back from moving forward.

My phone rings; a blessed distraction from this conversation. "You can check on your dog and I'll be back in a bit to see what kind of casserole you want for lunch." I hop off the bed and out the door, relieved to see that it is Gladys calling.

"You still survivin', toots? That old geezer got you ready to beat your head against the wall?"

"Oh, Gladys," I chuckle with relief. "It's so good to hear your voice. We've been locked away from the world forever. At first because Cos was worried someone was trying to hurt us and then we got lost in this world of caring for Truman. He's a lovely man, but–"

"A pain in his saggy old patootie, that's what," she finishes the sentence in a way I don't wish to utter.

"Yes. Definitely a challenge." I push back the tears that have been building for days; my frustration and sadness over the inability to do anything normal.

"You'll be interested to learn – Boysie brought my scone in today, along with some interesting news about your case."

"Oh? I thought he'd decided there wasn't anything new. Truman asked me to call him yesterday." *And the day before, and the day before.*

"He probably didn't want to say anything until he knew for sure. Now he does. They sent the footage off from Vem's security camera on her moaning studio. They have many fancy ways to enhance those things now, you know. I bet they could put one of those cameras on me downtown and they'd be able to look at your place clear up on the hill."

"What did he say, Gladys?" I snap.

"They found that two cars came up the dirt road that day. The first one belonged to Finnegan. He arrived at ten-thirty and left at ten forty-two. I told Piper that boy was no good. Didn't I tell her? No one wants to listen to old Gladys."

"Who owned the other vehicle?"

"Not so much owned, as used. The other vehicle was a rental. Turquoise car came from the Portland airport. A woman named Berit Campbell rented it. That was that lady you asked me about, wasn't it?

Your sister, maybe? Toots? You still there?"

My tired mind goes into overdrive. "What time was she there?"

"Boysie doesn't know if she was driving. We just have a license plate number, but they haven't been able to determine the people inside yet. Because of the angle of the camera, it's taking a little longer. Not a priority for the FBI, apparently."

"Why would Berit want to blow up my house? What's in that for her?"

"You're the detective, toots. I'm just the computer lady. Anything else you need from me?"

"No, not right now. Thank you, Gladys."

Ever since Finn asked Piper to change her last name, I've encouraged her to give him the benefit of the doubt. I asked her to give him another chance because he was young and foolish. *Now who's foolish, Lanie?*

I quickly reheat last night's repulsive, gray lump, covered in cheese and breadcrumbs. Benjamin Harrison's Biscuits in Suet Gravy ala Truman. I pour a large glass of milk and bring the tray to Truman's room.

"Be a good boy, now. They're telling me I'll be back to the estate next week sometime and we'll watch your favorite George Washington biography together." Truman hangs up the phone and leans back on his pillow. "I sure miss that guy."

"Just one more incentive to go home," I say firmly, setting the tray over his body.

He surveys its contents, as usual, for items he might send back. "You know milk makes me sleepy, Lanie. Don't you want me alert for our afternoon Presidential Match card game?"

"I'm going out for a bit today, Truman. Vem is home if you need anything."

He stares at me blankly. "You're just gonna go off and leave me? All by myself?"

"I'm afraid so. I won't be long, though." I turn and leave before he notices that I forgot his caramels – the ones the doctor told him he shouldn't eat anymore.

I'm almost giddy, leaving the house for the first time in weeks for something other than the fulfillment of Truman's needs. I don't even bother to look in the mirror. If my hair is messy, I don't care. I have somewhere important to be.

I drive my car to Vem's driveway, even though it is just steps up the hill. I don't want Truman to know I'm close by and call me back before I've accomplished what I've set out to do today. I look at my watch and realize Vem is just finishing up a Moaning for Almost-Mothers class, so I wait patiently while the last of the very pregnant women leave.

Vem steps out on her porch and waves. "Practice your joyful moaning all the way home!" she calls before noticing me. She jumps off her porch and runs to my car at superhero speed, barely giving me time to get my window down.

"Lanie? Why the wheels? Are the ones nature gave you in disrepair?"

"I want Truman to think I'm already gone. Just a couple of quick questions for you first, though. Do you remember when Berit stayed with you? Did you show her around?" She looks up at a bird or a tree, something that easily distracts her. "Vem!" Do you?"

"Yes. She wanted me to show her my moaning studio and then she saw your new home and asked about that. I told her the entire story about how you were gifted the land as a thank you for solving a big mystery."

"What was her response?"

"Well, you know she doesn't have much of a personality. A twitch here, a nod there. But I remember feeling like she disapproved. That was her scent: disapproval."

"And did she say anything else to you?"

"Just that it would be a lovely place for a day spa."

"Thanks, Vem. I'm meeting someone. Please keep your phone handy in case Truman needs something while I'm gone."

She looks at me with dismay. "But when you

went to pick up his prescription, he demanded that I cut his toenails and massage his feet with butter. Greasy butter, Lanie."

"I promise it won't be long!" I call as I back out of the driveway.

The Piney Falls Police Station is located inside the same building as the city library. Something that still makes me giggle. Boysie is in his office when I arrive. I can never tell if he is putting up with me because I am his mother-in-law's friend, or if he has genuine respect for me. He glances up when I walk through the door before returning to his paperwork. "Miz Anders, thought you might stop by. Kind of surprised it took her this long to call."

I am a little ashamed that I'm part of the local gossip mill and that Gladys is my primary source. "It is an important piece of news. Have you had any luck locating Berit?"

He shakes his head, still not bothering to look at me. "Not the woman nor her car. It's like they vanished into thin air."

I sit down on the chair facing him and push it up close to his desk. "What about Finnegan? Have you spoken to him about his visit to our property?"

He looks up and puts his pen down. "This is an official police investigation. I'm not obligated to fill you in until we've got all of our ducks in a row. Even then, it's just out of the kindness of my heart."

I put my elbows on his desk and look him directly in the eye. "One of those two put an explosive
device on our property. One of them planned to kill
Cosmo and Truman, maybe even me. If I'm in
trouble, I need to know."

Boysie studies me for a moment. "Has someone
been bothering you, Miss Anders? We still have a
patrol car drive by your property at least once a
day."

"No, it's been oddly quiet since this all happened.
But other than Cos going to the bakery and me
running errands for Truman, we aren't out much. I
have to think that the explosion had something to do
with my searching for facts about my father's visit."

He folds his hands in front of him. "Yes, that is
something I've been meaning to ask you about. You
say this man – Gavin Anders – visited our community looking for information about you?"

My father has been the furthest thing from my
mind these past few weeks. "He contacted everyone
in town, it seems; even your mother-in-law. He just
didn't contact me. And he bought a house from Finn
using my name on the title instead of his."

"First, I'm hearing about a house. Maybe you
should poke around there and see what you find?"

I look at him, incredulous. "I should look? Isn't it
your job to–" I stop before finishing that sentence. It
will work better if I do this on my own. "You're

right. Its time I looked at this property. Thank you, Chief Lumquest."

I don't have the keys and I barely know where this place is. But my mind is racing on little sleep and lots of adrenaline, a sometimes-lethal combination. All the way out of town, I think about the possibilities. Maybe my father is still alive, living in the house and laughing at the chaos he's created. He and Berit.

When I find the spot, I pull off the road and stare at the weather-worn siding. At one point, it was a beautiful home. Two stories, with a gabled window and a brick structure going up the side for a fireplace. As I get out of the car, I wish Vem was beside me. She would sniff the air and tell me instantly if I was walking into trouble.

I step up to the front porch and peer cautiously through the windows. Nothing inside. To my amateur eyes, it appears that the place may not be structurally sound. I'm casing the perimeter of the house, looking for any easy-to-spot clues, when I see a barn. It's not far away, and in much better shape. As I approach the big, barn doors, I notice tire tracks flattening the green grass. Someone has been here recently.

Carefully, I tug on it until it slides. There is a strong smell of mustiness and oil as it opens. My eyes take a moment to adjust to the light, but when they do, I come face to bumper with a turquoise car.

CHAPTER TWENTY-NINE

Deceit

I CAN'T BELIEVE my eyes. "Stop it, Lanie. There are many cars in Piney Falls. Probably at least five are turquoise." Concentrating hard, it's difficult to come up with one. People who live here seem to have an aversion to vehicles that aren't brown or silver.

Slowly, cautiously, I walk to the car and touch the hood. It's cold. The doors are coated with a thin layer of dust. Swiping my recently manicured fingers across one, I recognize the color and texture of the dust; it's what clings to our vehicles on our road when we haven't had rain. Bending down to look underneath, I can see oil dripping on the ground. I peer inside the windows; there is a single folder on the passenger seat. The door is locked.

I look around the empty barn; nothing jumps out as a tool that would help me break in. This is one day that Vem and her superhuman strength would have come in handy.

I reach into my coat pocket and find my phone. To my dismay, there is no signal here. I decide to take pictures of everything I've seen and send them to Boysie when I'm closer to town. As I head back to my car, I pause when I am at a place where I can take a good shot of the entire property.

Even though it's broken down and abandoned, there is something sweet and homey about this farm. It doesn't feel like a sad, lost part of history. I can understand why someone would want to purchase this land and spiff it up for their own family. Maybe Gavin Anders wanted to fix the place up for the two of us to start over as father and daughter.

Once I get closer to town, I pull over to make a few calls. "Boysie? Just wanted you to know I found what I think is the turquoise car. It's at the farm-house my father bought."

"I'll head out and examine it personally," he replies. "I changed my mind. It's probably not a good idea for you to be out there by yourself in the future, Miss Anders. Leave the police work to the police, and you tend to your life."

Before I can hang up from that call, Piper buzzes in. "Lanie?" she whispers with urgency. "Can you come now? I need you. I'm at Cheese with Your Burger."

"I'm on my way back into town, hon. Give me ten minutes."

When I pull into the parking lot, I can see them through the large window. Piper is twirling his blond hair in her fingers as he stares at her adoringly. My instincts tell me to yank her away from him. Maybe this is how a mother feels, seeing her vulnerable child in their first adult relationship.

They are giggling obnoxiously loudly when I enter. It irritates everyone in the restaurant as well, by the looks of the tense faces I see as I pass the other customers. I slide into the booth across from them as Finn whispers something in Piper's ear.

"That's bad, Finn," she responds unnecessarily loudly as she playfully slaps his shoulder. She turns to look at me and immediately I can sense there are problems. "Oh, hi, Lanie! Just stopping by for an afternoon snack?" she asks innocently.

"Salutations!" Finn adds enthusiastically.

"I stopped by the bakery and Doris told me you were taking a long lunch. I need your thoughts on some bridesmaid things. Maybe a particular type of bra that will work under those dresses." I sit back proudly, knowing how difficult it can be to come up with something on the fly.

Piper's nose wrinkles like she's just smelled the worst burnt scone of her life. "That's really weird, Lanie."

"Yeah, sounds like something I'm not gonna want to hear," Finn says with disdain. He leans over and kisses Piper in a loud, sloppy manner (that I will later describe to Cosmo as "urp-producing," before standing.

"Catch you both later. Tomorrow night's movie night, right Piper?"

She sticks her thumb in the air. "For sure! See ya, babe!"

When he is out of earshot, both of our faces are instantly serious. "What in the –" I begin.

"I never had the chance to be an actress in a high school play, but I always imagined I'd be good at it." She turns around and scans the nearby tables before continuing. "Ever since we got back together, he's been acting funny. I'll ask him to do something with me and he'll have to go into the other room first and check something on his phone."

"I'm really regretting the advice I gave you, hon." I shake my head. "This may not be the person you want to spend time with, after all."

She shrugs. "Maybe. But more importantly; today he got a call during lunch on the business phone. He left his cell here, and I've watched him enough to know his code. Something in me said I needed to investigate. You're always telling me to trust my instincts, right?"

"You're an intelligent woman," I confirm.

"When I opened it, I found this," she slides her phone over to me, where she's taken a series of photos. They are all messages from Finn's phone:

Birdie541: *Dude, you gonna drop the package?*

Finnster: *I'm pretty busy. Work's got me tied up.*

Birdie541: *We made a deal. You know what happens when/if you don't.*

And a few days later:

Birdie541: *Heard there was a big boom.*

Finnster: *I just did what I was told.*

My insides feel hollow. "Is that all?"

"That's all I could find before he came back. I'm trying to keep things normal while we're investigating. So I can get everything we need."

I reach over and grab her hand. "You are so very brave. This all has to be eating you up inside. This isn't just a random person. It's your first serious boyfriend."

She pulls her hand back. "I can't think about my own feelings right now. We've got to figure out who blew up your house and what happened to your sister. What do you want me to do next?"

"Oh, Piper, are you sure your heart can take this?"

She leans forward, looking me squarely in the eye. "Lanie, you're constantly telling me how strong I am. Let's solve this. Then we'll worry about my tender little heart."

We both laugh. It starts slowly and eventually evolves into a full on, tear-producing, belly-laugh.

We both have a lot of bottled up emotions that need to come out, and laughter is the only way to make that happen right now.

The patrons of the restaurant are once more staring at our table. Piper glances at her phone when we've each wiped our eyes for the millionth time. "I've got to get back to work. Doris has a book-club meeting and Cos wants me to do some freezer inventory." She stands and kisses me gently on the top of my head. "I'll call you when I have more information. We'll get through this."

The next morning, Cos and I drive Truman back to his farm. It is both freeing and concerning, leaving this elderly man alone in his home for the first time in two months. His neighbors stocked his refrigerator with groceries and changed his linens. All that remains is for two adults to part from another with the fear and tension of parents leaving their child on the first day of school.

"The list of phone numbers is on your nightstand as well as in your phone. You've got several folks who are ready and willing to jump to your aide," I begin. "Cos is very busy with the bakery and trying to rebuild," my eyes dart back and forth, not wanting to look at Cosmo as I spout this lie, "but he can come if needed. We all can. I know it's time for your afternoon nap, but Marveline will be here in forty minutes with soup for dinner, so we'll leave the door unlocked. Your neighbor Betsy will come by later in the evening to make sure you're ready for bed."

"Never liked Betsy much," he grumbles, as Cos helps him hobble into bed. Cos also sets a crutch in an easily-accessible spot, even though he's far past needing it.

"You said she changed her perfume last time you saw her. Now she smells like apple pie, just like James Garfield," Cosmo insists as he places a glass of water on his nightstand. "Text me after she leaves and let me know how things work out tonight. I'll wait up till I hear from you."

I look at them both with concern. That will turn into an hour-long discussion. "Well, we should let you get some rest, now. Piper said she'd make you a batch of plum-and-date scones for us to bring out on Saturday." I tug on Cosmo's arm, wanting to get him out as quickly as possible.

"Okay then, buddy," Cosmo says wistfully, keeping his feet planted in place. "It's been nice having you around. Hope I did right by you, after you put everything into my dream home." He lets out a sigh and I'm afraid he is going to break down completely. "'It is easier to do a job right than to explain why you didn't.'"

"Martin Van Buren," they say together. Cosmo sticks his hand in Truman's and they share a

meaningful embrace before my fiancé walks hurried-
ly past me and outside.

"Bye, Truman!" I wave quickly and scurry after
Cos, hoping he doesn't call after me, asking for
another glass of water or a last-minute foot rub.

"Are you okay?" I ask, slightly out of breath as
we get into the car.

"Relieved. Guilty. Guilty that I'm relieved." He
starts the engine. "And you?"

"It wasn't our fault; none of it. The only thing we
can do now is move forward and figure out who did
this. And–" We both stare at our feet. I don't want to
say it out loud. "We have to talk about rebuilding,
Cos. We've put it off for the entire time Truman was
with us. Vem wants to sell the place she's been
renting us. We can't stay there forever."

"I've been giving that some thought." He pulls
out of the driveway, unwilling to look at me.
"Maybe we should just sell the land and buy
someplace already done. There's too much bad juju –
or whatever November Bean would call it – surrounding that property. Maybe we could fix up that
farm house your father bought you. Seems a shame
to just let it sit there unused."

My heart sinks. The last thing I want to do is give
up our beautiful location. From the A-shaped
windows we were planning, we would have a view of
the Pacific Ocean on one side and the luscious

mountains on the other. My two places of serenity. "I'd like to give that a little more thought before we act on it. That land was a gift to us. How would it look to the people of Piney Falls if we were to turn around and sell it?"

He takes a few minutes to respond. When we first began dating, I was infuriated by his lengthy pauses, but now I understand that he always wants to respond thoughtfully. It's something that makes me love him all the more. "You're probably right about that. We'll give ourselves a deadline. Before the wedding."

"Before the wedding," I repeat. "While we're out here, let's stop at the winery and go over a few of those details with Marveline if she's got time."

CHAPTER THIRTY

Sassy Lasses Winery

"I WASN'T EXPECTING guests today." Marveline adjusts her rainbow-colored caftan as we stand uncomfortably on her porch.

Hands in his pockets, Cosmo rocks back and forth anxiously. "We were in the neighborhood dropping off Truman, so Lanie wanted to talk to you about some wedding plans."

Marveline's eyes dart back and forth between Cosmo and me. "I suppose I could sit with you on the porch for a few minutes." She motions for us to join her at an ornately designed, cast iron table on the massive porch of historic Naybor Manor; the centerpiece of the Sassy Lasses Winery. "I just uncorked a nice vintage last hour. I'll return momentarily." She leaves momentarily, returning with three glasses and a bottle of Mandeline Merlot as she pulls the door shut tightly behind her.

Although she lives in a historic showpiece, Marveline is an introvert who is always reluctant to invite people into her space. All of her events are held outside, and the doors to the mansion remain locked at all times.

"We didn't mean to bother you. I had a few thoughts about our reception. You talked about renting a tent and I'd like to make sure it will be the right size for our guests." I gaze beyond Marveline's head, to the far side of the porch where a gentle breeze makes her wind chimes sing. I never tire of the beauty and serenity of this property. It is the perfect location for our wedding.

"How many guests will you be expecting? We have access to tents of all sizes." She touches the corners of her mouth, wiping away excess lipstick. "So far, I haven't heard what size of an event this will be."

I look at Cosmo expectantly. I asked him months ago to give me a list of customers from the bakery along with friends I may have forgotten. So far, he's only shrugged when I ask for the final number.

"What?" he says innocently. "I've been meaning to get you that list. You have to admit, we've had more than a few activities keeping us occupied."

I turn back to Marveline, realizing that other than looking at wedding dresses, I've done nothing to prepare for my wedding. "We have set a date with you, right?"

She picks up her phone and scrolls through until she finds her calendar. "I have you down for August

21st. All the flowers should be in full bloom. Late afternoon?"

"Yes, late afternoon," I say absently. "You may have to guide me through this. I've been shutting down November's ideas for so long that I haven't developed any of my own."

"Well, I was thinking we could hang purple and gray paper lanterns in the tent. Give it a real, cozy feel. As far as centerpieces go–"

"Well, I'll be damned," Cosmo exclaims.

I sigh. "You don't have to be sarcastic. You'll be happy when we get all of these details worked out."

"Not that. Look." He points to a figure walking our way from the barn. When he reaches the porch, he pulls off his cap, revealing a familiar face.

"Royal?" I ask, stunned. "What are you doing here?"

"I don't want any trouble," Cosmo says, pushing himself back from the table. "I kicked you out of the bakery because those tables are meant for paying customers. You never even bought a coffee." He folds his arms defensively across his chest.

Marveline clears her throat. "Royal is here at my behest. Ever since Truman's accident, I needed someone to fill in doing his chores on the property. Royal has worked out nicely." She blushes, just slightly.

Royal glares at the two of us and then glances at

Marveline. "Didn't know you were expecting visitors today. Just finishing up in the barn. I'll be back at six for dinner."

"Wait," a smile creeps over Cosmo's face. "Are you two–"

"Cos," I caution.

"This situation is making more sense," Cosmo continues. "Nobody's gonna fault either of you. Just needed to get a read of the room." He chuckles but quickly forces the corners of his mouth into a somber expression.

"Royal asked for my guidance. He's curious about the wine business so I've been tutoring him after he's done with chores," Marveline says matter-of-factly. "Tonight, we're pairing wines with food. It gets lonely out here and I don't mind sharing my expertise."

"Since we've had this unexpected meeting, I'd really appreciate it if you sat down and answered some questions," I say. I know he won't be rude in front of Marveline, especially if they have some kind of blossoming romance.

He looks at Marveline uneasily.

"These two have helped me with all sorts of issues. They are treasured friends, and now they're allowing me to host their wedding," Marveline encourages him. "If they have questions about something, it would be to your benefit to answer."

Reluctantly, Royal sits down in the fourth chair at the table. I can smell Marveline's strong perfume on his flannel shirt.

"Gavin mentioned he was looking for a place. I told him about Finn's. That's all." he grumbles.

"Maybe not," I begin. "But I think you do know something about his daughter. Did you meet with Berit?"

He purses his lips and mulls that question over for a few moments. "What would you say if I did?"

"First off, I would want to know where she is now."

Royal gazes out across the lawn. "Last I knew, she was headed down the coast for a little vacation. Haven't heard from her in a while."

"My next question would be, what did she want with you in the first place? Did she ask you to do something illegal?"

"I don't do nothin' I don't want to do." He looks away from us, putting his hands in his armpits. "She came out here asking about Mr. Ladieux, just like you did. She said some people were after him, and she wanted to make sure he wasn't going to be hurt."

I look at Cos, unsure of how to proceed.

"If she asked you to do something illegal, Mr. Granger, we can help. You're not going to have problems with us," Cos says.

Marveline clasps her hands in front of her. "I

can't have someone on my property who is in trouble with the law. If you are into something you shouldn't be, we need to resolve this now. Our 'arrangement' will go no further unless I know your dealings won't compromise my business."

I stare at the two of them with curiosity; a gruff-looking man with little personality, and an elegant woman who runs a winery. Not exactly candidates for the Watermark Channel Romance of the Week. If there is really more to this relationship, Marveline is attracted to fixer-uppers.

When Royal doesn't respond, I huff. "Let's start at the beginning. She came to you, that first day. What did she say?"

"She got my number from her dad's phone. Said she was retracing his steps. Asked if she could come see me and talk about things."

"Do you remember what date that was?"

He pulls out his phone and finds the call from Berit. "Oh, 'bout the twenty-first, three months ago now."

"That was two days before she showed up at the bakery. We were all busy with the festival," I say to Cos. I turn back to Royal. "And then she came to your place? You must've had a million questions."

"She wasn't the friendly sort; all business. Said she was concerned about her father getting involved with shady types and she asked for my help to make sure he hadn't done something wrong."

I gulp. "And why did that matter to you?"

He leans uncomfortably on one foot. "Said she knew her dad was consorting with some folks who'd caused him trouble. She wanted to make sure they paid for what they done. I know what that's like; I had a brother who was picked on. I made sure every single one of them got what was comin' to them."

"What did she want you to do?" Cosmo asks.

"She wanted to know everything I told Mr. Ladieux. So, I spilled. I told her about the property Finnegan Lowery needed to sell." He fiddles with his shirt, noticing the buttons are misaligned. "Then I gave her the contacts I had for all of her other needs." He adds.

Cosmo leans forward. "Exactly what other needs are you talking about? What was this woman doing in our little town?"

Royal's eyes narrow. "Like I said before, Mr. Hill. I don't know what I don't know. When someone offers me money for a simple job, I take it. I don't ask questions after that."

"And the job? Give us details of the job, please!" I beg. There has to be more to the story than what he's telling us.

"The woman wanted to make her own purchases. I sent her to a certain person I know who sells just about everything you can't find in a typical store."

"Drugs? Berit wanted happy pills?" I sniff. "Those certainly didn't work."

"No. The lady wanted something that went 'boom.'" He chuckles; an evil laugh that Marveline doesn't seem to catch as she chuckles along with him out of shear politeness.

"This Berit person sounds like a real character. I wouldn't want to become her enemy," Marveline remarks, sipping her wine.

I grab Cosmo's knee and he puts his hand on top of mine. "We're not going to play games here, Royal. This is a small town. You've heard about what happened to our home. Who gave her explosives?"

"That woman isn't the type to get her hands dirty. I'm pretty sure if she was going to set up something like that, she wouldn't do it herself. Too bad about your place. I don't have direct knowledge of who did it. Just gave Miz Campbell some names. Guys who would help her with her project. Like I said, I don't know anything about what happened to your place or who might've done it."

"Where is she now?" I pound my fist on the table. "Where is my sister?" It's all coming together: Berit wasn't just here to reconnect. She wanted me dead. She wanted Cosmo gone.

"You're the one she hated?" Marveline is just now catching on to the story. "Oh, Lanie, dear. That's just awful. You could've been hurt badly, or worse. I know what it's like to have a troubled sister." She fingers her chunky silver necklace and looks at Royal absently. "You never told me you were involved with seedy types. That's something we'll need to go over before I give you any more responsibilities here."

Royal looks at both of us women helplessly. "I don't know. Really. She told me to lose her number. It's been a couple-a months since I heard anything. Didn't exchange addresses for Christmas cards."

"We could get you into a lot of trouble, pal. There has to be someone who knows where she is." Cosmo takes a scrap of paper from his pocket and motions for Marveline to give him the pen she's been using to write down our wedding details. "Give us the name of Mr. Explosives R Us, or we go to the cops and tell them it was you who arranged the explosives."

Royal has a look of betrayal on his face. "You promised right off you wouldn't do that."

"Well, I grew up in a cult," Cosmo says dryly. "One thing we learned to do really well is lie."

There is silence as the tension mounts. "Do it now," Marveline finally commands. Royal writes down the name and number and slides it across the table. Cosmo looks at it and stares at Royal with shock. "Are you sure that's where you sent her? We know where you live. And I've got just as many friends in this community as you do."

I reach over to Cos and look at the paper. "No. You're trying to pull a fast one." I shove it back in his face. "The correct number, please."

"I told you. That's where I sent her. My lady friend here is threatening to end my employment. I got no reason to lie."

"Who is it?" Marveline asks impatiently. "I don't have all day here."

I gulp. "It's Christian Finch. Piper's biological father."

CHAPTER THIRTY-ONE

Lanie

"PIPER, WE'VE GOT something unpleasant to tell you." I look at Cos, who grabs my hand with his sturdy fingers and grips it tightly. "We didn't want you to hear this from someone else."

We're in Cosmic Cakes and Antiquery on a busy Tuesday morning. Neither of us slept much last night, each thinking about what was to be said today and how it might affect the one person we've tried so hard to keep whole.

"What is it?" Piper searches my face and then Cosmo's. "Are you closing the bakery? Breaking up? Having a baby? Tell me!"

"None of those things, hon. Cos and I were out at the Sassy Lasses Winery yesterday after we took Truman home. I realized I've really got no ideas for our wedding. Luckily, Marveline has a knack for wedding planning."

Cos touches my arm gently. "Focus, Lanie. We're getting there."

I take a deep breath, cleansing all of my negative

thoughts and worries for my dear young friend. "It was while we were there that we ran into Royal Granger."

"He and Marveline are apparently up to some ugly business," Cosmo says dryly.

"Cos!" I shoot him one of my warning glares. "No funny stuff today." I take Cosmo's hand in mine, and place both of ours on top of Piper's. The door to the bakery jangles and a group of local business executives arrive for their morning coffee. They all wave at Cosmo and he waves back with his free hand.

"I should get this," Piper says, attempting to stand. I hold her firmly in place.

"Nope. Doris can handle them. She likes to hear whatever gossip they're spreading every morning," Cosmo insists. "This is more important."

Piper's eyes narrow with concern. "What is it? You're scaring me."

"Piper, we received information that your biological father, Christian Finch, is here in town. Cos made some calls this morning and discovered that he bought explosives. He may try to contact you, too."

"We know that was a hard time for you, kiddo; when you learned your biological parents gave you to another couple to raise. And, this guy comes from the Fallen Branch cult and whatever offshoots are still running. He may be dangerous." Cosmo leans forward. "You need to be on the lookout."

Her face turns a funny color. "Oh, that. I know he's here. He's already contacted me."

"What?" Cos and I say in unison.

"When did this happen? What did he say? Does he want something from you?" I ask in rapid fire.

"You both have nothing to worry about. He wanted my help with a project, and I told him I wasn't interested. All of this time has passed and the only time he contacts me is when he needs a favor?" She rolls her eyes. "I don't think so."

It is a slight relief to know he hasn't tried to worm his way into her life. We know very little about her biological parents, but what we do know is that they gave up their own child to keep the cult running.

"There's more, unfortunately," I continue. "Christian been in contact with my sister, Berit. That series of messages you showed me on his phone the other day? We think he might have conspired with someone to blow up our home and right now Berit and Finnegan are the two with the strongest motive."

She shakes her head in exasperation. "He keeps telling me how he sees our future together; starting our own family and leaving our families of origin behind. Al the while, he's involved in dirty deals with your dad and Royal Granger." She pulls her hand in and tucks them both under her armpits, leaning back in her seat. "I've realized he can't be trusted."

"We're not convinced Finn knows everything. Berit is very conniving. Because of his connection to my father and then to Berit, he may have felt pressured to help them no matter what the circumstances." I look at Piper cautiously. I'm still not sure whether she's interacting with him entirely for our benefit, or falling in love again.

"These are all threads. The knot in the middle is Lanie's dad. Once we figure him out, we'll be able to weave it all together. Finn may not be as awful as he looks, "Cosmo offers helpfully. "He's just a dumb kid."

"Hey!" Piper protests.

"You know what I mean. He's not on your level. There's probably someone else better down the road." Cos looks at me and winks. "You'll find your Lanie."

"For now, you want me to continue pretending I'm all in, right?" she says a bit too excitedly.

"Yes, for now. Keep looking at his phone, too. We need to know if they are planning something else. We also have to find out where Berit is. She has to be hiding somewhere close." I pause for a moment. "Piper, what did your father say to you, exactly?"

"He wanted to know if I remembered him, first off. Why would I remember him? I was just a baby when he gave me up. What a dumb thing to say."

"What else did he ask?"

"He wanted to know if I was interested in a relationship. He said he'd been keeping tabs on my life and was proud of me. His wife left him last year and he has no one else around. He said, 'We could make a good team; you and me, girl.' It creeped me out."

"There's no doubt he was trying to play you. But if you want family around, don't turn him away so quickly. Maybe he really does want you in his life."

Piper shakes her head with gusto. "I don't want HIM, Lanie. I have you and Cos. You both have been my family since the first day I met you. I've never felt more connected to two people than Cosmo Hill and Lanie Anders."

Cos wipes his face, trying to do it without my seeing. "You know how we feel."

Another large group enters the bakery. This time they are all teenagers, coming here to hang out after school. "Okay, NOW I really need to go. They can get very nasty if they have to wait too long." Piper stands up and kisses my head and then Cosmos'. "Love you both – so much."

Cosmo's phone rings. "It's the insurance company. They've been slow to send us a check because the investigation is taking so long." He puts the phone to his ear and listens quietly. "I understand. Thank you. Please get back to me when you can." He gives me the look that I know only means bad news.

"What now?" I ask with exasperation.

"Police found an accelerant in the downstairs bathroom. They think we might have–"

I gasp. "We set off explosives in our own home? We tried to kill Truman? They can't be serious. Why would we do that?"

Cosmo puts his hand on my shoulder reassuringly. "I'm sure it's just routine. No one believes we'd blow up our dream home before we've even spent one night there."

My mind starts to spin. "What if this is all part of it? Someone wants us to look guilty?" Now it is my phone ringing. "It's Boysie," I say, putting the phone to my ear.

"Miz Anders? Just received a call from the insurance company. They want me to question you regarding the explosion."

"Boysie, you know me better than that. Why would you think I was involved?"

"Just routine. You did tell me you found that car on your property. The one that was seen in the area before the explosion. Have to dot the i's and cross the t's. You'll come in tomorrow?"

I let out a very loud sigh, wanting him to hear my irritation. "Yes, I'll come in. It's not like I don't have other things to do."

Cosmo rubs my back again. "It's okay. We'll get through this. Nobody in their right mind thinks we've done anything wrong." He raps his knuckles on the table. "It's pretty clear to me what needs to come next. We've got to find out what was going on in your dad's life leading up to his trip out here. You've got no leads on Berit, but if you could find out what happened right before his death, it might give you more insight into both of them."

"I already called Gladys last night. She was more than happy to come in early this morning and get busy on that." My blood pressure is returning to normal as I regain my composure. "We should stop in before we go home, and see if she's found any information. You know she can work the dark web like nobody's business."

Cosmo tilts his head. "Gladys isn't my favorite person. Her gossip drives me nuts. I've got plenty to keep me busy here. You visit with her and I'll come get you when I'm ready to go home." We stand and kiss each other lightly on the lips before I head to the counter to retrieve Gladys's standing order of a Pluto Peach scone.

When I arrive, Gladys is pacing back and forth in front of her desk. She looks up when she sees me and scowls. "What took you so long, toots?"

"Did I miss your call?" I'm caught off guard with her standing and not in the pre-nap position. I hand her the scone and sit in my usual chair while she devours it.

"This old gal's been very busy this morning," she says through voracious bites, "talking to this person and that. I've got more information on your father than you can shake a stick at. Your head just might pop when I tell you what I've learned."

"Okay, pop away." I cross my legs and lean back, way back, in order to avoid the crumb shower coming from her mouth.

"Well, first of all, your father is much beloved in his little community of Bownton. Folks there can't stop talking about all the good things he's done. Built a home for unwed teen mothers, founded a community center and started monthly ping pong tournaments. They just adore ole' Gavin and his do-gooding."

"Berit mentioned that."

"Folks believe he funded those places through his gambling. Your father had two addictions: one for the game, and one for pleasing the community. They fed off each other."

"You have been busy today! Did they say much about his family life?"

"He ran off and left his wife. Lots of rumors about why. The majority were are that the wife resented his projects and gave him an ultimatum – charity or me. They never divorced though. The girl, well, she was trouble from day one."

I lean forward, safe in the knowledge that she has

finished chewing. "What did they know about Berit?"

"She was a real bully. Took kids to their knees if they looked at her sideways. Parents in the town knew her father did these nice things for others, so they let her get away with her nastiness. Beat up kids, stole from local stores, and did what she wanted. Her own mother overlooked the behavior. Maybe she was scared of her, too."

"That sounds like what I've learned about Berit." I think back to my conversation with Minerva. She said things weren't good between Gavin and his daughter. "And then she just turns up out here, wanting to check up on her father?"

Gladys nods. "Could be. Or maybe she's checking up on you. Making sure your father never contacted you because she wanted his love, if any daughter was gonna get it. Your father, in all of his wanderings, used a different last name. Ladieux."

"Gladys, do you think Berit was here the whole time my father was here? Watching him, making sure he never made contact?"

"Have to wonder, toots. Never made sense to me he'd travel all the way to this side of the country without so much as a 'boo.'"

"If Berit were to follow him, how would she make sure he never made contact?"

Gladys puts her orthopedic shoes on the table.

"I'd imagine he knew she was here at some point. Decided he wanted to protect you, so whatever was going on, he got wise to it and purposely led her off your trail."

"And then he went back home before his death. Did he make any deathbed confessions? Did he say anything to anyone?"

"Well, here's the thing." She motions for me to come in close, like there is a reason for us to share a secret in this lonely building. "I found a friend who swears your father wasn't in Connecticut when he died. Says he never left Oregon."

CHAPTER THIRTY-TWO

Five Months Ago

"MY ONLY REQUEST is those little hotdogs wrapped in dough. Touch of cheese and some hot sauce if that wouldn't be too much trouble," Cos looks to me for my approval. I try not to show the horror I'm feeling inside. I saw this as a semi-formal event, even if I wouldn't be able to get him in a tux.

"Of course. That's a good start. And I'm sure Ms. Wench has some good ideas, too."

The gray-haired woman nods, pushing her copper-framed glasses up her nose. "We have entire menus planned out, or you can pick and choose. How many will be attending your wedding? That's where we need to start."

"Less than fifty–" "One-hundred-and-fifty–" Cos and I say simultaneously.

"Cos? We talked about this. We've got the list planned out already."

He looks down at our kitchen table, which is covered in what's left of the assorted scones he brought from the bakery. "I've been meaning to talk to you about that, Lanie. Do we really need to invite the entire city council? I don't know half of those people."

As much as I love this man, some days he infuriates me. In fact, every day we are planning our wedding is infuriating. Last month when I asked him to look at invitations with me, we sat down on three different occasions and each time he acted as if I was speaking in French.

"We went over this again and again. According to Gladys, this is THE summer event in Piney Falls and everyone who is anyone expects an invitation. Which skipped invitation will make someone unwilling to help the next time we need a favor?"

Cosmo shrugs helplessly as his knee begins to bounce, a sure sign he's agitated. "I suppose. It just seems like we're paying for a lot of food for a lot of strangers."

"You know the saying," Ms. Wench half-sings. 'Happy wife, happy life.' Let's start things out on the right foot!"

"Yoo-hoo, neighbor!" Cos and I look at each other with dread. Vem will not offer helpful suggestions to the caterer. The opposite, in fact.

"Ma'am, what you're about to hear in no way reflects upon our character or our future decisions," Cosmo warns.

"Cos!" I protest as Vem comes barreling into the kitchen dressed in her best lavender jumpsuit and matching glasses frames.

"Whatcha guys doing? I thought you were coming to my Moaning for Money class this afternoon? You could use a few extra moans in that department, if you know what I mean." She elbows me in the side before noticing our guest and extends her arm and body across the table. "November Bean. Neighbor extraordinaire."

Ms. Wench stands and smooths her skirt slightly before extending her hand in return. "Josephine Wench. Caterer for the Anders-Hill wedding."

Vem looks at both of us with hurt in her eyes. "You're not going with my menu? Crab and peanut butter spring rolls are the hot topic of my after-moan coffee hour!"

"Just looking at all of our options, Vem," I soothe. "Why don't you take a seat, we're almost done."

"If you were asking me, I'd suggest finding someone to get busy building your house. It's been almost three months and you've done nothing. I'm not one to be pushy, but I told you I was planning to sell this place. You guys need to make plans, pronto." She sits down uncomfortably close to Ms. Wench and grabs her face. "You heard about their tragic home fire? Still no suspects after all of this time. One day,

Cos and Truman are creating a masterpiece and then, KA BLOOIE!" We all jump as she yells dramatically, throwing her hands in the air.

"Ever since then, I can't get the two of them to discuss hiring a contractor and rebuilding." Vem continues in her regular voice. "I suppose you come across this a lot in your business. Feet-draggers."

Ms. Wench clears her throat and sets papers in front of all three of us. "Some ideas for you to mull over. I do have another appointment, so I'll be in touch again soon. So nice to meet you." She brusquely ushers herself out.

"Not cool, November Bean. Not cool." Cos says after following Ms. Wench to the door and waving her goodbye.

"If you won't listen to me, my only recourse is public humiliation," she retorts. "You guys need to make some plans. I'm glad the wedding is finally moving forward, but at this rate, you'll be spending your wedding night in your car."

I stand and begin clearing the dishes. "She's right, Cos. We've got to face our fears and move on with this project sooner than later." I begin to pick up the plate with the remaining scones, but Vem bats my hand away and moves it in front of her.

"How can we rebuild when we have no idea who did this? The trail just went cold. We can't find Christian Finch. Piper hasn't gotten any more intel from Finn. Someone is still out there, watching and waiting." Cos puts his hands in his jeans pockets and rocks back and forth as he looks out the front window. "They could be hiding in the woods right now, following our every move. The best criminals are the ones who have patience. I have a feeling this guy has plenty of that."

"No more listening devices. I check the perimeter daily," Vem says through mouthfuls of scone. "Berit's going to make a mistake soon and then BAM! We'll get her."

"Gladys is still on the lookout for more information on my father," I offer. "He died in Margery Falls, on the eastern side of the state. The funeral director said my father was cremated and Berit picked up the ashes the next week." I sigh, putting the dishes in the sink. "That's more than we started with."

"Being stuck as you are, maybe you need to move things along. Maybe Berit's henchman needs some encouragement," Vem says.

Cos walks back into the kitchen. "You may be right, November. If we ever want to move on with our lives, we've got to smoke the criminal out."

"What are you both talking about? Poking the hive with a stick? It doesn't sound safe," I say with concern.

"Poking it – but all the while being safe," Cos

puts his hands in his pockets and begins to pace as he thinks. "The great detriment of a small town is gossip. But it can also be a tool. What if we were to spread rumors that we knew who burned our place down? That an arrest is imminent and all of their known associates are being watched?"

"We'd have to get Boysie's okay first. I don't think he would like us making official announcements on his behalf."

"Not official. Rumor mill. You'd tell Gladys. I'd have Piper start whispering to people at the bakery. That's all it would take. Of course, we'll tell Boysie first, but then we man our battle stations and wait."

"And how will you do that? What are you manning? And could I get a glass of milk? These scones are a little dry today, Cosmo," Vem forces a cough.

"Those are yesterday's scones and not meant to be eaten four at a time," Cos admonishes as I set a full glass of milk in front of her.

"Almond only, sorry," I say pre-emptively. She shrugs and chugs the glass down.

"Piper will continue watching Finn's phone. I'll set up cameras on November's house and on a few trees so we know exactly who is coming up this road. November, you'll write down the license plate of everyone in your moan classes so we can rule them out, hopefully. Gladys will watch the dark web. Boysie will do – whatever Boysie does." Cos looks at me and smiles. "We've been handling this all wrong, Lanie. Sitting here being victims these months. It's time we get proactive."

Seeing him so fired up has me excited, but also nervous. "Seems a little dangerous, Cos. Especially since we don't know who we're dealing with. Is it Royal? Piper's dad? Berit? They're all suspects in my book."

Vem stands up and wipes her face on her arm. "I'm in. Cos, let's get busy on those cameras. You can set up a surveillance room in my house."

"This isn't your production, November Bean," Cos warns. "But that's a nice offer. Thanks." He leans over and kisses me. "I'm going to get some supplies and check on things at the bakery."

After explaining our plan to an enthusiastic Piper, I stop to give Gladys a script. "You sure you want me to say all of this?" she asks skeptically. "To tell people that you know who set the explosives and you're coming for them before the police get to them?"

"Every bit. And you are excellent at making things dramatic when they aren't. So please do that, too."

"What's that supposed to mean, toots?" she asks accusingly.

"Just that you're good at colorful embellish-ment," I stammer. "Gladys, we've researched my father to death and not found much. I think it's time to look into my mother."

"Thought you'd never ask," she smiles and pulls a ream of paper from her drawer. "Didn't want to offer it 'til you were ready, and you and Cos have been prickly ever since the explosion. I guess I understand that."

I stare at the stack of printouts with both horror and admiration. I hesitate to think what she knows about me. All of my many conquests at conventions. I bet she has them all written somewhere, along with their addresses and social security numbers.

I begin to leaf through and she slams a gnarled fist on top. "Easier if I just tell you," she snaps.

"Go ahead," I reply with uncertainty.

"Lavender Ladieux, given to her mother's sister to raise as her own."

I gasp. "I never knew that. My mother was raised by her aunt?"

"This is going to take us all day if you keep interrupting, toots. I've got to get my nap in before I head home or I'll never make it through dinner."

"Sorry, Gladys. Please continue."

"Lavender Ladieux was raised with her cousins. Didn't get on with her aunt very well. Ran out at night. Such a pretty girl, they all said. Everyone commented on her looks. Probably where you got yours." She sighs, examining my face. "Finally, at age fifteen she ran away for good. Her aunt never went looking for her. She ended up leaving with a teacher from school. It was a real scandal in that little town."

The hairs on my arms raise. "Who was that teacher?"

"I'm getting to that. She apparently worked in a dance hall and didn't go to school much. It was a big surprise to most in the town that she even knew her teacher well enough to run off with him. But behind closed doors, blouses fly, if you know what I mean. She left town with her history teacher, Gavin Anders."

"My father? Gladys, I don't know what to say." I can't imagine my mother as a teenager, flirting with her teacher. That doesn't jibe with the image of the serious woman who didn't allow me any sort of connection to the outside world.

"That's not the worst of it. There were rumors there was more to the two of them running off. Rumors that Lavender killed a man and threw him in a fire pit. Her former boss. She and your father did a good job of covering it up. But not good enough."

"Why is that?"

"Because she didn't realize the family of this Mr. Kowalski wouldn't give up until they found his killer. They were ruthless, just like he was. Even if it was a young woman, even if she was harmless, they would find her."

"And did they?"

"Well, toots, that's where things get sticky." Gladys folds her hands over her sagging chest and looks at me like a cat who just caught a bird. "This man's daughter tracked them down, but she didn't harm them, at least not the way you'd think. She pestered him, stalked him. Relentless, you might say."

"How did my father handle that? Did he have her arrested?"

"Oh, no; to the contrary. He married her. Your father's second wife was Jeannie Kowalski, the daughter of the man who was murdered."

CHAPTER THIRTY-THREE

Piney Falls

"I NEVER MET someone as alluring as you. I'm not just saying that. I mean it." Finn wipes a bit of ketchup from the corner of Piper's mouth before setting the napkin down on the table. He playfully nibbles on her nose. She returns the favor.

"Thanks," she giggles. "You say that every day. But honestly, I never tire of it. There's no guy in Piney Falls who could hold a candle to you. They come in to the bakery all the time, trying to ask me out. But none of them are Finn Lowery." Piper looks deeply into Finn's eyes.

"You two realize there is someone else at the table, right? I said nothing when you exchanged a shoe, but that thing you're doing with your nose is making me queasy." I tap my fingers impatiently on the table, hoping to bring them both out of their love-induced coma. "I'd also like to mention that you are the owner of this restaurant now, and your customers and staff look for you to set an example." I stare hard at Finn, trying to get his attention. It's no use. His gaze is stuck on the lavender contact lenses of one Piper Moonlight.

A baby drops its bottle on the floor, causing commotion in the next booth over. It's enough to bring them both back to the real world. "Lanie," Piper looks at me with embarrassment. "I'm so sorry. Something comes over me when I'm with this guy. He's got charm."

I can't help it. My eyes roll on their own. "Finn, I've been meaning to ask you about your sister. I haven't seen her around, and you mentioned that she purchased the business with you."

He raises one pierced brown eyebrow. "Faythe? She decided the restaurant business wasn't for her. She still helps on weekends, and she's my silent partner, but her heart is somewhere else. She's going to beauty school in Tellum now."

Mentally, I check her off of my list. She doesn't sound interested in arson.

"It's been exceptional meeting you lovely ladies for lunch. We need to do it again soon. Perhaps next week on your day off?" Finn touches Piper's chin and mocks a kiss. "Lanie, you'll come again, too? Piper loves you so much."

"Absolutely," I say with a hint of sarcasm that neither one of them seems to detect. We both watch him walk back to the counter where an employee has been waiting patiently to ask him about the schedule.

"You are really laying it on thick. I appreciate your dedication to this project and, more so, your patience."

Piper's face turns a shade of gray I've not seen before. "Umm, yeah. I've been giving it my all." She pulls Finn's phone from her pocket and sets it on the table in front of me. "I'll keep watch today while you go through the messages."

Something is off with her, but I don't have time to dig deeper, so I peruse his phone for messages. Since we started Operation Rumor Mill, Gladys and Piper have done a good job of spreading the rumor that Cosmo and I know exactly who burned down our dream home. Now we watch and listen to see who is upset by this news. I stop briefly when I see a thread from Piper. She's telling him that Christian Finch has been calling her, bugging her for something, but she wants no part of him. I keep going until I see a new string:

Birdie541: *They're coming for us. We're going to stop them before they get too close.*

Finnster: *I appreciate your assistance in the sale of my home, but I'm done helping you. I have a business to run.*

Birdie541: *You made the deal. There's no way out for you now. I can crush you in ways you can't imagine.*

Finnster: *Blocking you.*

"This isn't good. I think it's Christian, threatening him. I'll take a picture of the phone number and have Gladys run it."

"Hurry up, Lanie!" Piper insists. I take a quick picture and hand the phone back to her. "You don't know for sure that it's Christian."

"I'll be waiting for you in the car." I slide out of the booth and out the door, waiting for her to complete her normal routine. Piper has become an expert thief, so good I often ask myself if she has done this before and just hasn't told me. While they canoodle in the booth, she slips her hand in his pocket and removes his phone, transferring it to her other hand. When he gets up to leave, she goes through his messages and takes pictures of anything she thinks I might find of interest. After he's gone back to work, she goes to tell him goodbye and slips the phone back in his pocket. I don't know if he's that clueless, or she's that good, but it is a process that works every time. She kisses him goodbye and the routine begins again on her next visit.

When she gets into the car, she plops down breathlessly. "What?" she asks, noticing that we aren't moving.

"You. You're quite an amazing young lady. Helping us the way you are. Not letting your emotions overrule an important task."

"Well, you know I would do anything for you

and Cos. You're my family."

"About that, is Christian Finch still bothering you? Cos and I have been trying to track him down, but he seems to move around. We want to tell him to leave you alone."

She fiddles nervously with the zipper on her coat. "Yes, he thinks we're going to run off together and be a happy family. He comes into the bakery when Cos isn't there. People talk, and I've heard rumors that he's dealing drugs. There's just something creepy about him, Lanie."

"He was in a murderous cult and abandoned his daughter for them. He's dangerous." I put the car in gear, remembering that Cos and I have an appointment with the jeweler. "You don't have to talk to him if you don't want. I would be happy to speak with him. Next time he comes in, get his phone number. He doesn't know me and I'm not as ferocious-looking as your boss."

"Would you? That would make me feel so much better."

I don't tell her I have an ulterior motive for obtaining this information. "Cos will be out with me, picking out wedding rings. Maybe he'll stop in when he sees the boss leave."

Today is the day we take the next step in our relationship. I was too young to remember when my mother wore her wedding ring. In *Bride of Barry-*

more, Tulip Sloan was engaged to be married and wore a huge diamond. When my mother explained what that was, I became enamored with the idea of having a ring to connect you to another person.

"I can't wait to see what you choose!" Piper begins to laugh. "Lanie, you wouldn't believe this, but Cosmo has been studying jewelry online when we're slow. He's looked at kings and queens, rap stars, and the rich and famous. He takes notes and prints off pictures. It's rather adorable."

It makes me warm inside to think of Cosmo working so hard. It also hurts a little, knowing the stress it's caused him. He aches to get this right, and so do I.

"What do you picture Cos wearing, Piper? Something with a diamond? A simple gold band?"

"He's a simple guy. I'm going to say: go with a simple ring. Or – you could have something made especially for you?"

I shake my head furiously. "The thought of that gives me hives. I've never been interested in complicated jewelry, even when I could afford it."

I drop her off, then round the corner to the jeweler where I'm meeting Cos. There is a strange-looking man pacing in front of the store. He appears as though he hasn't slept in days; unshaven and wrinkled. His hair is long, his body is thin and frail. "Are you alright?" I ask as I walk to the door.

His eyes widen when he sees me. "You're Lanie."

"Yes, I am. Do you need something to eat? A warm place to sleep?"

"I – I was supposed to come here to rob the place. Scare you and Cosmo away. But I want out of this gig. My daughter won't have anything to do with me until I'm on the straight and narrow."

I swallow hard. Now I see the round face and full lips, familiar to me on a much different human. "You're Christian Finch, aren't you? Piper isn't interested in a relationship with you, Christian. At least until you stand before a judge and admit your crimes." It's hard to keep my temper in check, knowing almost certainly that he was involved in destroying our home and injuring Truman. I want to grab him and shake him. "I can go with you when you turn yourself in for blowing up our house. That's a start."

"No way, lady." He puts his dirty palms in the air. "I'm not going down for any of this. I just said I was done. I'm gonna tell Royal I want out and I'll pay off my debt some other way. I'm thinkin' my daughter might help me out. She's doing pretty well for herself." He starts to back away from me. I'd like to grab him and hold him there until Cosmo arrives, but I don't know what kind of weapons he's got. I reach into my pocket for my phone, to call Boysie. "You're not calling the cops on me."

He begins to fidget and back away from me. I grab for his sleeve and miss. "If you want your daughter to be proud of you, this is the time to make changes!" I yell as he hurries away. "We'll find you, Christian Finch! You can't hide!" If I was a star athlete, I would consider chasing him. But Lanie Anders does not run under any circumstance. I stare in frustration until he is no longer visible.

There is nothing more I can do for now. I take a deep breath, pushing away the frustration I'm feeling as I enter the jewelry store, where Cos is waiting. "Today is the day you're early!" I say with just a hint of exasperation.

"What?" he asks. "I wanted to be on time for this important event."

We hug uncomfortably, both nervous about what lies ahead.

"Did you get a number for Christian?" he asks.

"Yes. They're still in contact. I'm going to call Gladys when we're done. More importantly, I just saw him. He was going to cause problems for us and changed his mind. We've got to put a stop to this. I need to speak with Boysie about him and see if we can set up a sting operation of some kind."

Cos tips his head to the side. "One thing at a time. We're here to get our rings. Let's focus on ourselves and deal with this later."

I nod reluctantly.

It surprises us to see Urica Jolloby, Gladys's best friend and art gallery owner, behind the counter of the jewelry store. She wears her usual tie-dyed dress, and her gray hair is piled high on her head in coiled dreadlocks.

"Urica? What are you doing here?"

"Filling in for Jonas today. He's home with a nasty cold. I know a little something about jewelry and I'll be glad to help you." She leans across the counter and motions for us to come closer. "Gladys tells me you've set up quite the operation. Says you've got some cameras on top of the moaning studio and everything. She says November set up a room, just like the FBI has, where she watches all the people who come and go. She says–"

"Gladys was only supposed to share specific information," Cos says with disgust, remembering our plan for her to spread rumors. "I should've known better than to let her be a part of this operation."

I touch his hand gently. "It's okay. Urica, here, will make sure the news of our discovery gets where it needs to go. Right, Urica?"

She smiles, displaying two gold teeth on either side of her bottom jaw. "What do you need me to say? You kids know I'm along for the ride."

"For now, we need you to help us pick out wedding rings." I move to the glass cabinet where a dizzying display of glitz reminds me I'm no longer the type of person who would fawn over such decadence.

I point to a ring with two yellow diamonds and a ruby. "Can I see that one?"

"Them's real high-quality diamonds. I admired that one myself." She sets it on the counter and I pick it up gently, examining the simple desiqn. This is the first time I've perused this part of the jewelry store in all of my half-century of living.

"Cosmo Hill, what're we looking at for you?" Urica asks, pulling a tray of glittery men's rings out of the display and setting them on top of the counter.

"I, I–" he stutters. "Give me something easy. Lanie, can you pick something?" He puts his hands in his pockets and begins rocking back and forth. I can hear his phone buzzing. We promised each other we wouldn't speak on the phone while we were completing this important task. It buzzes again. And again.

"Cos, just answer. It must be important. Maybe Doris is having some problems closing up."

He looks relieved as he grabs his phone from his pocket. "'Lo?"

"Okay. Yep. You can tell Lanie." He holds the phone out to me, even though I've got rings on three different fingers and Urica is explaining her grand-daughter's idea to make wedding rings from old silverware while I admire them.

"I'm kind of busy right now, Cos. Can you take a message?"

He shakes his head and insists I take the phone. Reluctantly, I grab it from his hand with my bejeweled hand.

"Lanie, I've got them. The car, I saw it drive up to your place. Actually, two someone's. The first was earlier, and I had to watch it on replay, but now I'm seeing it live. I'm running over right now." All of her words jumble together.

"Slow down, Vem. Deep breathing, remember? Who did you see?"

"Earlier, I saw Truman. He came up to the place and stood for a while, writing something down and then he left. But now, there's another car." She's out of breath and running.

"It's okay, Vem. You don't have to catch them. You've got them on camera, that's enough. We can have Boysie run the plates and–"

"I'm – close enough. Oh, boy. I can see clearly now. I know who it is. Fudge and knuckles, Lanie, it's–"

"Vem? Vem? Are you still there?"

CHAPTER THIRTY-FOUR

More Pieces to the Puzzle

"VEM? ARE YOU here?" I tiptoe over November's expensive, pea-green carpet. For a person with an unusual look, her house is like something from a New York style magazine. I stop briefly to gaze at her portrait of Tulip Sloan. In the six-foot, lifelike painting, the '40s movie actress is draped across a maroon velvet couch. Her lips purse in a pouty pose she must've held for hours so the artist could get it just right.

In fact, whoever made it must've been completely enthralled with her. Judging by the date scribbled by the artist's name, I know Tulip was nearing the end of her life and deeply immersed in a world of drugs and alcohol. The soulful eyes represented are of a young starlet, not a seasoned actress whose days melted into nights and into days again, until they were all the same. I've read enough about her, watched so many of her movies that I feel like I sometimes know this woman better than I know myself.

"Did you find anything?" Cosmo has searched the entire house, leaving bits of mud from his hiking shoes all over her impeccably groomed carpet.

"I was – I guess I got lost in the portrait. Sorry." I blush. It's not like me to forget myself.

"She's in trouble, Lanie. We may not have a minute to spare!" Cosmo isn't one for dramatics. The time I had a subdural hematoma, he sat by my hospital bed day and night without saying much of anything. The nurses said it touched them how a man of so little verbiage was so in love. It's concerning now that he is completely on edge.

"Let's look in the surveillance room, Cos. Maybe we can retrace her steps." Vem is indestructible. I can't imagine anything happening to her that she couldn't kick, moan, or meditate her way out of.

I guide Cosmo to a small room on the second floor, hidden behind a secret door. "What was this place originally used for?" he asks. "Was she planning on kidnapping someone?"

"She wanted a secret command center to use when the aliens came. Didn't you hear that story?" I type Vem's usual codes into the keypad on the door: moan555, moaninbabe22, howwwl99. Nothing works. "Cos, can you think of something else she might use? Something that should be obvious?"

He rocks back and forth, his hands in his jeans pockets. "It's gotta be toilet paper related. She likes passwords she thinks really stick it to her ex. When we were building her moaning studio, she wanted the code to get in to be something like tpkingtped72."

"That's it. She likes to recycle everything, including passwords." I punch in tpkingtped72and the door slowly opens. There are several monitors with pictures from all angles on her property, including one facing the road and one facing the plot where our house once stood. It's a kick in the gut, seeing the charred remains of our home. When Cos and I go for our walks, we purposely avoid walking by it.

"We need to take the rest of the charred wood down. I guess the police finished whatever they were doing."

"Mmmhmm," Cosmo says noncommittally. He moves to the computer keyboard. "I'm gonna see if I can back this up." He fiddles with the keyboard for a few minutes before he magically pulls up a different day. November is practicing Monday Wail and Yoga in her garden. The camera is pointed at her and she begins to undress.

"Make it stop, Lanie!" Cos leans back in his chair and puts his hand up to his eyes. "Whatever I did in my life to deserve this, I'm sorry."

"Move!" I command, sitting down. Vem taught me all the particulars of this system but at the same time was lecturing me on trying to find more information on my roots. One sentence began with,

"Click here and then hit the back button, just like you're using your own back button to forget about your family."

After I fiddle with it for a few minutes, I'm able to navigate to this afternoon. A car pulls into what would have been our driveway and parks as someone takes pictures. I can see November at the bottom of the screen, engaging in her, "I'm moving with purpose" jog as she approaches the car. She has one hand on her hip and the other is grasping her phone.

"Something bad is going to happen." Cos points to the screen. Sure enough, someone gets out of the passenger side of the car and runs around to Vem. He hits her over the head with something, catching her as she falls. He throws her into the backseat before she can right herself. The car speeds away.

"Oh, Cos. I feel sick. How could I be so callous? Thinking Vem would be safe from my sister and whoever she is plotting with?"

"We're going to call Boysie and between the three of us, we'll find her." He rubs my shoulder supportively. "Who do you think got angry when they heard we found the arsonist?"

"I don't know. Gladys and Urica told everyone in town. And then Piper found evidence on Finn's phone that whoever is blackmailing him knows. We came up with this brilliant plan, but no way to really track the letches down."

Cosmo smiles reassuringly. "It would take an army of aliens to keep November Bean away from her best friend."

Cosmo calls Boysie, explaining the situation, while I look around. I haven't been upstairs in her home for months. Everything is immaculate and in its place. I walk into her bedroom, a peach wonderland. I remembered it more of a chartreuse, but it wouldn't be out of character for her to change everything to match her mood.

She has a large desk sitting next to a gigantic window with several small pieces of paper stuck to the top. "Tell Lanie she needs to wear more blush" reads one. I giggle to myself, a bit ashamed to be finding amusement in this dire situation. "Order vermillion-colored jumpsuit and glasses on a Thursday." Oh, to visit her mind. The next one makes me jump. "Cos! Come here!"

He comes running in, a look of tension on his face. "I just got off the phone with Boysie. He's sending a team out. He's worried, too. This whole situation has the entire department on edge. What did you find?"

"Here's an interesting one–" Cosmo picks up a random note. "Bird seed, squirrel dung and almond milk. I was right; she is vitamin deficient," he quips.

"No, not that. This is strange–she's been in contact with Minerva, the woman I spoke with about

Berit. She was a family friend." I hand him a bright-pink sticky note with a familiar phone number.

"Why would November be in contact with her? Being nosy again?"

I rub Cosmo's arm comfortingly. "I'm sure she's trying to help. I'll call her as soon as Boysie leaves."

We wait for what seems like hours for Boysie and his team to arrive. When they do show up, they thoroughly comb through Vem's large home for any clues to her disappearance. Boysie asks us the same questions over and over, until he's satisfied he's learned everything we know. After an exhausting day, we close up the house and turn out the lights. I want to break down and cry as we shut the front door.

"Cos, will you make a sign for the Moaning Studio to inform her students she's temporarily out of service?"

"You're awfully calm, Lanie. I thought you'd be having a complete breakdown by now."

"I know," I say, wrapping my arms around my middle. "I'm not sure why. Maybe she's sending me a signal right now, but I feel like she is okay. We're going to make it through this, Cos." I take his hand as we walk to our place, not daring to glance back toward her empty home. When we reach the front yard, Cos splits away and heads for the garage to find something suitable to make a sign.

I pull out my phone and call the number, the same one that Vem wrote on a note on her desk. "Who's this?" A suspicious voice on the other end of the line says.

"Mrs. Jensen, this is Lanie Anders. We spoke recently regarding my father, Gavin Anders."

There is an awkward silence. "Did something else happen?" She doesn't seem shocked to learn Gavin Anders is my father.

"I think you've been in contact with my best friend, November Bean. She may have been asking more questions. She can be very persuasive."

"I remember. She's a peculiar sort. It wasn't about your father. She wanted to know about your mother. Said she had a theory and wanted to prove it."

"What questions did she ask?" The thought of November acting as sleuth for me both warms my heart and concerns me deeply.

"She wanted me to tell her everything I knew about Lavender Ladieux."

If November had just asked me, I would have told her. "My mother was adopted. Taken in by her aunt and uncle, Rose and Charles Ladieux, and raised as their own. She lost her mind after my father left her and never regained her sanity."

"I should have been completely honest with you when you called the first time." Minerva sighs. "I was afraid you'd be angry if I told you the truth, but your friend convinced me I should be honest." She pauses. "I knew your mother – Lavender Ladieux – quite well. We grew up as sisters even though we were cousins. She was such a pretty thing. I was jealous, if I'm being truthful."

"My mother – had–" I stammer. "She never mentioned siblings."

"Of course she didn't. We drove her away, my mother Rose and I. Out of jealousy, I suppose. It made us both feel better about our sour situations. Lavender was working at the dance hall, bringing in good money, supporting us. We weren't at all grateful."

There are a hundred questions swirling in my mind. "The dance hall where the man was murdered?"

"Yes, Lou Kowalski's Dance Hall. The story was that he got drunk and fell into the fire pit. But people gossiped that Lavender stole from him and, when he confronted her, she pushed him in. She and Gavin disappeared after that. Oh, that got tongues a-wagging." She laughs. "It took me a long time to recognize my part in her running off. I was lost in an evil world of a different kind. It was shortly after your mother left that Jeannie Kowalski and I began a friendship. She'd lost her father; I'd lost a sister. It seemed like a reasonable thing."

The hairs on the back of my neck raise. Ever since Gladys told me that Jeannie was my father's second wife, I've wondered if there were more to the story. "Did Jeannie know Lavender?"

"Oh, yes. She knew her from high school. Never had anything good to say about Lavender. Jeannie and I bonded over our jealousy of that poor girl."

Jeannie must've tracked them down. Either through Minerva or by some other means. But her marrying Gavin wasn't a coincidence. "You said my mother had her reasons for being crazy. Did you stay in contact with her?"

"We connected twice. After I came to my senses and realized Lavender was a victim too, I asked Jeannie to help me find her. I wanted her to know I married Ralph, who was the door man at Lou Kowalski's Dance Hall. If it hadn't been for her, I never would have met him and had forty-three glorious years of marriage. He was a very successful businessman, you know. He owned a chain of fish restaurants on small boats called Ax's on the Water. On his very first boat, he couldn't afford an anchor so he made one from an old ax he'd kept as a souvenir from the Dance Hall. That was the reason for the name." Minerva stops to blow her nose.

"When Jeannie gave me Lavender's number, I called and told her thank you. She hung up on me." She pauses, her voice cracking. "We hadn't treated her well. My sister Frances came with me when we tried to visit after Rose died of alcoholism. We thought she should know. When Lavender realized who we were, she slammed the door in our faces. And, Miz Anders, there's one more thing you should know–"

"Yes?"

"Your mother's birth was a secret. At that time, it was unheard of for a woman to raise a child out of wedlock, especially her type."

"What type is that?" My voice is shaking.

"Hollywood. My aunt was a very famous actress. My aunt, your grandmother that is. Her name was Tulip Sloan."

CHAPTER THIRTY-FIVE

Family Ties

"MIZ ANDERS? ARE you still there? I've got chair aerobics in fifteen minutes. I don't have much longer to visit."

The phone and my arm are resting on the counter. I didn't realize they dropped, but they did. For a moment, I'm lost, unable to comprehend what's been said. I'm floating, maybe not even breathing. I pick it up slowly and bring it back to my ear. "I – don't know what to say. You're telling me that Tulip Sloan is – was – my grandmother?"

"We never spoke of it as a family. Not in a formal sense. My mother didn't want Lavender putting on airs. Mother and I whispered, though, when she wasn't around. I was very easily led in those days; by a horrible man and then by my mother. Having my mother's attention meant agreeing with her ideas that Lavender was the enemy. I'm truly sorry for all of it."

"She forced me to dress like Tulip Sloan. I performed at the mall every weekend." I think about all the times we watched Tulip Sloan's movies, learning every bit of dialogue, my mother collecting old magazines with any mention of her famous parent. She was obsessed with this woman. I'd always thought it was just a part of her illness, but it was so much more. It was her only connection to her roots.

"I saw the newspaper articles," she chuckles. "When my sister, Frances passed away, I found them pressed in a nice remembrance book. You were the spitting image of your grandmother."

"I wish I'd known about Tulip. I was just a child doing what my mother asked of me. Our lives revolved around this woman and I had no idea that was the reason. No idea at all."

Minerva clears her throat. "Mother said that at the time of Lavender's birth, Tulip dated the actor, Johnson Hobarth. Handsome fella. Tulip never breathed a word to Mother, but we always assumed he was the father." She pauses for a moment, I suspect she's trying to give me time to digest this earth-shattering news. "Tulip died of a drug over-dose when Lavender was still a young child," she continues. "Mother went alone to her funeral. She didn't want the press to see Lavender and decide for themselves who she was. Even after Tulip was gone and their agreement was over, Mother was still trying to honor it."

"I suppose Johnson didn't know either. That was

the way things worked." I've read many books about movie stars in the forties who hid their children. Often, the birthfather had no idea.

"Never. Back then it was normal for Hollywood folks to give birth to secret love children and leave them with family. Tulip made Mother promise she'd never breathe a word. Of course, being the loyal woman she was, Mother told no one but me."

"She was doing her sister an enormous favor. It would have been difficult to raise the child of a movie star in silence." My words don't match my feelings. My poor mother was treated as a burden her entire childhood.

"We lived a pleasant life in our little town. Aunt Tulip bought us a big house and when she asked mother to take in her baby, she offered to give us a monthly allowance. Such things weren't spoken of, you know. When my father moved out, he took the bulk of Tulip's money from our savings. If it weren't for Lavender, we would've been on the street."

"Remarkable." I think back to the times my mother would be at work and I would dig through her cubby holes in the basement. She collected every single gossip magazine from the 40s and kept them in one spot. Tulip Sloan's face covered almost every issue and each story seemed more outlandish than the next. "Tulip Sloan, Sexy Screen Siren cuts her own hair with Gardening Shears!" "Tulip Sloan, Star of the Upcoming Winds of Wallaby, Caught in Swimming Pool with Studio Head!" I read them for hours, drinking in the tales about the woman I was forced to portray. All the issues I kept after my mother died perished when my house in Chicago burned down. I wish I could read them again with the knowledge I have now.

My mind sifts through these memories for a moment, before I remember there are more answers needed. "Tell me about Jeannie Anders," I say.

"She was so kind and interested in me. I was broken; even though my mother wasn't of sound mind, she was all I had. When she was gone I was eager to find someone who cared. From the first day, Jeannie asked me questions about Lavender. I was flattered she wanted to know so much about me and my family so I told her everything. Jeannie admitted she'd always had a thing for Gavin. One day she announced she'd tracked him down and was moving to be near him. He was naïve, just looking for the next damsel in distress. In a long letter, she confessed that, after she'd married Gavin, she went to Lavender's home. Jeannie couldn't help herself, she wanted to confront the person who'd killed her father. She told Lavender everything I'd said in confidence. Everything about her mother."

I gulp. My poor mother was trying to hang on to her sanity and Jeannie Kowalski came in and pushed her over. "That's when she began her obsession with Tulip Sloan movies."

"As much as I loved Jeannie, she was devious. It's so obvious now, the reason she initially befriended me was to find out what I knew about Lavender's whereabouts. We developed a deep friendship, despite her early motives."

"Can you tell me why Jeannie and Gavin separated?" I ask.

"She became too much for him and, just as he did to your mother, he walked out." Minerva taps the phone with her finger. "After Jeannie died, I started wondering if she began that rumor herself about Lavender killing Lou. No one had ever said a word about it until Jeannie came up with the story. My Ralph always said Jeannie didn't know what she was talking about."

"I know you need to get to your class, but there is one more thing. How did Jeannie die?"

Minerva makes a humming sound. "Guess there's no harm in telling you. Gavin felt Jeannie blackmailed him into marriage. She said she knew what really happened to Lou and threatened to go to the police about Lavender being the killer. Gavin knew Lavender was sick and he didn't want her to suffer through that. That's why you and your mother had no contact with him."

This makes more sense than anything I've heard

up until now. "He really loved us?"

"Yes indeed. Jeannie didn't like 'losing to Lavender' as she put it. She was convinced Gavin would try and find you, so she followed him everywhere. That day, he was picking up furniture for the youth shelter at a former drug den. Jeannie was watching from her car with the window down. As they lowered the couch down the porch steps, a gun fell from the cushions and a volunteer stepped on it, causing it to discharge a bullet right into Jeannie's head."

"You spoke with my friend, November. You said she had a theory about all of this. Do you remember what it was?" As much as I discount Vem's wild ideas, there is always a kernel of truth to them.

"Couldn't hardly make heads nor tails of that woman. At one point in the conversation, she began howling. I just about hung up on her, but my mother always said, 'We do what we must.' I decided I could tolerate her if it would help you. 'Berit's the rotted root,' she mumbled. I agreed. After her funny noises, she says to me, 'Miss Minerva, I'm gonna tell you what I think: Lanie's parents ruined her childhood. But it wasn't just Lavender's twisted tree and Gavin's absence; it was a lack of good people outside of the family. I know that from experience. After my divorce, I was hollow and broken. I came back to my hometown thinking that would make me whole. It wasn't until I met Lanie that I was able to heal fully.

We're not blood, but our roots have become permanently intertwined.'"

We sit in silence for a moment. "Thank you for your time, Minerva."

"Before you hang up, there might come a day when you're interested in connecting with those of us from your mother's side. I could send you that information if you like."

Emotions are hitting me from every side. My concern for November – who has been the closest thing to a sister I've ever had – finally understanding my mother's obsession with Tulip Sloan, and all of this family suddenly appearing in my life for better or worse. I'm completely overwhelmed, but this is an opportunity I don't want to throw away. "Okay."

As soon as the phone call is done, I find Cosmo in the garage where he is painting a sign on an old piece of tin he'd been keeping to make a *Mr.* and *Mrs.* shield. He had an idea to paint it and display it in front of our table during the reception. When he sees me, he looks up with worry. "It's more important to use this for November right now. I'll attach it to a tree down at the bottom of the road and keep the lookie-loos out until we're certain everyone is safe. You know what kind of goofballs she attracts–" His voice cracks.

"Oh, Cos." I rush to his side, pulling him in close. "I'm worried, too. She was doing something for me – for us – and now her life is in danger! I'll never forgive myself."

We hold each other while he sobs quietly in my hair. "Dammit, if we find that woman, you won't tell her a word about this. She'll be sprinkling me with scented compost for the rest of my life, trying to rid me of my sorrow over her disappearance."

"My lips are sealed." I hug him a little tighter. "It makes me love you all the more; knowing you can care so deeply for someone who drives you mad on a good day."

He strokes my hair and kisses me one more time. "There is something we need to discuss."

I pull away, remembering why I came down here. "On my end, too. I just had an enlightening conversation with a relative. But you go first."

He raises his eyebrow at the thought of me communicating with another relative, but says nothing more on the subject. "When November called, she said there were two cars. The first one, this morning, was Truman. She said he got out and looked around and wrote some things down before leaving again. I'm gonna have to call him and get an answer about that."

Seeing Cosmo's heart breaking on top of everything else is more than I can take today. "I know how much he means to you. He's been such a big help with the house. Maybe there's a logical explanation?"

A police car, one of two that the town of Piney Falls owns, speeds up our hill and over to November Bean's residence with the lights spinning. Chief Lumquest lumbers out of the car once again and pulls out his phone. At the same time, he motions for us to come to his side.

"Yes, Mother. We'll be there for dinner at six. I bought the smoked turkey yesterday." He shakes his head and puts his finger to his lips. "We're having a staff meeting, so I need to hang up. Won't forget." He puts his phone in his pocket and shrugs. "Didn't figure you'd want her to know just yet. She'll have half the town out here combing these woods."

"That might not be a bad idea," Cosmo says. "The more help we have, the better."

"Doubtful the kidnapper stuck around. They're probably long gone. Knowing the financial means Miss Bean has, they will be looking for a ransom soon, I'd suspect. But I came back to tell you what's happened. Royal Granger just robbed the hardware store downtown. Took all $150 they had in the cash register. He slipped away from us, but the Tellum police are assisting and we'll catch him. Just want you folks to keep an eye out."

"I'll take care of him if he shows up," Cosmo says menacingly.

"Boysie, I just got off the phone with my aunt.

She says Vem was questioning her about my mother. Maybe she came across information that was dangerous to both of us."

"Your aunt?" Cos asks in disbelief.

"Mother says you don't have no relatives other'n that sister we can't find." Boysie yanks up his pants, the successful result of a recent two-week ice cream fast.

"Your mother-in-law doesn't know about this call," I retort. "Please listen. The woman I've been speaking with, my Aunt Minerva, says that my grandmother was Tulip Sloan. This could all have something to do with the kidnapping. November spoke to her recently and they both agreed Berit was up to no good."

Cosmo's jaw drops. "Why didn't you tell me first? Before blurting all this out in front of the police?"

"I was getting to that when Boysie showed up." My phone buzzes and I see that it is Piper. Something in me says it's important to pick up. "Hello? Are you okay, hon?"

"Lanie," she whispers. "I just checked Finn's phone. He got another message from his mystery caller. They want him to meet at the farmhouse to take care of business."

My stomach drops. "What does that mean?"

"I don't know but they gave him thirty minutes

to get out there. Or else. He's in the bathroom. What should I do?"

"Don't return his phone. We don't want to put Finn in danger. Cos and I will handle this." I look at Cos and motion to move away from Boysie.

CHAPTER THIRTY-SIX

All Tied Up

C OSMO IS GOING at least twenty miles per hour faster than the speed limit. "All these years, all this time – Your mother knew about her connection to Tulip Sloan?" He asks, his voice as revved up as his driving.

"I just thought my mother was lost in her madness," I say not daring to glance at the landscape whizzing by. She was trying to re-create her own mother in me. If only she would have told me. I would've tried to help her." I can't take this anymore. "Cos! Please slow down! If we die before we get there, we're of no use to Vem."

He lets up slightly on the gas. I get a glimpse of the speedometer. Now we're only going ten over. Maybe if I distract him, he'll slow down a little.

"That whole pretend life she created; she was trying to tell me something. When I left for college, I never returned. By then, she only spoke in movie quotes. I tried getting her help, but she refused. She died alone. She'd been re-enacting a scene from *Life's*

Sweet Aroma, dancing in the street in her Tulip Sloan replica dress when she slipped and fell. The bus driver saw her too late." My voice shakes a little as I speak. I thought I'd put these feelings away long ago.

"I know it's hard to share." Cos relaxes his shoulders and with that, we are back to an acceptable speed. "We needed that out in the open before our wedding. I've shared my darkest secrets with you and you've been pretty closed off."

"I know, babe. I've kept it shut away for too long. The sadness and shame shaped my entire adult life. I put everything I had into my job and didn't bother with serious relationships, seeing how my parents had failed so miserably. It wasn't until I met you that I understood how worthwhile real love could be."

He looks quickly at me with his worried face. "You should've stayed behind. That's a lot to process today." He speeds up once more. "You can stay in the car if you want. We're almost there."

I grab the door handle and hang on tightly. "November's safety is the most important thing right now."

As we pull over on the side of the road, Cosmo turns to me. "Why your father had to come out here and involve you in this mess is still a big question mark in my head. He could've phoned you to tell you he was sorry. We could have avoided all of this. You sure you want to go in?"

"Berit was involved somehow." I stare at the cows chewing their cud in the field next to us, oblivious to Vem's peril. "That woman has got something dark inside, mark my words. We don't have time to spare. Let's rescue Vem!"

CHAPTER THIRTY-SEVEN

A Rescue And A Beer

"**D**O YOU THINK we should wait for Boysie?" Cosmo asks as he parks the car just off the road, out of view of the old farmhouse. "I mean, he trained for these types of scenarios. We've been in some sticky situations before, but never anything where we didn't have the element of surprise on our side."

"Vem's life could be in danger. Another few minutes might be too long."

Cosmo nods in agreement. "What's the plan, boss?"

"I could go around back while you kick in the front door. That gives us a slight advantage." I start getting out of the car when Cos grabs my arm.

"Finn's not the brightest guy in the world, but Royal is another matter. If things go bad, you get yourself and November to safety. I can fend for myself. Understand?"

"Tulip Sloan's granddaughter isn't about to take on a battle she can't win." I smile, trying to exude confidence I don't feel.

"I haven't come this far to miss marrying the woman of my dreams," Cosmo says with the smile that drew me to him those long months ago.

Exiting the car, we hug the thick bushes as we make our way up the driveway. When we part – me heading for the back door and Cosmo for the front – we give each other a knowing nod.

In the silence of the country surroundings, I can hear his foot kicking against the front door. I turn the knob. Locked. I hadn't planned on that. I don't have superhuman strength to break a door. In the seminar, *Breaking the Locks on Your Success*, Zebulon Morton used breaking into a home as a metaphor for opening your mind to success. He told us the weakest part of the door is just above the lock. I didn't sleep with him because he had two other dates lined up, and I wasn't about to stand in line when there were plenty of people waiting in the bar.

I take a step backward and concentrate. I can do this. I lift my foot and focus all of my strength on this small area. Just as I'm mid-thrust, the door swings open.

"Lanie! Were you going to save me? You're about ten minutes late."

I fall forward, into November Bean's arms. "I was so worried. Did they hurt you?"

She kisses my head and holds me at arms' length.

"No sirree. November Bean is bombproof. They knocked me out, so I was temporarily off my feet. But they made one big mistake."

"What's that?"

She beams. "Underestimating the power of the Bean's bean. I pretended to still be conked out as they hauled me in. When Royal left to make a phone call, I released my hands from the restraints and took this one down." She points to a man who is hog-tied on the floor behind her. "Not much upper body strength. I could've done it mid-moan."

She stands aside, motioning for me to enter. I can see Finnegan Lowery's reddened face as he struggles in vain to get his hands free.

"Finn! I thought we intercepted that call!" I bend down to view his terrified face. "Did you think this was all a game? Involving my father in your sick plans?"

"Royal came into the restaurant when I didn't answer his text. He forced me into the car with him. He's been blackmailing me to help him for months. He said the sale of the house was illegal and he would go to the cops if I didn't help them." He struggles, trying to get his hands loose. Neither Vem nor I make any move to release him.

"Where's Piper? Did you hurt her? If you did, you'll be missing some limbs before you're untied!" I warn.

"She's safe. She was in the bathroom when he took me. She probably has no idea."

Relief sweeps over me. If anything happened to her, I don't know what I'd do. "What is the purpose of all of this? Blowing up our home? Kidnapping November?"

"Pointing the finger at you, Lanie," Vem responds matter-of-factly. "This wimp and Royal were going to make November Salad. Royal is off right now planting evidence at my house that I had discovered you started your place on fire to collect insurance money. They'd set the scene that you lost your cool and brought me out here to–" she makes a slicing motion with her hand. "And that would be the end of me."

"Why does Royal hate me so much? I've done nothing to him."

Cosmo rushes into the kitchen, glancing first at a squirming Finn on the floor, then November before his eyes finally rest on me. "The door had a piece of wood jammed against the handle on the inside, or I would have been in sooner. I see you've got everything under control." He puts his arm around my shoulder and pulls me in tight.

The three of us look at Finn. Cosmo tugs on him by his bound arms until they reach the center of the room. Finn squeals in protest. "Talk, punk. We need to know everything before I excuse the ladies and make mincemeat out of your face."

"I – I needed a loan to buy Cheese with Your Burger. The bank wouldn't lend me the money, so a friend said I should contact Royal because he knew some loan shark. We were gonna meet again in a week. When he came to me, he said he'd just met some sucker looking for a project. He told me we could sell the place for an inflated price to this rube and he'd take half."

Cosmo puts his foot on Finn's head. "That doesn't explain kidnapping. You'll squish like a grape."

"Cos!" I protest. "Hear him out." He moves his foot, but stays close by.

"We sold it to this Gavin Ladieux for twice it's worth. The guy said he and his daughter would fix it up nice and use it to benefit the community. I thought that was the end of it, but Royal insisted I still owed him. I'm his and if I don't do what he wants, he'll expose me. He comes into the store the next week and tells me he's got another job for me, helping him put an uppity woman in her place."

"I just don't understand that kind of hate."

"Not everyone is spectacularly loving and kind the way we are, Lanie," November says. "Royal's always been twisted."

"I tried to stop him," Finn continues. "I told him I was going to the police. He laughed in my face. All

I wanted was to own my restaurant. It shouldn't have been so messy."

Cosmo reaches down and begins untying Finn. "We've got to find him and put a stop to this nonsense."

The sound of sirens coming down the road are a relief to all of us. They speed on by the farmhouse, continuing down the highway. "Well, that was unexpected," Vem quips. "Now what?"

"We go back home. You can stay with us until we figure out how to get the truth from Royal." Cosmo presses lightly on my back. "We should all get out of here. I don't feel good about waiting around for Royal to show up."

"What about me?" Finn asks, while brushing the dirt off his white dress shirt.

I put my hand on Cosmo's chest, reminding him to be polite.

"We'll give you a ride back to town. But you stay away from Piper. Or I won't be so nice," Cosmo growls.

"Yes, sir," Finn mumbles.

After we leave Finn at the police station, where he confesses to his role in Vem's kidnapping, I text Piper, letting her know we're home with Vem and will tell her the entire story soon. I look in the refrigerator, trying to find something edible, though none of us are hungry.

"Beers?" Cosmo asks. We all agree and settle on the couch to review our day. We're only there a few minutes before there is a knock on the door. Cosmo jumps up. "You two wait in the bedroom," he warns.

"Not a chance," Vem replies, assuming a defensive stance. "He wasn't able to take me down before, he's certainly not going to do it this time."

"I'm not missing that show," I add.

Cosmo rolls his eyes and grabs a frying pan before walking to the door. He holds it above his head as he throws the door open, ready to strike whoever or whatever awaits.

"Hey now. An ex-con threatening an officer of the law doesn't look good on my daily report," Boysie chuckles nervously. "I guess you weren't expecting me."

"Come in, Boysie," I call from behind Cos. "We're drinking our dinner. Can I get you one?"

"No thanks, Lanie. I'm still on duty. Just wanted to stop in and give you folks the news."

"Good, I hope." November puts her hands on her hips. "Although I don't smell anything positive."

"I'm afraid not." Boysie stiffens. "We found the turquoise car that was previously in the farmhouse garage. It was parked on A Street and there was a body inside. The deceased was one Christian Finch. Looked like he'd been in quite a scuffle before he was shot." He shifts his weight uncomfortably. "Didn't take us long to figure out it was Royal Granger."

"When I ran into Christian, he said he wanted out. He must've told Royal and it didn't go over well. I'm sorry his life has ended today. He was ready to change himself." I shake my head.

"He was a troubled soul. Found lots of drugs on his person."

"We've got to track Royal down. Now. If you can't legally get into his house, I'm sure we can figure out a way to do it," Cosmo says excitedly. "Robbery, kidnapping, and murder? I want to know what this creep is planning next."

"Sorry to tell you, Cosmo, but that won't be happening." Boysie's face is somber.

"What do you mean? Did you already catch him?"

Boysie scratches his chin. "We'd been searching for him all day, ever since the robbery. Just so happens my deputy was taking his break, sitting at the corner of Fir Street and Mulberry Way when he saw Royal breaking into my mother-in-law's car. When the deputy yelled at him to stop, he drove off. I've told mother for years not to leave the keys inside."

I roll my eyes. "I've talked to Gladys about that numerous times. She says, 'Piney Falls is a small town, Lanie. You don't have to worry.'"

"A chase ensued," Boysie continues. "All three of the Tellum vehicles and both of ours. Mr. Granger took us on quite a ride before crashing into the big spruce off Spearmint Drive. Died instantly."

My chest falls. "Now we'll never know why he did this?"

Boysie shakes his head. "That's not necessarily true. In his car, we found all sorts of surveillance information. He'd been tracking you for months. Seemed a little obsessed with you both. It's a good bet he set the fire."

"So, this has nothing to do with my sister?"

"Not that we can find, Lanie."

Cosmo hugs me tightly. "That's good, right? Maybe your sister isn't the evil shrew you thought she was."

"My nose would disagree. She smelled of deceit," November adds helpfully. "You were right to distrust her."

CHAPTER THIRTY-EIGHT

Loose Ends

"YOU'LL NEVER KNOW why your father was here. That's gotta be so hard for you, Lanie." Piper puts my half-foam latte in front of me and sits down.

"I tried finding Berit's law firm because I wanted more answers from her. Unfortunately, it doesn't exist and there's no evidence she was even an attorney. She's just as much a mystery to me now as the day she arrived."

Piper looks outside at the last sprinkles of rain from last night's deluge. "Maybe it's better that way. You don't have to be tied to your past. You left everything behind for a reason and now you're getting ready to start your new life with Cos."

"You're right. No more Royal Granger, no more Berit Campbell. Just a wedding to plan." I grin. "And what does my maid-of-honor think of escorting me to lunch later?"

"I would, but–" she fumbles. "I'm going to go talk to Finn."

"What? Are you crazy? He could have gotten Vem killed! He isn't to be trusted, Piper!" When the words come out of my mouth, I instantly feel regret; His motives weren't evil. My desire to protect Piper got the better of me and now I realize he's not so bad.

"He only did that out of desperation. He wanted so badly to be a respectable business owner. That's why he was pushing me to change my name, too. I can understand that need to please." She looks away from me nervously. "I do like him. He gets me. But I'm telling him I need some space, at least for now. He's got one hundred hours of community service to perform for his role in all of this. That will keep him busy for a long time. I've got to stay focused on what's best for me."

"Okay, hon." I soften my tone. "You have a good head on your shoulders. I trust you to make good choices and I think he will too from here on out. A few months down the road, things may look different to both of you." I pause for a second, not sure if I should bring up the next topic. "How are you feeling about the death of Christian Finch?"

"Whatever problems he had, they were his alone. I never felt a connection to him. I'm sorry his life is over, the way I'd be sorry for anyone else in our community who'd died, but that's it." She clasps her hands in front of her. "Lanie, I was hoping you and

Cos could come to my place for dinner tonight. I have something important to ask."

She's caught me totally off-guard. "Sure. Any time I can skip cooking is a bonus. Should I be concerned?" There is a hard tap on my shoulder. "Ow!" I turn around to see November, resplendent in her orange-sherbet jumpsuit with matching glasses. "You can just say hello. That's how things work in the civilized world, Vem."

"Sorry, Lanie. I've been up since four, going over things in my mind. Trying to decide how to tell you this."

I glance at Piper, hoping for some clarification. She shrugs her shoulders. "What is it, Vem? We need a few days without drama."

November pulls up a chair and sits down uncomfortably close to me. "I was in the middle of something very important when I was rudely interrupted by a seedy criminal. A poor excuse for a kidnapper. If I were going to kidnap someone, I'd at least–"

"Vem," I interrupt. "Get on with it."

"I contacted Minerva. The woman you discovered was your aunt."

"I know that. Cos and I figured that out when we went to your house." The irritation in my voice is hard to disguise. "Piper was in the middle of telling me something. Is this important?"

Piper shakes her head furiously. "I want to wait until Cos is with you. Go on, November."

"Well, she wasn't entirely honest with you again." November looks around the room, as if she's about to divulge a secret of national security. "She was in contact with your father. Quite a lot, as it turns out. He left his wife and daughter when Berit was in high school. He discovered Jeannie had stalked him all those years ago, plotting to destroy his marriage to your mother. It made him sick."

"I knew that, too."

"What you don't know is that Berit is exactly like her mother. She was angry that your father left. She began harassing him, tracking his every move, just as her mother had done decades earlier. He was worried about you. That's why he came out here. He wanted to meet you, and warn you about Berit."

I lean forward in my chair, the anger about past events rising inside me once more. "Why didn't he tell me that himself?"

"Because when he arrived, we were in the middle of Piney Falls Proud Days. Well, getting ready for it. He told Minerva everyone around town raved about you. And he realized how busy you were with our event. He didn't want to bother you until it was finished."

"And then? When it was over? Why was he gone?"

"He discovered Berit was hot on his trail. He didn't want to endanger you, so he left quickly. Unfortunately, he was in his car at a rest stop when he had a heart attack."

Piper grabs my hand and squeezes it. "You see? He did care about you. And he left you that house. One tangible example of his love."

I squeeze hers in return. There is so much gratitude in my heart for these women and their concern. "Vem, he was that scared of Berit? As angry as she was, why would she just leave without telling me off? After she came all this way?"

"There wasn't anything here for her. Your father was gone. You weren't interested. I don't know. I'd need another sniff of her to tell you for sure." November says matter-of-factly. "It's over, Lanie."

"My father actually cared about me." I say out loud for the first time. "That one will take some time to digest."

Vem's phone buzzes. "Fudge and pickles. That's my security system. There's been some activity at your build site."

I stare sharply at Piper. "If this is Finn, you really need to end things. We can't have someone like that hanging around us."

Piper pulls out her phone and does a quick search. "Finn's at work. He just posted a picture of today's special: the French Fry and Cheese Sauce

Avalanche." She shows me a picture of an unappetizing mound of cheese and grease.

"We'd better get over there, Vem. Piper, will you tell Cos to meet us at home?"

"I'm on it." She gets up from the table and gives me a quick side hug. "I'll see you later. I'm sure it's nothing."

I smile wistfully. "I wish I could share your optimism."

November and I pull into her driveway and can see several cars parked at our property. "Should I call Boysie?" November asks.

"I suppose," I sigh. "Here we go again." We rush to the site of our former home, where there is a lot of activity. November sniffs the air. "Doesn't smell dangerous."

A familiar face appears from the crowd. "Morning, Lanie," Truman Coolidge says, pulling his star-covered cap off his head. "Thought we'd get a start before the next rains hit. Gotta take advantage of the sunny days when we get'em."

"What's going on, Truman? Who are these people?"

"Folks from the community. Some from Tellum, who came to Piney Falls Proud Days. People who appreciate what you and Cos give to us all. They've been looking for a way to show you how thankful they are." He makes a sweeping gesture behind him, and I spot several familiar faces. "With all this help, we'll have the outside walls finished by next week."

"Did you organize this?" I ask with wonder.

"That's why I saw your car on the security camera the day I was kidnapped!" Vem yells. "I knew you weren't one of the bad ones."

Truman nods. "You folks took me in when I needed help. I'm not the easiest character to handle. I decided when I got home that I'd get this thing rolling. Your house will be done by the time you two make your way to the altar. That's still happening, right?"

"It sure is." Cosmo's comforting voice says from behind me. "This is a really amazing gift, Truman. I don't know what to say, buddy."

Truman disappears for a moment before returning with a hammer. "Don't say anything. Just quit your gabbing and get to work."

Chapter Thirty-Nine

Wedding Day

I SHOULD HAVE known this wouldn't go smoothly. Our house was finished in four weeks; the catering, flowers, and set-up went off without a hitch. In the world of Lanie and Cosmo, that means something is looming on the horizon. I'd completely put this woman out of my mind with all the wedding preparations going on. She wasn't even a blip on the radar until this afternoon.

"It seems odd you'd show up to a wedding where you weren't invited," I say calmly to my half-sister, who is standing in front of me with a gun pointed at my veil. "Don't you have a law firm to run?"

Her face twitches slightly. "You already investigated me. You know I'm not an attorney. I work in sales, just like you."

"When you disappeared, I forgot about you. You were a short chapter in my life. I never went so far as to figure out who you really were, Berit." I don't want her to think I care, though Gladys had discovered she was fired from her sales position for stalking a co-worker who thwarted her advances.

"Do you know how many conferences I attended? Just to see you? I sold computer parts, and industrial cleaning supplies – you name it. I kept working in the office supplies industry so I could follow the great Lanie Anders."

"Why?" I ask, even though I already know this answer.

"Because you were a fairy tale Daddy couldn't erase from his memory. He put you on a pedestal. I had to understand why you meant so much to him that he was able to walk out on me and my mother without looking back."

I gulp. If she was truly following me, she saw some unsavory behavior; the old Lanie who would stop at nothing to be number one. "Well, I've changed since then. Those conferences and all of those people are part of my past. Shouldn't you be moving on as well?"

"Never," she chuckles. "Now that Daddy is gone, you're my project. I hired that idiot to set you up. I'm so glad I never fully paid for his services. Completely inept."

"Royal Granger? You know that 'idiot' is dead because of you. Kind of sloppy work, if you ask me."

I look around, hoping that someone will come in to tell me it's time to walk down the aisle. Since I made a big deal of spending some time alone, I'll just have to keep Berit talking. "You wanted to set me up because you were jealous? Of a relationship I never had with my father?"

She nods. "You need to suffer. Do you know that, after Daddy discovered Mother's truths, he left without saying goodbye? I called him twelve times every day and he wouldn't pick up. Once I had the money, I started tracking him, so I'd know if he was back in touch with you or your mother. He didn't make one move I didn't know about."

"By 'truths,' do you mean the fact that she stalked our father, the same way you stalked me? That she made it her mission to destroy Dad's marriage to my mother because she believed Lavender was responsible for her father's death? And that you developed an obsession with him that drove him away from you?"

"Daddy did all of his charitable work so easily," she says, ignoring my words. "Yet he couldn't find it in his heart to care about his own family. When I found out he bought that house, I knew it was some kind of misguided attempt to gain your affection," she snickers. "I was planning to have it burned to the ground with your frizzy-haired friend inside."

I gulp. The thought of losing Vem to this monster is more than I can take on an already-emotional day. "You have no reason to hate me. I never knew any of these things. If anything, I should be jealous of you. I have no clear memories of my father." I step to the side and she copies my move, not allowing me to come any closer.

"Daddy was planning to start a new life here, with you. He left Piney Falls when he realized I was following him. Still trying to protect Lanie, while Berit is left with nothing!" There are tears in her eyes and I'm concerned this burst of emotion will make her even more irrational.

"I'm just wondering what your end game is here. You kill me – and then what? Everyone you spent your life stalking is dead. What does Berit Campbell do then?"

She is thrown off by my question. "I – my ex-husband has a new wife. I've been researching–"

Out of the corner of my eye, I can see a quick flash of color. November Bean moves like the speed of light, betraying her age with her agility and strength. She takes the hem of her flowing multi-colored robe and pulls it over Berit's head, causing her to fall backward and in to November's chest. Taking advantage of this moment, I grab the gun from her hand and throw it to the ground, causing it to fire a bullet that hits the lovely table with my bouquet and ricochet into the door. My bouquet splatters beautiful lavender roses all over the floor.

November pushes Berit to the ground, sitting on top of her with her robe still over the wretched woman's head. "Not only did you have me kidnapped, but you left my guest house without making your bed. Unforgiveable!"

Piper and Faythe rush in to see the chaos. "What happened?" Piper asks.

"Berit decided to make a surprise appearance. Go get Boysie. Tell him I'm sorry, but he'll have to miss the wedding. We'll send some cake home with Gladys."

"Lanie? Is everything alright in there?" Cosmo is at the door as Piper rushes past him.

Maybe Berit was right about one thing: I have my roots in fairy tales. "Don't come in, Cos! You can't see the bride before the wedding!" I shout. "Everything is fine."

When Boysie arrives, Vem relinquishes control of Berit, but not before berating her again. "You are nothing like Lanie! Nothing! You couldn't hold a cucumber and date candle fermented for sixty-seven days to my Lanie!"

"This thing needs emergency services," Piper says, picking up what's left of my bouquet.

"I suppose I don't really need flowers. It's more about marrying the man I love." I try to hide my disappointment from Piper.

"Never fear, Lanie. I have a solution," November says, pulling something from her sleeve.

Thirty minutes later, I am composed and ready to

walk down the aisle. I pause at the rear of the beautifully landscaped garden, taking a deep breath. The sweet summer smells of the vineyard – flowering bushes, roses, and begonias, intermingle with the fresh, salty ocean air.

The people I've come to think of as my family are all standing, smiling encouragingly at me. Each one made me better somehow. I gaze from one warm face to the next, thinking how lucky I am to have them all in my life.

I've scanned every face but one. At the end of the aisle, surprising me in a gray tux with a lavender rose in the lapel, is a man so handsome he takes my breath away. Cosmo has tears in his impossibly deep blue eyes. Luckily, his best person, his sister Cedar, is at his side, handing him her laced handkerchief. Piper is standing on the other side of the wooden podium that Truman constructed for our wedding that was engraved with our silhouettes. She is tearing up too, though she tries to sniff and hold it in.

Truman offers his arm. "Ready?" he asks.

"Past ready," I proclaim. I walk slowly, wanting to drink in every second of this day. Urica reaches out and touches my hand as I walk by. Gladys pats my rear. "Finally, toots!" she grumbles. When I reach the end of the aisle, Cedar takes my arm on one side and Cosmo's on the other. She squeezes both of us before kissing me lightly on the cheek and placing my hand on Cosmo's, joining our families together.

Cosmo's eyes scan me from head to toe. "I've never seen such beauty," he whispers. He leans in close and his hand gets stuck on something.

"Vem's birch bark gum. It took an entire pack to keep those flowers together. I'll explain everything later."

He discreetly pulls the gum off his finger and we turn to face November, who, just thirty minutes ago, was sitting on top of an assailant. Now her expression is serene as she faces her biggest audience yet; 150 Piney Falls locals, something she's been preparing for her entire life.

"Friends, people I tolerate, and those we consider family; I welcome you to my wedding."

"Our wedding!" Cosmo mouths.

"I welcome you to our wedding," November corrects herself.

She opens her book and begins reading her speech as Cosmo and I gaze into each other's eyes. It's been such a long journey that it's hard to believe we're finally here. When it's time to read our vows, Cosmo reaches into his pocket and pulls out a crumpled piece of paper.

"Lanie, before you came, I was kind of a turd." There is a smattering of laughter. "I spent the first third of my life in a cult, the next in prison, and I was planning on spending the rest in a shell. Then this movie-star lookalike walked in and life took on new meaning. Now I can't wait to get up every morning and see what mayhem we're going to find together."

I look at him with tears in my eyes. "Cosmo Hill. Before you, I thought I had everything a woman needed: money, a good job, and a great wardrobe. When that life went up in smoke, I didn't understand how things would ever be good again." I touch his face. "Then I found you and this town. That's when I realized things can be messy and unpredictable and still be perfect. You bring out the best in me, Cos. Every day is better than the last."

When we are finished with our vows, we exchange the rings Urica designed for us. The matching gold bands have the intertwining letters "c" and "l" in tiny diamonds snaking around them. We kiss passionately and our guests rise to their feet, applauding.

"'Bout time," Gladys remarks as loud as she possibly can. "Never thought it would happen while I was still breathing."

Cosmo and I stand patiently for pictures in front of the old mansion as our guests are guided by Marveline to the reception area. When we finish, we walk silently, hand in hand to the large tent. Neither of us dares to speak without the fear of breaking down with emotion.

The atmosphere inside the tent is yet another beautiful scene. There are lanterns hung above every table, adding a warming glow to the already cozy atmosphere. Cream-colored roses, eucalyptus, and lavender peonies highlight the centerpiece on each table. The band Cosmo insisted upon is playing, and it is a lovely mellow sound; not at all what I imagined. While we were taking photos outside, our guests cooled off with popsicles made from Sassy Lasses wine and incased in a wrapper that matches the style of our rings. That was Marveline's brilliant idea.

In front of our seats is our two-tiered cake, covered in an intricately piped lace pattern of frosting, enhanced with edible gold foil to match the lace on my dress. "Piper, it's gorgeous!" I exclaim. One layer contains a vanilla sponge filled with fresh strawberries and light Bavarian cream. The second layer is a dark chocolate, espresso-soaked sponge cake with alternating layers of hazelnut chocolate mousse, and coffee butter cream. She gives me the thumbs up sign.

We sit down to our dinner of summer salad with spinach, strawberries and a sweet strawberry vinaigrette. For the main course we chose lobster macaroni and cheese and pulled pork sliders, each of us picking one dish.

Occasionally, we reach for each other's hand,

comforted in the knowledge we're joined forever. I drink in his beautiful face as he and Truman compare presidential weddings. The entire experience is surreal. When we finish our meal, I give Cos a knowing glance and we both stand.

"Before we cut our cake, we have an announcement to make," I say after I have everyone's attention. I motion for Piper to join us. "Not long ago, Piper came to us with a request. I'd like her to tell you what that was."

Piper clears her throat. "A friend of mine told me I should change my name. He told me people would associate it with certain bad things, and he thought I was better than that. At first, I disagreed with him. But over the past year, I've been thinking more and more about who I am and who I want to be. I realized I've outgrown being a Moonlight. That's why I asked Lanie and Cos to officially adopt me. As of yesterday afternoon, I'm Piper Anders Hill. The daughter of Lanie and Cosmo." I pull them both in tight for a family hug.

The room erupts in applause. I can hear Gladys, who is at the table nearest to ours, sputtering, "Why didn't I know about that?"

I move to the side, so our daughter can stand in between us as we cut the cake. Phones come out and everyone captures the three of us with our hands on the knife, slicing through Piper's strawberry wonder.

Marveline, who is unusually smiley, says, "Let's get a few shots with the professional photographer. Cake will be served in ten minutes."

We all squeeze into the frame, each in our own state of revelry. Our arms are locked together behind us; the Anders-Hill family is an unbreakable union. "Head to the side slightly," the photographer commands of me. When she finishes, she walks up to the table. "Mrs. Hill, I heard you acquired some property outside of town. Are you thinking of flipping it? My husband and I have been looking for a nice place."

"No, I'm sorry." I glance at my family: my incredibly handsome husband, and my unbelievably talented daughter. I'm overwhelmed with emotion. "Piper is taking over the property," I say through my tears. "We're going to expand our family bakery to serve local restaurants. That location will be our professional kitchen. She'll live upstairs once Truman gets the remodeling work done."

Vem comes immediately to my side and uses her striped robe to wipe my face. "We can't have you looking like a melted candle, friend!" She kisses me gently on the nose and sits back down.

Piper taps on her champagne glass with a fork. "I'd like to make a toast," she says, raising her glass. "To the most wonderful people I know. My parents, Lanie and Cosmo Hill."